MORE HIGH PRAISE
FOR SUSAN EDWARDS!

WHITE DREAMS
"Susan Edwards has the talent of hooking her readers in the first paragraph and selfishly holding on to them until the last page has been turned! Highly recommended reading!"

—Huntress Book Reviews

WHITE NIGHTS
"Tender, heartwarming, touching, *White Nights* is a story you can savor."

—Connie Mason, *New York Times* bestselling author

WHITE FLAME
"Susan Edwards has penned another winner.... Her sensual prose and compelling characters are forging a place for her at the forefront of Indian romance."

—*Affaire de Coeur*

WHITE WOLF
"Ms. Edwards's words flow like vivid watercolors across the pages. Her style is smooth, rhythmic and easy to read."

—*Rendezvous*

WHITE WIND
"Talented and skillful, this first-rate author has proven her mettle with *White Wind*. Ms. Edwards has created a romantic work of art!"

—*The Literary Times*

A DESPERATE PLEA

Holding her breath, Blaze brought the crystal closer to her face. She couldn't see what he looked like, just the shape of a face, but as though he felt her gaze upon him, he turned his head toward her and Blaze couldn't help her gasp of amazement. His face became clearer until that was all she could see. It was like looking into a mirror and seeing the face of another.

His eyes were a rich, warm green like the thick carpet of ferns growing in the deepest shade of the forest. His face was covered with hair as most trappers seemed to want to wear it, but his mouth was firm and his nose long and straight. But his eyes drew her again, mesmerized her. They were deep pools of soothing green.

"Who are you?" Her voice was a soft whisper.

The stranger stared into her eyes, then his image grew smaller. He held out one arm. Long fringe swung back and forth and his finger curled out and toward her.

"Help me."

SUMMER
OF THE
Eagle

SUSAN EDWARDS

LEISURE BOOKS   NEW YORK CITY

A LEISURE BOOK®

April 2007

Published by

Dorchester Publishing Co., Inc.
200 Madison Avenue
New York, NY 10016

ISBN-10: 0-8439-5335-7
ISBN-13: 978-0-8439-5335-0

Visit us on the web at www.dorchesterpub.com.

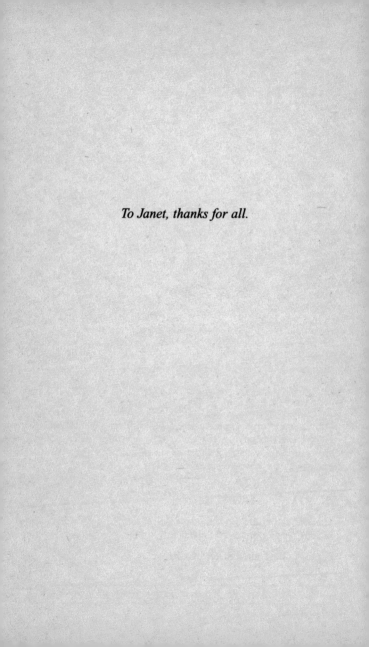

To Janet, thanks for all.

SUMMER
OF THE
Eagle

Skan, Wi, Inyan and Maka are Superior Gods. They are also known as Creator, Chief God and Great Spirit. Four Gods, yet they are as one. They are mysterious. They are Wakan Tanka.

PROLOGUE

The little girl danced and skipped along the shoreline of a deep blue lake. A small shallow finger of water trailed inland. She splashed through the water, sending glistening diamond-bright droplets flying around her.

Named after the stars in the night sky, Taya laughed and giggled. As she romped happily, her long blue-black hair flew around her head. Her legs were short and thin beneath her long, fringed doeskin dress, but her body held the promise of grace and beauty.

She breathed in the warm pine-scented air; her gaze absorbed the beauty of forest, sky and lake. Though she was young, she was a child of the land and, as such, she was at one with her world. A long shadow flew before her on the sandy soil. Taya ran, trying to catch it. She glanced over her shoulder and waved her hands at the magnificent white-headed eagle flying overhead.

1

The bird's wingspan was double her size, and as it flew low along the shoreline, she spread her arms as wide as she could and broke out into excited shouts. *"Miye kinyan! Miye kinyan!"* I fly! I fly!

Rising high, the eagle cut across the lake. Taya stopped to wait for the bird to return. Once more she took off running with her hands out to the sides, her gaze on the ground in front of her as her shadow and that of the eagle's came together: spirits of bird and child joining then separating as the eagle once again rose high into the sky.

Taya clapped her hands together and stood, face upturned as the eagle made another pass, this time coming in low to brush one wingtip across the top of her head. It gave a shrill, high-pitched cry as it rose once again into the air.

"Ina." When the bird took wing over the lake, she twirled in a tight circle, her arms out, the fringe beneath her arms flying and waving with each movement. Dizzy, Taya dropped to the ground. Out over the lake, a second eagle joined the first. This one was slightly smaller, a male, and it gave chase to its mate.

Sighing wistfully, the little girl watched the pair of regal birds soar together then dip down to drag their bright yellow talons over the surface of the lake then rise high. The sky was their throne, their cloaks made from the greens of the earth, lined with the shimmering gold of the setting sun and edged with the silvery-white of the clouds.

The pair of eagles made a last sweeping flight

over Taya, each tipping a tapered wingtip as though bidding her good night. *"Miye kinyan,"* she whispered as she stood to return home. With a happy grin on her face, Taya spread her arms wide and pretended that she too was flying as she ran across the deserted shoreline.

Eager anticipation settled deep inside her. Someday, she would fly. Strands of her silky blue-black hair swirled into her face, curtaining her vision. A sudden darkness that had nothing to do with the hair in her eyes made her come to an abrupt halt. She held herself still as she listened to the whispers that came to her on the breath of *Tate*, the Wind Spirit. Around her, the world seemed to pulse and vibrate, a warning that something was wrong. Instincts that came from more than just a child of the land hummed through her body and made her feel afraid.

She shoved her hair out of her face, her gaze locked onto the retreating pair of eagles. She opened her mouth to call them back but before she could utter a sound, an arrow flew out from the thick canopy of leaves. The feathered shaft rose into the air and struck the smaller of the two birds. The eagle gave a shrill shriek then plummeted like a stone. Shock sent Taya tumbling to her knees.

Around her, the world went oddly silent but for the anguished cry of the female eagle going into a blurring dive to chase her mate. A slow buzzing grew in Taya's ears as her mind tried to reject what was happening. Before she could react, think or even scream in denial, a second arrow zinged upward.

The arrow and bird crashed together, and the sharp arrowhead clove straight through feather, bone and flesh. The arrow continued upward then fell to the earth after the mortally wounded bird.

Taya screamed in terror, the sound shattering into fragments the beauty of pre-twilight. With each scream, the world came apart. The wind roared across the lake, churning and agitating the water, sending waves crashing to shore with enough force to shatter the smooth beauty of the shoreline.

Water parted around the little girl. Taya dug her fingers into the wet soil as though seeking to anchor herself to the earth. The wind struck the wall of forest with a fury that bent the tips of hundred-foot pines, cedar and spruce, and ripped branches from trees and slapped cone-shaped fruit high into the air.

Far away, the sun dimmed for a heartbeat in time, then it flared bright white, sending tongues of flames shooting across the seething clouds that boiled and gathered and swallowed the regal blues, golds and pinks of what had been a pretty, pastel sunset. Taya, unaware of the violence around her, continued to scream in shock and horror. Her eyes blazed with blue fire. Pain and fury shimmered deep in their depths and fueled the raging elements. A sudden slash of lightning followed by a crash of thunder spurred her into action. She stumbled to her feet and ran.

"*Ina.*"

"*Ate.*"

The howling wind devoured her cries for her mother and father. Lightning scored the sky, thunder drowned out all sound. Beneath her feet, the ground trembled. Animals in the forest scurried to safety, birds huddled together, their young tucked securely beneath their wings, but the child didn't cower or hide from the Thunder Beings.

Taya ran along the twisting shoreline and didn't slow when she saw a tall warrior step out from the cover of trees and brush, his attention focused on the gathering storm above his head. He didn't see Taya, didn't see her fall to her knees or hear her screams of outrage or see the fear in her eyes. The wind whipped and tore at the hunter's braids, his clothing and the quiver of arrows on his back. He pushed himself forward, fighting the storm. The air crackled with emotion and the beat of another sound:

Drums.

The heavy pounding filled the air with the force of blows, and the hard and fierce tempo matched the furious elements. The eagles' slayer glanced anxiously into the grove of trees as though debating whether to seek safety. After a brief moment of indecision, he leaned into the wind to go claim the prize of his hunt.

Behind him, Taya went sprawling twice more. Bright flashes of light illuminated the boiling mass of dark, angry clouds, and where forest and water met, the warrior stopped abruptly. When he knelt, Taya jumped onto his back and struck him with her fists.

"*Hiya!* No! Do not touch them," she screamed, her voice thick with rage, pain and fright. A loud crackle overhead drowned out her screams. The warrior whirled. Taya lost her grip and landed on the hard ground. She rolled onto her hands and knees, her gaze locked onto the slain bodies of two humans: a man and a woman.

The male had an arrow protruding from his heart, the female had a gaping hole in her chest. Blood ran in rivers down the man's chest and created a dark, ugly stain on the woman's soft, doeskin dress. Her mother and father. Taya's heart shattered into tiny pieces, and tears of grief blurred her sight.

"*Ina.*" She cried, her fists tangled in her mother's long, silky black hair. She turned to her father, brushed her trembling hands over his still face. His eyes were open but unable to see or hear his daughter's grief.

"*Ate.*" She sobbed as she shook her father's shoulders.

"Wake," she pleaded. She rubbed her wet cheeks against her mother's cold face and begged her to wake up, but neither woke; neither moved.

"What magic is this?" the warrior asked. His voice trembled as he grabbed the child by the arm.

Taya kicked, bit and struck him with clenched fists. Screaming, filled with a rage that she'd never before felt, she fought for her own survival. Even at her young age, she knew it was too late for her parents. Behind them, a tree burst into flame. Startled, the warrior dropped her, giving Taya the opportunity to grab her mother's knife.

At only six winters, she was perfectly capable of avenging the deaths of her parents. She whirled and charged the warrior, her hand held high, her voice shrill. "You killed them. *You* die." Her heart pounded to the primitive rhythm of drums in the distance.

The warrior looked confused and frightened, but not of her; after all, she was just a child. He easily twisted the knife from her hand then knocked her to one side as though she were nothing more than an annoying insect.

Taya felt herself flying. Flying like the birds. She landed hard, hitting her head on a rock. Pain pierced her head then she rolled onto her back beside her dead mother. She stared up into the sky where flames scorched a path through dark clouds and bright white jagged bolts splintered the heavens.

Beneath her, she felt the fury of *Wakinyan* as the Thunder Being shook the earth. Though the world above her was on fire and the air around her chillingly cold, she was no longer afraid. Like her parents, she lay perfectly still. Like them, she would die and go to the spirit world. Perhaps there she could fly.

Like them. With them.

Taya welcomed the calm, soothing white light coming at her, surrounding her, bathing her. All went eerily silent but for the heavy beat of drums in the air. Even that faded into silence, and suddenly, she found herself floating above the bodies of her mother and father. As the world spun, taking her away from her parents, she watched the warrior grab the little girl named Taya and run.

In the beginning, there was only Inyan. *He lived in darkness. He was soft and shapeless. Like a cloud.* Inyan *was power. He was all there was.*

CHAPTER ONE

Blaze woke abruptly. Her head throbbed painfully, her heart pummeled her ribs and her lungs, starved for air, burned. Jerking upright, she drew in deep, shuddering breaths and fought waves of nausea and dizziness. "Not again," she moaned into her hands. Her long, blue-black hair fell forward.

Tonight made three nights running that the terrifying dream had yanked her cruelly from sleep. Who was this child who haunted her? The first night she'd watched as though she was high above, observing a horrible event. The second night she'd felt herself falling into the dream, or maybe the events in the dream had risen to engulf her. She didn't know; it didn't matter. One moment she was watching the events unfold, then she was there, seeing everything happen yet unable to stop any of it. Tonight, she'd become that happy, contented child with no knowledge of what was to come and the child's fear and grief had become her own.

"Ina. Ate." Mother. Father.

The echo of the child's screams had tears slipping from the corners of her eyes. The little girl's sorrow and pain rose from deep inside Blaze. Sharp and stabbing pain made breathing difficult. Rubbing a palm over her heart, Blaze knew she was feeling the echo of the child's pain, the child who'd felt the arrows tearing and ripping flesh and bone apart.

Blaze shook and trembled. Worse than the pain in her chest was the overwhelming sense of sorrow and loss. In tonight's dream the man and woman lying dead on that wet, sandy shoreline had been *her* beloved parents, but that wasn't possible. Her mother had died giving birth to her and her father still lived. So who were these people?

It all seemed so real: the orange-red flames shooting across the sky, the seething blue froth of the lake, the jagged white spears of light raining down around her, trees exploding, sparks scattering into the air. Even the acrid scent of burning seemed real. Everything had been intense, and the ground had vibrated with a fury she'd never known.

Using one of the furs she slept on, Blaze swiped it across her head, wiping the sweat from her skin. Her doeskin dress was twisted around her body and the inky blackness of the cave was hot and stifling. She felt trapped in the small confines of relentless darkness. Shifting, she straightened her dress and tucked her knees high beneath the long, fringed skirt as she curled into a tight ball and focused on steadying her breathing and calming her trembling body. After a while, she rolled onto her back to stare up at the low stone ceiling where a small natural opening allowed smoke from the fire pit to escape and gave passage for the light from the moon and stars to enter.

A current of cool air entered from the entrance of the cave and mingled with air that slid in from a hidden crevice in the back. The fresh air dried the sweat of night terrors from her skin but did little to stop her trembling.

Blaze closed her eyes and sought to bring soothing images of *Ina Maka*, Mother Earth, into her heart and mind to dispel the nightmare. Wiping all thoughts of the dreams from her mind, she called forth an image of herself leaving the cave. She climbed—higher and higher until she stood at the very top of her stone mountain. Normally, visualization came easy for her, but tonight it took all her concentration, which she welcomed, as it also kept the nightmare at bay.

She saw herself standing on the edge of the tall cliff with the sleeping earth spread out below her, and a thick carpet of bright glittering stars overhead. Beneath her feet, she felt the hum of ancient life. Her hair floated in the gentle breeze and the long strips of fringe on her skirt and beneath her arms swayed gently as she turned in a slow circle.

Peace and calm slid through her as she held the image in her mind. The mountainous rock that provided her with shelter also provided comfort and a source of power, one she could physically stand upon and draw strength from or visualize as she was doing now.

Calmed by the images, each muscle in her body relaxed and she gently drifted. Behind her eyes, night gave way to day and from her perch on top of the world, she watched the graceful brownish-black body of an eagle soar overhead, then dive down to the water, strong yellow talons nabbing a silvery fish.

The *anunkasan*, or white-headed eagle, was her totem animal: her protector and companion when she traveled to the spirit worlds. It was also the bird that haunted her dreams, and without warning, the images in her mind shifted and plunged her back into her nightmare.

Blaze moaned and rolled her head from side to side, trapped by the visions cascading through her mind. She knew what was coming, yet was helpless to stop it. "No. Please no," she begged. She didn't want to be here, to see this, but a force stronger than her own will held her tightly in its grasp.

In her dreamlike trance, she stepped closer to the edge of the cliff and looked down, saw the child; then she was falling in slow motion, watching the ground coming at her. Blaze sucked in her breath as the sensation changed to one of soaring. She was flying through the air and below her the little girl stared up and held up her hands. Blaze flew close and touched the child and felt the child's joyful cry.

I fly. More than words, Blaze felt the happiness— but it hadn't lasted. The joy and innocence of that moment in time were ripped from the child cruelly.

12

Crying out as she felt herself falling into a whirl-pool of blues and greens, Blaze found herself back in her bed on the cave floor. She blinked. "So real," she whispered, her voice a thin thread of torment. The sheer joy of that child running through the water with her arms held out to her sides made tears of regret stream down her face.

Angrily, Blaze brushed her tears away. Not once in her childhood had she ever felt that wondrous, absolute joy, the feeling of being loved and cherished.

Closing her eyes, Blaze tried to put the dream from her. Her body ached with exhaustion. She needed sleep but each time she closed her eyes, the nightmare returned with the same determinedness of a badger digging after his prey. Admitting she'd get no more sleep that night, Blaze crawled out of her bed. The fringe of her deerskin skirt brushed against her shins as she stood and paced.

Beneath her bare feet, the cool packed earth helped ground her, but it wasn't enough. Slipping outside, the cool night air soothed her overheated skin as she made her way down to the lake. Kneeling, she cupped water in her hands, drank deeply then splashed the coolness on her face, neck and arms.

Sitting back on her heels, Blaze stared out at the calm, silvery surface of water glittering with reflected moon and starlight. How at odds this peaceful setting was from the lake in her dreams that had boiled, churned and thrown waves sky- and land-ward. Blaze sighed. What did the dream mean? Why was it coming to her? Three nights running the nightmare splintered her mind into pain, horror and grief.

Blaze sat back and rested her head against her knees. Of everything in the dream, it was the overwhelming sense of grief that lingered for the remaining dark hours and nagged at her during each long day. In the space of two heartbeats innocent joy had been destroyed. The echoes of the child's screams made her heart shatter into tiny pieces. Jumping to her feet, Blaze took off at a fast pace, trying to outrun the images of her nightmare.

The shoreline jagged out into the water. Blaze waded through the shallow cove, her fingers brushing against the trunk of a tree. Life hummed beneath her fingers and she gave the bark an absent pat. *"Mitakuye Oyasin.* To all my relations," she murmured. A shadow swept over her, sliding into the dark forest with a dismal and complaining cry.

Hinyan.

Owl. She stared into the forest, unable to see the owl: the symbol of the darkness within where secrets lay hidden. Blaze drew in a deep, shaky breath. "Secrets. So *many* secrets." She leaned against the tree and tipped her head back.

Something soft brushed her cheek. Reaching up, she caught a small white-and-brown striped feather and glanced up into the dark treetops. She couldn't see the owl, but she felt the bird high above. Had the bird not given a cry as he passed, she would never have known he was there.

"Pilamaya. Thank you."

A small splash of water drew her attention. "You are restless this night, my child."

Blaze glanced to her left and spotted an old woman from her village seated on the ground next to the lake. Low-hanging branches with leaves swinging gently back and forth like a curtain shielded the woman from view.

"*Unci.*" Blaze bestowed the respected title of *grandmother* on the woman who was mother to the chief of their tribe and wife of the old shaman. She lowered her gaze to the ground out of habit. Her eyes with their strange coloring sent children running to hide behind their mothers' skirts. Even the bravest warrior was afraid to look her in the eye. "I do not mean to disturb you." She turned to go.

"You do not disturb this old woman. Come. Join me, *Cunksi.*"

My daughter.

The softly spoken words so startled Blaze that she stared at Wise Owl in confusion. "Do you not see to whom you are talking?" She kept her voice respectful. The woman had never been unkind.

"I see well enough, child. Why do you not sit?"

Blaze tipped her chin, allowing the light of the full moon to fall directly on her face. "Why are you not afraid? Why do you not run?" she asked softly. In all fairness, Blaze didn't blame her people for being afraid. She remembered the first time she'd gotten a mirror in trade from another tribe who traded with trappers. She'd stared for a long time into eyes unlike anything she'd ever seen.

Each of her eyes was a multitude of colors—a wheel of blue shading into greens and browns with a second layer of transparent yellow sunbursts and blue streaks covering a third of her eyeball like an incomplete web.

Wise Owl chuckled. "I am too old to run, child. Do you mean to harm me?"

Tears forming in her eyes, Blaze shook her head. She tried hard not to be resentful that so many chose to judge her by looks, not her actions. "I have never caused harm to another—at least, not on purpose." She bit down hard on her lower lip, fully admitting that sometimes she herself found her unique abilities scary.

"I do not believe you will harm me, so I ask again: Will you join me, *Cunksi?*" The woman patted the ground beside her, her eyes dark, fathomless pools.

Cunski.

Daughter.

Blaze fought back a sob. In all her seventeen summers, she could not remember anyone ever calling her daughter. Feeling weary from lack of sleep, troubled by dreams and just plain heart-sore, Blaze sat beside the woman and drew her knees up to her chest, smoothing her calf-length skirt down over her legs to keep the chill of night at bay.

The tree with its swaying branches created a private shelter for the two women. Blaze wrapped her arms around her knees. Silence cloaked the two women, one wearing the wrinkles of time proudly, the other young and troubled. Time passed. Over the horizon, the full moon glowed and shone down upon them, bathing them, and all around them, in silvery light. Finally, the old woman spoke. "Tell me, *micinca*. What keeps you from your bed this night?"

My child.

If the old woman only knew. The temptation to unburden herself to the quiet wise woman was too much for Blaze to resist. As was the custom of her people, she took her time responding, choosing her words carefully.

"Dreams, *Unci*," Blaze replied. She didn't want to hurt or insult the woman by refusing counsel, yet she'd learned the hard way to keep to herself. Once again, silence fell. Frowning at the shimmering lake, Blaze understood that it was up to her to say more. She twirled the shaft of the owl feather between her fingers.

Each night she saw more of the child, Taya, but was it a nightmare or were these visions? She just didn't know. "A child. I dream of a child," she said softly. Glancing at the silent woman beside her, she added almost defiantly, "She was happy."

A gentle breeze tugged the woman's gray hair. "Children should be happy."

Blaze leaned back against the trunk and rested the feather against her heart. She smiled sadly. "And loved." Her voice held no bitterness. She accepted the life she led, and the relationship between herself and her father.

"This happy child troubles you. Why?"

17

Picking up a skinny twig, Blaze snapped it in two. "Her happiness does not last," she whispered, frustrated and afraid. She laid her head on her knees. Pain seared through it. A soft breeze lifted the long blue-black strands of her hair; it was a soothing balm against the back of her neck, her face, her bare arms. Beside her, the old woman remained silent.

"I am afraid," Blaze mumbled. "For this child. Something terrible happened to her, but I do not know if it is real." She lifted her head. "Is it a vision of the future? Can I help this child? I do not understand why she comes to me. What does she want of me?" She picked up a small stone and, frustrated, rubbed her fingers hard over the cool, rough surface.

"Dreams are messages of the spirits. Listen to your heart."

Blaze lifted her head. "I do not want them to speak to me. I want peace. Is it too much to ask?"

"The path of a *winan wakan* is not a smooth and easy one."

"A holy woman? Me?" Blaze actually laughed and dropped the now gleaming stone. Her people grudgingly accepted her as a *pejuta winan*, a medicine woman, but only because their *wichasha wakan*, their shaman, had said they must. But he'd died four years ago, and without him, there was no way her people would ever accept her as his replacement. They were afraid of her, and allowed her into their lodges only if her father, the tribe's *wichasha pejuta*, medicine man, was also there.

Wise Owl raised the stone Blaze had polished with her touch and held it up. "You cannot hide from the truth. It is in your heart."

"Why are you not afraid of me?" Anyone else would have looked at her as though she'd sprouted two heads or was some evil spirit.

"It is not for me to question the gifts given to you. I only speak the truth."

Deep inside, Blaze knew the old woman was right. She was more than just a healer and the pebble in the woman's hand was proof. One of her many gifts was the ability to connect with the ancient life trapped inside rocks and stones. She could sense whether a stone held healing properties, and as she'd just done without giving it a moment's thought, she could use her mind and fingers to create beauty where before there had only been dullness.

She stared at her hands. She had knowledge and abilities that no one else had or even knew about. She had so many secrets, many even her father knew nothing about. "What is in my heart does not matter," she said simply. She could forgive her people for being afraid of her, but her father's hatred cut deeply.

Tears pricked Blaze's eyes. Her own father could not accept her for who and what she was, yet this old woman seemed to have no trouble accepting her. There was no fear in her eyes. Just kindness.

Wise Owl rose. She patted Blaze gently on the head, smoothing hair from her face. "You must have faith and trust, *cinca*."

"I have always followed our ways. Do I not respect and honor all things and speak kindly no matter what is done or said to me?"

Wise Owl sighed. "I did not ask if you followed the way of our people. Having faith and trust in what is, accepting what is, is often a hard lesson."

For a long silent moment the two women gazed at one another. Blaze gave in to a tiny bit of defiance and stared hard at Wise Owl. She waited for the older woman to glance away from the blue and yellow fire of her eyes, but to her amazement, the old woman grinned.

"My husband was right when he said you had spirit." She reached down to gently cup Blaze's face in her old, worn hands. "Listen carefully, child. Much rests on your young shoulders. The truth is in you. To find it, travel the wheel of the south. Seek the child. Learn the truth and find your answers." She wiped a tear from Blaze's cheek. "In innocence you were born, and in faith you will grow to fulfill your destiny." She paused then pulled something from around her neck.

"Follow your heart and you will find strength and protection." Wise Owl pressed a tiny bag dangling from a leather cord into Blaze's hand, then turned and slipped into the deep shadows of the forest.

Holding the gift tightly in her fist, Blaze turned to stare out over the silvery water where the face of the full, round moon floated low over the lake. She fingered the pouch that had been softened by time and handling. Slowly, she pulled the top apart and upended it. A small clear crystal stone fell into her palm and caught the rays of the moon. Attached to one end was a thin band of leather that had been threaded through a tiny hole made in the stone.

She gasped and ran her fingers over the six-sided nearly translucent surface. The life of the stone vibrated deep in her heart, pulled at her very soul. Holding it up, she held her breath as the moon and stars winked at her from inside as though trapped in the smooth, polished crystal.

Her fingers found and touched the stone she wore around her neck, hidden beneath the fringed yoke of her dress. It felt warm through the deerskin. She pulled it out and held it up. The stone was a carved deep blue crystal in the shape of an eagle, with its wings folded tight against its body and its beak open as though in a silent cry.

Holding the two stones side by side, Blaze stared in wonder at the soft glow that surrounded both crystals. Raising her arms high over her head, she stared at the stones. The blue crystal seemed to blaze with fire, while the clear crystal glittered like snow falling from the sky. Fire and ice. Her fingers tingled with the heat of the blue, and the cool of the clear.

How would this crystal help her on her journey?

"What is it you want of me?" She asked the question of everything: stars, moon, sky, earth. She asked it of the gods, the spirits and all her relations on Earth.

Pale light bathed her slim body and washed her dark hair in its silvery light. South was a place of self. A place of strength, faith and protection. Her feet were in the south, her head in the north, a place of wisdom. "I seek knowledge, *Waziya Ouye*, power of North. I have many questions and no answers." She tried to clear her mind of all chaotic thought and focus all her energy into being receptive, but the turmoil in her mind kept her from being able to concentrate clearly.

She took a step to her left and turned slightly. "*Wiyopeyata Ouye*, West power, power of the setting sun, you've sent dreams. What do they mean? Who is this child? What is she to me?" Blaze fought down the images, even the happy ones, for they loosened a gushing stream of raw grief that hurt unlike anything she'd ever known.

Quickly Blaze turned. "*Wiyoheyapata Ouye*, East power, you command the rising dawn. My mind is confused. Point me in the direction I must take."

She ended her prayer circle facing south: "*Itokagata Ouye*. South power. I seek your strength and protection as I journey the wheel of south." Kneeling, she touched the ground beneath her. "Mother Earth, hear me. I am your daughter. Teach this daughter what she needs to know, protect this child who comes to me in my dreams."

She waited several heartbeats then stood, her head falling back on her neck. Once again, she lifted her hand. "Father Sky, you share the world with sun, moon and stars. You are all-powerful. You know all, see all. You *are* all. Tell me what I must do."

Blaze sent her senses flaring outward. Answers came from everywhere: the appearance of an animal, a sound riding the back of the wind, a shadow passing in front of the moon. The answer was here, somewhere. She waited for something. Anything.

But received nothing. No sound. No voice in her head, not even a comforting whisper of wind or rustle of leaves. Blaze felt abandoned and angry, then immediately felt ashamed. The Great Spirit was all-knowing. Mysterious. *Wakan Tanka.*

Her shoulders sagged slightly. Answers came in their own time, and it was obvious that there weren't going to be any quick-and-easy ones for her tonight. With a long sigh Blaze tucked her blue stone back down her dress so that it hung hidden between her breasts. The clear crystal went back into its bag and she hung that around her neck as well. Warmth seeped into her skin as she resumed walking along the lake.

Hidden beneath the thick canopy of trees, her village slept. The darkness hid danger and concealed her presence, yet Blaze had no fear of the night or of any animal roaming through the woods: they were her brothers and sisters and cousins. She didn't even fear her own people, for they were too afraid of her to approach.

Guards were posted in the forest to keep her village safe from raiding warriors of other tribes. They didn't acknowledge her, nor she them, but she knew they were there just as she knew they saw her. Had she been any other woman out wandering in the dark, the warriors would have escorted her back to their lodge. But not Blaze. She smiled sadly.

Blaze, they avoided. They thought themselves hidden, concealed, safe from her evil eyes.

Her gaze swept over the dense woods to her left. No, she couldn't see Walks Like Turtle in that clump of brush, but she felt him. Staring where she knew the warrior stood, she felt his fear and quickly turned her head.

Their fear of her angered her at times, but mostly it made her sad. She'd never harmed anyone, and indeed, she'd used her healing abilities to help many of their people. But because she was able to heal in ways that even she didn't understand, they all feared her. Even her own father treated her as an outcast.

She rubbed her eyes tiredly. Coming to a fallen log that snaked out into the water, she nimbly walked out to the end and sat, fists on knees and chin on fists. Alone and lonely, she stared out over the lake. The wind brushed against her as though offering comfort. It caressed her, enfolded her. It soothed and calmed and remained one with her as she watched the moon fade and the sun rise.

Luc Cordell's pack pulled heavily against his shoulders, his belly rumbled with hunger, and he was tired. After three weeks of wandering up and down streams, trapping, skinning hides and eating his own miserable fare, he was eager to return to base camp. Unfortunately, the stubborn pack mule refused to move. Shifting the rifle in his arms, he gave the rope a sharp tug.

The mule planted its front hooves, kicked back

its rear hooves then shook its head from side to side. The piled-high load of furs and supplies strapped to the back of the animal shifted dangerously to the side. Luc gave another tug. The mule jerked his head hard and high, yanking the lead rope out of Luc's gloved hands. Luc felt the heat of the rope burn and swore at the hole in the palm of his glove, and the reddened skin beneath that told him too late he needed new gloves.

"Look you *exécrable*, stubborn—"

A loud bray cut him off. Man and beast glared at one another.

"You miserable beast." Luc jabbed a finger at the animal. "One more. One more stinking trap. If I can do this, so can you!" Luc snatched the rope and pulled. The mule pulled back. Luc lost. "Fine. Stay here." He tossed the lead rope over a branch and tied it tight even though he knew the stubborn animal wouldn't go far. Sensing victory, the mule munched happily at the tender shoots of green grass at the edge of a sluggish stream.

"Lazy beast. I should let the wolves have your worthless hide," Luc muttered as he picked up his rifle and swung his pack over his shoulder. Shoving his way beneath low branches, he followed a faint deer trail that edged along the stream, half hidden by the deep, shadowed thicket. His last trap. The thought cheered him considerably. This was it for him. After more than eight years in the business he was calling it quits as soon as he turned over the pile of hides his stubborn mule would love to shake off.

He sighed. His father and uncle were not going to be happy with his decision to leave the family business. Selling furs gained by trapping or trading with the Indians paid very well, but it wasn't the life Luc wanted. Unfortunately for him, each time he broached the subject of his leaving to return home to New Amsterdam, his father asked him to stay one more year.

Luc swiped low branches out of his way. One year had turned into two, then three. "No more putting it off," he said firmly. He was heading back east, though he wasn't sure where exactly. Maybe back to the city of his birth. He still had his mother's town house, and if that proved too painful to live in, he'd find a new place to settle.

Gossip among trappers boasted of many new settlements on the western border. Anything was better than wandering the godforsaken land and coating himself with the stench of death that permeated his clothing and followed him from trap to trap.

He ran a hand over his scraggly beard. He didn't even know what he looked like anymore! Luc inhaled a deep breath and tried to remember the city smells of home then burst out in a fit of choking.

"Merde!" He stumbled back from the horrendous stench that slammed into him like a brick wall. His eyes watered as he continued to cough and choke on the thick cloud of skunk. No need to wonder what animal this last trap had caught.

His eyes burned and his nose ran. The skunk that he couldn't yet see hadn't been dead long judging from the god-awful stink. It made breathing difficult.

"Dammit." Luc stood with hands jammed onto his hips.

Now what? If he abandoned the trap his uncle would tan *his* hide. If he fetched the steel trap and dealt with the lung-burning, nose-numbing skunk, he'd stink for weeks. He took another step back, then another and another. "Hell with it." He spun around and headed back the way he'd come. His uncle could take the cost of the trap out of his share of the business.

Returning to the now docile mule, Luc began the long trek back to base camp. The mule, piled high with mostly square packs of beaver pelts, along with fox, mink and a handful of buffalo robes, plodded happily along as though knowing they were done for the day. Luc followed the winding stream as it burbled and tripped over large boulders. Green ribbons of land edged the stream with patches of thick ferns growing in and around the trees. Splotches of bright summer blooms added color. Sprinkled along the path, sunlight kept the shade light and the air warm. Quiet beauty escorted him across the untamed land.

He drew in a deep breath of fresh, sweet air. As he walked, his eyes continuously scanned the shadows of trees and thick vegetation for any sign of trouble, his rifle laying across his arm, his knives, both of them within easy reach. Luc ran a hand down his side and through his buckskin shirt and felt a long puckered scar, a souvenir from a Chippewa scout he'd caught poaching his traps.

One of Luc's first hard-earned lessons: never relax and let your guard down. He'd learned the hard way that this country held plenty of trouble, from both the two-legged and four-legged variety.

Each passing hour put him closer to camp. This time tomorrow he'd be on his way home. "I'll miss this, Mule." The animal shook its head as though it didn't believe him. "Tell you what I *won't* miss." Luc gave one soft ear a light tug. "Won't miss you, you stubborn ass."

The mule bared his teeth and let out a long, loud bray. Smiling, Luc admitted that he probably would miss the stubborn beast dubbed simply as Mule. He would also miss the sheer magnificence of this wilderness, the pitting of his strength and will against that of Mother Nature. Living here, in the untamed land, made a man appreciate everything.

Born in New Amsterdam, he'd lived in a town house with his Dutch mother until her death shortly after he'd turned fourteen. His father, a French trapper, spent most winters with him and his mother telling wild stories to Luc in front of the winter fires.

His father had portrayed a world of vivid and vibrant color. The wildness, the life of the Indians and the freedom to just walk and go where one wanted had made Luc yearn to see his father's world. He'd dreamed of wrestling with a bear, hunting elk, collecting beaver and fox pelts, and most of all: seeing savages. His mother had of course refused to let Luc go with his father, even though one of Luc's younger cousins was already in the business.

But when his mother died right before his father and the rest of his family were due to set out for a new season of trapping, Luc had gotten his wish. He'd been thrilled with his first sight of Lac Superieur, and each year since, he found himself heading farther into the unexplored western frontier.

The world of trappers and trapping was exciting. There was so much to do he didn't have time to miss his old life or to be bored. He loved the outdoors, didn't mind the backbreaking work and relished the days, weeks or even months that went by without contact with another human. He'd always be grateful to the work, the time alone and the soothing yet wild beauty of this land that had helped him over his worst grief.

Pitting himself against the untamed land and surviving life in the wilderness left no room for weakness, self-pity or grief. Luc had thrived on the freedom to do as he liked, to go where he chose. He'd enjoyed the simple, down-to-the-roots lifestyle and had discovered more about himself in those first few years in the wilderness than in all his years living in the city.

Formal schooling enabled him to read and write. Life as a trapper taught him to survive. He glanced down at his worn breeches, a bit tight in the thigh and butt. Maybe he could sweet-talk his sister into making him a new pair. She'd sewn his dusty buckskin vest. In the summer heat, he wore no shirt beneath. His arms were bare and his chest gleamed with sweat.

"Ma would not have been happy, Mule." His mother had always called him her "golden boy." As well as his golden hair and deep green eyes, he had an easy charm and manner with those around him, and a will of iron. She'd had big plans for him to go become a lawyer or doctor and marry a girl worthy of his wealth. Luc sighed. Once upon a time, he'd embraced her vision of his life. These days he wasn't sure what he wanted.

Stopping, he drank fresh, clear water from his cupped hands, splashed his face, then just dunked his head in the stream. Rising to his knees, he shook the water from his head then smoothed the long, golden strands back and wiped his palms on his breeches. He stared down at his rough, calloused palms. Nothing of the golden boy remained. His hair hung halfway down his back, his once smooth jaw sported a scraggly beard, and his body had grown several inches taller. Muscle had filled him out and he was a deep shade of brown from his face to his toes.

Yes, the land had made a man of him, but now it was time for that man to do something with his life. Each year more trappers poured into the area, all competing for the prized pelts. The French and English waged wars over territory, and each year, small trading companies sprang up like thistles in a smooth, soft meadow to cause trouble to any who stepped in. The challenge was still here, as was the hard work, the reward, and his love of the land, but Luc wanted to make a difference in another way.

Picking up a smooth round stone, he took aim at a knot in a tree across the stream that was widening with each mile. Drawing back his arm, he sent the rock soaring through the air. At the soft thud of it hitting the tree he grinned, then smacked himself in the head. "Big accomplishment. You can hit a target with a stone." He shook his head at his own silliness. He could use a knife, rifle, bow and arrow, and throw rocks with deadly accuracy, but those weren't skills he'd be likely to need when he returned to city-living.

The jingle of harness and dull clanking of traps banging against each another brought Luc to his feet. Mule, tired of waiting for him, had taken off at a leisurely trot.

"Dammit, Mule! Get your ass back here. Rotten beast." Deciding it wasn't worth fighting the animal who sensed they were close to camp, Luc shrugged his pack back upon his back and grabbed his walking stick, adjusted his rifle and followed.

As the sun traveled across the sky, Luc left the stream to follow a path through a thick forest. He no longer had to pay attention to landmarks like a tree that had died, or one that had been hit by lightning, or outcrops of granite; he knew the way without even thinking. If a fire had destroyed the woods, he'd still be able to find his way to camp—and he'd had to do just that late last summer.

As he walked, the trees grew thinner. Beyond swaying branches he caught glimpses of blue. He was close. He quickened his pace and grinned when he spotted a thin stream of smoke rising into the air. Cupping his hands over his mouth, he gave a loud cry that echoed through the trees at the edge of another lake. The amazing number and sizes of the lakes in the region had once amazed him. Mule stopped to nip at a patch of tall grass growing next to the stream. Spotting people running toward him, Luc broke into a run.

"Luc! *Bienvenue à la maison.*"

Luc swung his fifteen-year-old stepsister, Kangee, around in his arms. "*Bonjour,* my little sister." He smiled into Kangee's brown and blue eyes and repeated the greeting in Lakota. "*Hola, miya tanke.*"

Kangee folded her arms across her chest. "In the time you have been gone, you have forgotten how to speak to me." Her dark eyes were full of exasperation.

Narrowing his eyes, Luc shook his head. "I said it correctly," he argued.

Shaking her head, Kangee held up one finger. "I am not your older sister." She held up a second finger. "You are male. You must call me *tanksi* as you are a male referring to your *younger* sister. *Tanke* is for a male referring to his older sister. And *miya* means me, not my. When you address me in Lakota, you should say *mitawa tanksi.*"

Luc rolled his eyes. Rules of the Lakota language were complex. Much depended on the speaker's gender, the gender of the person one was addressing with the age and relationship also thrown in. With the influx of French trappers, many of the natives of the land knew French, especially as many of the trappers married into the tribes or lived among them during the long, harsh winters.

"Say it," she demanded.

"*Chipie*," he added in French, calling her a brat. Kangee's French was much better than his Lakota, and she took her role as teacher seriously.

When she didn't so much as crack a smile, he sighed and exaggerated the pronunciation by drawing out the word. "*Mee-ta-wah.*" He tugged his stepsister's long braid and pulled her back to him.

"You will study hard while you are home." Kangee wrinkled her nose. "You have also gone long without a bath."

Luc deliberately pulled her close, pressing her into his shirt. "Skunk, sister of mine." He didn't have the heart to tell her he wouldn't be here long enough for her lessons in the way of the Sioux.

Kangee retaliated by digging her fingers into his side. Luc pulled away, barely managing to stifle his laughter. Damn, she knew he was ticklish.

"Brat," he muttered, his eyes glinting with brotherly vengeance. But the sounds of shouting drew his attention.

"Saved," he murmured.

"Yes, you are spared. This time," Kangee said, a giggle in her voice.

"Luc! Luc!"

Luc turned to greet his twin half-sisters. With a

loud roar of happiness, he reached down and scooped them into his arms. "Argh, it is ze rugrats," he growled, rubbing bearded jaw against the face of one eight-year-old, then the other.

The twins giggled and squirmed in his arms. "Monstre! Monstre!" It is ze monster man," they shrieked back.

To their delight, Luc spun them around in a fast circle until he got dizzy and fell to the ground still clutching them. Laughing, the girls collapsed on top of him. "I'm going to miss you, brats," he whispered softly in French. The thought of leaving his young sisters made him sad, for he accepted that, when he left, he probably wouldn't see them again. For a moment his determination to leave wavered. How could he leave his sisters? His father? Even his stepmother.

Eagle Woman treated him no differently from Kangee or the girls. Luc would never forget the day he and his father arrived at the Indian village where Eagle Woman gave his father a very warm welcome and had presented him with two small daughters born less than a month before. Luc, still grieving over the loss of his mother, had been angry and resentful to learn that his father had had a mistress.

Luc had felt betrayed—not just for himself, but for his dead mother who'd lived most of her life alone while his father lived the life of a trapper. But when Eagle Woman put her infant twin daughters into Luc's arms and called him the son of her heart, Luc's resentment faded.

He'd fallen in love with two of the sweetest bundles of life he could ever have imagined, and also found he could not hold a grudge against the woman who'd given his father such precious gifts.

And after he'd been introduced to Kangee, the precocious girl of eight who thought of him as her long-lost brother, his heart had truly been snatched away. Kangee idolized him, and what male could hold out against the pure love of a young girl's heart? His father and Eagle Woman had married in a simple ceremony that very night, making them all a complete family.

He held the twins close to his chest. The two had stolen his heart as infants, and leaving them now would break it. Standing above him, Kangee narrowed her eyes. Luc shook his head, wishing he hadn't voiced his regret aloud. His heart already felt ripped in two. Standing, he focused his attention on the twins who were running back toward a man and woman walking along the shoreline.

"You cannot leave." Kangee's voice was low. "Your father needs you here with him."

Luc put an arm around her shoulders and pulled her close. The top of his sister's head didn't even reach his chin. She was small and dainty and exotically beautiful. Her long black hair hung in a satin sheet down her back. She wore a belted hide dress, the yoke beaded in an intricate design. Her skirt was decorated and fringed.

She was smart and clever and had the pick of any warrior she wanted, yet she remained single. What type of man would she choose for her husband—and he had no doubt the choice would be hers. It was almost tempting to stay around to find out. Instead, he sighed with regret. "It is time. My heart is no longer in what I am doing."

Kangee nodded fiercely. "It is not right what you do."

"I do that job with care, sister of mine."

She glanced away in shame. "I know you do. Others do not."

Kangee's stand on trapping was no secret, and in Luc's heart he agreed—which was part of his decision to leave. He was tired of taking life for no other reason than to provide pelts for hats, or fur wraps or other luxury clothing.

The twins, Anika and Adrie , were miniatures of their Lakota mother with their long blue-black hair and warm, sun-bronzed skin. They ran back up to him, each holding a tiny hand of their five-year-old sister, Skye. His father had insisted on naming the twins after his Dutch aunts, twins themselves.

Skye had been named after his father's deceased baby sister who'd died in childhood. She stood with her hands behind her back. Her eyes, always so serious, were a mosaic of blues and browns. *"Mitawa tiblo."*

"Yes, your eldest brother is home." This time he used French. He wasn't giving Kangee reason to scold or correct him. He bent at the knees and picked up his youngest sibling, then stood to greet his father and stepmother.

"*Bonjour, mon pere. Bonjour, ma mère de terre.*" From his first day among his stepmother's people, he'd called Eagle Woman his earth mother. The title fit and came easily to his lips, giving her the deserved title of mother without taking it from the woman who'd given him life. Luc had also learned that the Lakota did not call each other by given name but by relation. Names were sacred and never abused thoughtlessly.

"*Hau*, my son. It is good to have you back among us." Eagle Woman hugged him warmly then stepped back with a twinkle in her jewel-like eyes. "I think you have been too long in the wilderness."

Luc laughed. "Skunk," he repeated. He eyed his father. "Caught one in the last trap. Left it behind."

Conrad Cordell slapped Luc on the back. His shaggy, graying brows shot straight up. "Would have done the same. Still, you get to tell your uncle," he said. He was nearly as tall as his son but wider in the shoulders and hips. Father and son shared the same sharply brilliant green eyes.

"Worth it, *mon pere*." Luc used a mixture of Lakota and French. French was more natural, but he tried hard to please his earth mother.

Eagle Woman laughed. "Wise choice, my son. I for one do not wish to smell skunk for the next week!"

"Let's get that mule unloaded. We're losing daylight, and your uncles and cousins have arrived." Luc's father grabbed the bridle of the mule and pulled the animal away from its grazing. With a glance at Luc it went meekly.

37

"Rotten beast," Luc grumbled. "Uncle Albert and Uncle Will aren't due for another two weeks. Luc's family usually met up several times during the season. They had several places they cached the furs until it was time to sell them. Luc hid his disappointment at the news. He'd wanted to leave immediately. No point in making it harder by putting it off. The problem was, his Uncle Albert was the undisputed head of the Cordell clan and held the reins in his iron-fisted hand. Family was important to him, and Luc would have a hell of time leaving now.

"Arrived last night. Got themselves a good load and need more trade supplies." Conrad eyed Luc's loaded mule. "Did good, Luc. This will make Al happy."

Luc fell into step with his father. Along with trapping, they relied on trading with the natives to get the valuable furs. That was his Uncle Al's area of expertise. Al traded glass beads, mirrors, awls, axes, ivory combs, tobacco, knives and colorful cloth and ribbons for furs—and for the right to enter and trap without fear of attack.

Conrad absently rubbed Mule's ear. "Come morning, you and Travers will head north. Al's taking a load downriver. Get us more supplies. We'll all meet up end of July at Eagle Woman's village."

Luc frowned. His cousin Travers wasn't skilled enough yet to be on his own. If he left, Travers would be left without a partner. "Uncle Al might need help. Travers could go with him," Luc suggested. He drew a deep breath. "I'm planning on heading east—"

Conrad shook his head. "Al's got his pals. Besides, that brother of mine has no patience." He eyed his son. "Travers needs you, son. Next season he can go it alone and you can go where you please. Al's got no patience with the boy."

Luc felt trapped as neatly as that skunk. His cousin had only been with them for one season and still had a lot to learn about surviving in the wilderness. "Uncle Al's got no patience for anything or anyone," he grumbled.

"Got that right, boy." Conrad slapped an arm across his shoulder. "Take pity on young Travers. He looks up to you. This'll give you both more time to get to know each other."

"*Mon pere*," Luc began, then stopped. His father was right. Travers wasn't much younger but he respected and looked up to Luc. He and Travers got along well—like brothers. Luc sighed. This morning his decision to leave the family business had seemed simple, but now he felt guilty. Like he was cutting off not just his own limb but that he'd be letting down others. And for what? There was no one else. No one place calling to him. Just a bottomless well of unrest.

"What is it, Luc?" Conrad stopped and stared eye to eye with his son, his big rough hands gentle on his shoulders.

Luc remembered how hard it had been to get used to his father's displays of affection. Growing up, his father had been a stranger, one who showed up periodically to tell tall tales that appealed to the boy Luc had been, but he'd never been a father. More of an uncle or a very interesting stranger. That was how Luc had always thought of the man who'd sired him. But now he could honestly say he loved this man and would miss him. Yet his father, even if he didn't realize it, needed to concentrate on his own family, and as much as Luc was welcomed and loved, he really didn't belong—but if his father knew that, he'd be hurt.

Hearing his father whistling off-key, watching the man scoop his youngest daughter into his arms, his other gentle hand guiding Mule, Luc realized he couldn't tell his father about his decision to leave now. Selfishly, he wanted to spend one last happy evening with everyone. Tomorrow was time enough to make his announcement.

With all his power, Inyan *was not content, for what use was power unless one could exercise that power over another. Thus,* Inyan *created life by opening his veins and spilling his blood.*

CHAPTER TWO

Wi shared the crystalline blue heavens with *Skan*, the Sky God. Beneath the deep blue dome of their domain lay the lush, ripening earth. Rich blues and reds, vibrant greens and bright yellows in all shades imaginable were cleverly woven together to form the tapestry of life. Each of the Superior Gods was represented in the vast array of color.

The Sun God claimed red as his color. It blazed from him, a ball of fire, the color so intense that few could gaze upon him. Heat radiated from him and would warm the earth below whenever he rose high into the sky. Today marked his longest day over this part of the world. It was the first day of summer. It was his season, his cycle, his time to rule. The rich colors below pleased him, as did the signs of life. To behold such beauty was a gift.

"A gift of my making."

The smug voice of *Maka* made *Wi* sigh. "Without my light and the warmth I bestow upon you,

you would be barren and cold." He stared down at *Maka*, the ancestress of all living things. Her deep blue lakes dotted the land, and thousands of tiny falls of water glittered like a shower of gems.

"Or too hot. All upon me would wither and die, there would be no color, no beauty." *Maka*'s voice held a haughty note. "Without me, there would be no one to see or enjoy your beauty." Her remark reminded him that at one time his heat had scorched the land. Moon had been created to give the earth relief from his unbearable heat.

"Enough," came the voice of *Skan*. His voice softened. "She needs us. It is time for her to learn the truth."

"The dreams cause her pain," *Wi* said. "Is there no other way?" Though he asked, *Wi* knew there was not. This child of his heart had to find her way alone. There were choices to make, truths to learn, and mysteries to unravel.

After a lively meal of succulent stew served with flat corn cakes, Luc and his father headed out toward a small rise in the land where his uncles were camped for the night. Mule was once again loaded and unhappy, now with twice the amount of furs he'd carried during the day. The animal would be turned over to Albert who'd take charge of the booty.

When they reached the small encampment, Luc's father strode over to join his brothers. Luc unloaded the mule and secured him for the night. "Not going to miss you," he muttered, knowing perfectly well he would. The stubborn beast shook his head and gave a soft bray.

Joining his cousins Travers and Alex around a small campfire, he drew out his knife and began sharpening it.

"Guess you and I go north, eh Luc?" Travers's tools were laid out in front of him, but he just stared into the fire.

"That's what I hear." Luc grimaced, kept his eyes on his sharpening stone and the blade of his knife. He added a noncommital grunt.

"I want to go with you and Travers," Alex said.

Travers barked with laughter at his sister. "Pa ain't gonna let you go, Alex. Not this year, not next year. Not never."

"Not fair." Alex shoved her knife back into the tooled leather sheath. "I came out here to join the business, not to sit around with a bunch of women tanning hides, sewing and cooking."

"But you sew so well, Alex." Luc fingered his clean shirt, the one Alex had made and presented to him earlier. He ducked to avoid the pebble tossed at his head. "Hey, don't blame me. I'd take you with me."

"Then ask, Luc. Ask Pa. He'll listen to you."

"Won't, Alex, and you know that." Luc did feel sorry for his cousin but he happened to agree with his uncle. Alex was far safer with Eagle Woman and her people than out tromping around in the wilderness. It wasn't the four-legged beasts her uncles and cousins were worried about, but the ones with two legs, whether white or red.

From the rear, in her baggy britches, boots, buckskin shirts similar to his own, and with her short, dark hair, she looked like a male. But from the front, there was no doubt that Alex—short for Alexis—was all woman.

He glanced over at his father and the others. Both his uncles were burly men with barrel chests, short stocky legs and thick, coarse hair that bushed around their heads. Luc and his father were taller, with slim but muscular builds. The men were engrossed in conversation with a group of rough-looking trappers from Big Bart's outfit. Several Chippewa scouts sat in a silent circle on their own.

Luc tried to listen to what was going on, but the trappers spoke in low, hushed voices. Still, their vigorous hand movements said there was something important afoot. Suspended over the fire, a hunk of venison sizzled. Fat and blood dripped into the fire, the flames flaring with each greasy contribution. The bottom of the roast looked burnt, the top raw.

Luc rubbed his eyes to ease the stinging from the smoke that had decided to change directions. He shifted to the other side of the fire. The acrid scent of burning meat made him grimace. His uncle Will was a lousy cook, either burning the food or serving it raw. The meat being cooked tonight would be packed for meals on the trail. Luc would not miss his uncle's sorry food.

Another glance at his father left Luc frustrated. He'd wanted to spend his evening with his sisters and parents, but Albert had insisted on a family meeting. So far, Luc and his cousins had been excluded from the talk. Luc was feeling antsy. The meeting taking place showed no sign of ending anytime soon, as the men were now sitting, passing around flasks of whiskey. Luc noted that his uncle Will didn't share his goods but drank freely from everyone else's flask.

Overhead, twilight was falling. His uncles' camp was on a slight rise in land with the stream winding below in a dark, fathomless ribbon. From where he sat, he could just barely see the smoke flap of his father's tipi. Though Eagle Woman's people lived in lodges during the warm summer months, when she traveled with his father, she used a hide tipi. Luc shoved his sharpened blade back into his tooled leather sheath and strapped it to his shin.

Beside him, Travers flipped his own knife into the air then caught it. Every so often he glanced down toward the tipi with a frown on his face. Sighing, he eyed Luc. "Don't suppose your sister will welcome me if I come visit?"

Coughing, Luc pulled out a second knife. This blade was already razor sharp. He didn't look at Travers. "She's probably busy with the twins. Bedtime and all. Tells her sisters stories every night."

"Tells me stories, too," Travers grumbled.

"Yeah, like she's too busy or too tired to talk to you," Alex tossed in, sisterly glee in her voice.

Travers grabbed his knife by the blade and tossed it. The sharp tip dug into the ground just in front of

Alex. He smirked. "Do something useful and sharpen that."

Luc narrowed his eyes. "You know the rules, Travers. We each take care of our own tools and chores. That knife might save your life. Take care of it yourself."

Travers frowned. "Hey, she makes you clothes. Seems fair that she helps me out once in a while."

Alex glared at her brother. "Don't need you to stick up for me, Luc," she said. She grabbed the knife and with a quick flick of her wrist sent it flying. It landed with a thud in the trunk of the tree, inches from her brother's head.

Travers jumped to his feet. Luc followed suit. He grabbed his cousin by the arm. His glare included Alex. "Knock it off, both of you."

Alex got to her feet and shoved them apart. A good deal shorter, she was slim as a willow but tough as a reed. The sheen of temper in her gray eyes made both men back away. "Think I'll tell some stories of my own to your sisters—like, men are rotten." She brushed past them and headed down the hill toward the tipi.

"Good job. Pissed her off for sure," Luc said.

"Women!" Travers stowed his gear and stomped off in the opposite direction.

Sighing, Luc knew he'd been right. Travers had a long way to go before he could survive on his own. Eyeing the roasting meat with disgust, he turned to his uncles. "Meat's burning, Uncle Will."

William Cordell glanced over his shoulder. He

said, "Done when I says it's done." And he went back to his drinking and smoking.

Luc walked over and gave the spit a good turn. There was no use ruining perfectly good meat, though the hunk looked like his uncle had used it for target practice.

Albert and William ambled over. Albert wrinkled his nose at the burning carcass, then eyed the butchered hide tossed over a shrub. "Figure after all these years you'd be better at dressing your catch."

"Don't care what it looks like, Al. Just gonna eat it." William plopped down and rested his head against the same tree where Travers had sat.

Glaring at his brother, Albert pointed a stubby finger. "I care about the hides, William. You're getting sloppy again. Ruining too many. Not a tenderfoot anymore," he complained.

William fell into a sullen silence. Albert could be a mean son-of-a-bitch, especially when it came to business.

"Got to beat Dangerous Dan's outfit this year," he went on. He fixed them all with his bushy brows raised, his lips drawn into a tight line. "Hear that? I want to beat his ass this year. No more sloppy work." He ran a hand through his wild, bushy hair.

"Getting Jim and the rest of Bart's group to help us is cheating but clever," Conrad said. "Not sure I trust them, though. Pretty scrubby bunch, that one. Don't trust them scouts neither."

Albert waved aside all concerns. "Long as we win, it don't matter. Lot's riding on this bet." He glanced around, frowning. "Where's my boy?" Once more he touched his head. And where the hell is my hat!" His gaze roamed the camp.

Luc shrugged. "Travers left." He noticed that the other trappers and scouts were gone, too. He wished he'd left when his cousins had, but he'd wanted to catch his father on the way back to talk privately.

"I can see that for myself, boy! Called this meeting for a reason." He glared at Luc as though it were Luc's fault that his cousins had given up on him, but he paced, something Luc knew he did when he was about to hand out orders. Sure enough, he began outlining Luc and Travers's routes for the next two months.

"Shouldn't we wait until Travers is here?" he spoke up.

Albert fisted his hand and slammed it into his palm. "He ain't here, boy, now is he? You tell him. The two of you leave at sunrise."

Luc stood. He *was* leaving at sunrise, just not to head north as his uncle wanted. He was heading east.

"Where you going, boy?" Albert gripped a flask in his big, meaty hand.

"Bed." He'd talk to his father in the morning.

"Sit your ass down. Not finished. Heard Dan has got a mighty fine haul going so far. Big Jim found some new waterways. Lots of beaver. Got me some maps." He tossed Luc a hand-drawn map on a small square of parchment. "Don't give it to Travers. Son of mine will lose it for sure." He dismissed Luc and turned to William.

"William, you and me are gonna—"

Luc reached across and handed his uncle back the map. "Going to have to give this to Travers yourself, uncle. Come morning, I'm leaving. Going back home."

Silence fell over the group. Everyone looked shocked. Luc knew it was due more to his interrupting his uncle than his announcement. Red-faced, Albert stood, swayed a moment then stomped over to Luc and thumped him hard in the chest. "Not going anywhere, boy. Yer part of zis family. Cordell men stick together. Got too much invested in you to let you go running back home."

The usually smooth, fluent French had begun to slur with drink and temper. "And fer what? Got nothin' back there. Better off here. Land'll make a man of you."

Luc put out a hand to stop another thump. "I'm not a boy, uncle," he said quietly. "I make my own decisions. I'm done with trapping."

The moment the words were out of his mouth, a huge weight floated off his shoulders. He was truly free. He was doing it. He was going home. He wasn't sure exactly where home was at the moment, but it wasn't trekking from here to there in the wildness and never arriving anywhere.

Crossing his arms on his chest, his feet spread wide, he glanced down at his father. "I'm sorry, *mon pere*. I wanted to tell you earlier."

His father walked over to him, then clapped him on the shoulder. His eyes were dark and sad. "Knew this day was coming. Been seeing it in your eyes and didn't want to admit the time had come."

"You're not mad?" Luc felt another vast load leave him—this one from his heart. He'd been afraid that he'd hurt his father's feelings or cause a fight between them.

Sputtering angrily, Albert fisted his hands. "Conrad, don't encourage the boy. He can't quit. Not *now*."

"Boy's made up his mind, Al." Luc's father fingered a small green stone hanging from a cord around his neck. "Can't blame the boy when I feel the same." Conrad sighed. " 'Fraid this makes two of us, Al. I'm taking my family home. Eagle Woman misses her family, and truth to tell, my heart's just not in this anymore." He smiled sadly at Luc. "Never saw much of my first wife, missed seeing my boy grow up. Don't want to be away from my girls."

Luc and his father slapped shoulders in a tight, hard hug. Luc said, "My mother gave me a good life, and I always looked forward to your visits. But it wasn't the same, like what the girls have with you. They deserve to have you with them every day." He wasn't bitter or resentful. Just happy that his father understood, and happy for his sisters. They adored their father. "I'll miss them. And you."

Albert's voice rose to a roar. "It's the middle of ze season! I forbid either of you to leave." He jabbed another finger into Luc's chest. "And you, zis is all your doing."

Luc's father grabbed Albert's hand. "Leave the boy be, Al. You heard him: He wants out and so do I. You can keep the traps, keep our share of this last haul. Got yourself more trappers working for you. Losing us won't make any difference."

"Conrad! We are family. Raised you and William. We've always stuck together. The Cordells against the world. I'm not going to let you go!" He kicked one wood fork adjacent to the fire. The spit fell, and the fire flared as the meat went up in flames.

Albert's face was red with anger, but Luc's father was calm. "Mind's made up, Al. See you in the morning before you head out." He turned to Luc and jerked his head. Luc fell into step, wincing at the sound of cursing behind them.

He felt bad. "I'm sorry, *mon pere*, I didn't mean to break it this way."

"Tried to tell me earlier, didn't you?" Conrad led the way along the edge of the pine-covered hillside.

"Yeah, but I just couldn't do it." Luc shoved his hands deep into the pockets of his breeches. The two men walked shoulder to shoulder in companionable silence. Dried leaves crunched beneath their feet, and the air was heavily scented by the pines.

They continued snaking around brush and the thick trunks until they stood on the very edge of the gulch. The valley spread out in purple hues below. Luc's father shoved his hands down onto his hips.

"I'll miss you, Luc. Been great having you at my side." He glanced at his son. "Don't make up for all the years I missed, boy, and for that I'm sorry."

Luc laughed. "Ma would never have lasted living out here, and you and city life are like oil and water." It was sad but the truth.

"True. Guess you take after your ma. Fine woman, my Annie. Fine woman."

Luc heard the regret and sadness, and sought to give his father some measure of comfort. "She was content," he said. And it was true, he supposed. Growing up, Luc had never truly understood how his mother could be content away from her husband. But she was.

"She had you, boy. You were all that woman ever needed."

Luc glanced sideways at his father. "She loved you." But he knew his father was right. His mother hadn't seemed to need a man in her life. Between her charities and her son, she'd been plenty busy.

"Yeah, loved each other, we did. Luc—"

Luc stopped his father. "You have a new family. This is where you belong. I don't." He watched his father rub the stone hanging around his neck.

"What about Kangee? Girl's sweet on you."

Luc rolled his eyes. "Kangee is sweet on every man she meets," he said dryly. At fifteen, his stepsister was eager to start her own family.

"Was sure hoping the two of you would hit it off." Luc's father shrugged. "But I guess I can't have everything." He continued to absently finger the stone around his neck. "Girl can sure cook, though. Her mama taught her well."

"Eagle Woman is special, and so is Kangee. They

both deserve husbands who can share their lives completely." Luc met his father's startled gaze then frowned. He hadn't meant to let on that he knew just how special his father's family was.

Luc's father stared, stuck the stone back beneath his shirt. He remained silent so long, Luc figured he was upset. "Don't worry. I won't say anything," he muttered. He didn't want his father angry—not now, not when he was on the brink of leaving.

"How long have you known?"

Relief flooded Luc. He stared up into the sky. The stars were becoming visible as the light of day faded. "A while." He leaned against the tree at the edge of the ridge, its roots a dark tangle jutting from the earth. "Was out in the woods. Saw you and Eagle Woman." He shook his head and added, "Don't mind saying you scared the hell out of me when you turned into a wolf." He rubbed his shoulders against the bark as he remembered just how shaken that experience had left him. That was the stuff of nightmares, or stories meant to scare children. No one could change shape—but he'd seen it with his own two eyes and still wasn't sure how he felt about it. It just seemed strange. And unnatural. Yet undeniably real. He let out his breath. If his father was happy, then that was good enough for him. He didn't need to know or understand more than that.

Luc's father stared out toward where smoke still curled up into the sky from his tipi. "You didn't say anything."

"No. But she knew." Luc shrugged. "Eagle Woman sat me down the next day and told me that she was a SpiritWalker, and that you, through her, were one as well." He pointed to the stone around his father's neck.

Conrad sighed. "Is that why you want to leave?"

Luc debated lying, then sighed. "Part of it. Not all. The whole thing is a bit strange." He winced. "Okay, very strange—but it works for you. A blind man could see that you're happy, so that makes me happy too." In truth, he found it very unsettling to know that there were people who could shift shapes by merging their spirits with that of animals.

He kept to himself the fact that many nights he'd lain awake, waiting and watching for his parents to return from their "walks." He'd seen owls fly and swoop overhead, heard the crashing of wolves in the brush and their playful barks and known it was his father and earth mother. One year, while staying with Eagle Woman's people for a few weeks, Luc had come across a bear rolling on the ground a short ways from their village. Eager for the hunt, he'd lifted his rifle. Then the bear had gotten up and ambled off, changing into a warrior. Luc had been shaken and found it harder and harder to trap and kill. Deep inside was the fear that one day he'd take the life of a SpiritWalker. Or, God forbid, one of his own family. How could he ever know?

His father's voice called him back. "Son, I didn't mean to exclude you. Guess I was afraid that if you knew the truth you'd hit the trail faster than a jackrabbit, or that if you stayed, you wouldn't love your sisters the way you do."

Smiling, Luc shoved his hands onto his hips. "Love them with all I've got, *mon pere*. Never wanted to be what I wasn't. Still don't."

"What *do* you want, Luc?" His father now stood in full shadow. A warm breeze rustled the leaves above their head, and the branches of the thick brush at their back.

Luc shrugged. "Not sure. Guess that's why I got to go. Need to find a place where I fit. Where I belong." Drawing in a deep breath, he rolled the tension from his shoulders. "Can we wait until tomorrow to tell my sisters?" He didn't expect his father to not tell Eagle Woman; in fact, it wouldn't surprise him to learn that she had known long before Luc had. She often felt or saw future events.

"We'll tell everyone tomorrow." Conrad gave his son a determined look. "Think you can stay another day or two—give your sisters some time with you before you go?"

Now that it was settled, Luc agreed. "Okay. Going to walk for a bit. See you back at camp." He needed a few minutes alone before he faced his earth mother and sisters. He wanted to be able to burst into the tipi and be "ze monstre man" without any tears. He left his father standing at the edge of the gulch. As he walked away he heard low chanting. He didn't turn his head, didn't need or want to see his father fall from the ravine as a man and soar away as an owl.

Neither Luc nor his father saw the face hidden

deep in the shadows behind the thick shrub or the wide eyes of the man who'd heard every word spoken between them. His gaze stayed focused on the owl soaring across the dark sky.

Far below the sphere of fire that was *Wi*, a pack of wolves lay sprawled in a patch of morning sun at the base of a rocky cliff. Two fluffy gray and black pups frolicked and tumbled over the sparse brown grass, another settled at his mother's breast, while the last pup lay trapped beneath his mother's front paw, her tongue roughly bathing his face while he yipped and struggled for freedom.

A large eagle swept in low over the pups. Immediately, the pack came to life. The alpha pair, along with the rest of the pack sprang to all fours, teeth bared, hackles raised. The bald eagle let out a shrill cry and soared out over the stream.

Sitting a short distance away, Blaze watched. Though nature often took a course that was heartwrenching, she understood the cycle of life, of one form dying so another could live. Last year the eagle had been successful in snatching a young pup from the wolf pack. She sighed with relief that this year the pack was guarding its young better.

Spotting her, two of the pups ran over. The mother watched intently but didn't move. Blaze had a way with animals. They weren't afraid of her, and often showed up when they were injured or sick. Like the mother wolf who'd needed help delivering her young.

Completely unafraid, the pair jumped into her

lap. Blaze sighed and hugged the furry bodies briefly and smiled. How could one not smile when holding a warm, cuddly pup? Their lack of fear, their innocent trust and their unconditional love eased some of her heartache while at the same time was a harsh reminder that these innocent creatures gave of their own free will what her own people could not.

She nuzzled her face against one pup. "My own people are afraid of me. They fear the very gift that brought you into the world." She set the wiggling pup down and watched the pair run back to their pack.

Blaze rested her cheek against her drawn-up knees. Her head and body ached with exhaustion, but no matter how tired she became she would not give in to the need to sleep. She didn't dare close her eyes for fear that the images would return to haunt her daytime hours.

A low whine drew her attention. The mother wolf appeared beside her. Blaze smiled sadly. "You are right. Sitting here feeling sorry for myself is of no use to anyone." She reached out and stroked the wolf's head. "I just do not know what to do. What do these dreams mean?" The animal walked back to her children then turned to stare at Blaze with wise eyes.

The child is the key. The words swept through Blaze's mind. She drew in a deep breath. She remembered her conversation with the old woman and called back to mind the dreams. It had started with an innocent child, and at the end, that innocence had been shattered—the child had changed forever.

But did this child exist? And if so, where? How could Blaze find her? *Follow your heart.* Blaze put a hand to her chest and felt the small leather bag given to her by Wise Owl. She pulled the clear stone from the pouch and held it up to the sunlight. She studied the patterns in the smoky-white center. Last night it had looked completely clear. In the sunlight, she saw four tiny golden flecks that hung like stars trapped in the crystal.

"You are a special stone," she murmured as light fell on one flat surface and radiated through the crystal, bringing it to life. She felt something in the crystal, some greatness, a power that seeped into her and sang in her veins.

Ancient life.

"What is your purpose?" she asked as she watched the center come alive. She focused. Visions often came to her on shiny surfaces, things she could see and others could not. Many times a vision was her first warning that she was needed in the village.

She focused on her questions. The clouds inside the crystal seemed to move and change color until, finally, there in the center of the stone, there sprang the image of a broad-shouldered, narrow-hipped buckskin-clad trapper with golden-brown hair. One of the stars pulsed over his heart.

Holding her breath, Blaze brought the crystal closer to her face. She couldn't see what he looked like, just the shape of a face, but as though he felt her gaze upon him, he turned his head toward her and Blaze couldn't help her gasp of amazement. His face became clearer until that was all she could see. It was like looking into a mirror and seeing the face of another.

His eyes were a rich, warm green like the thick carpet of ferns growing in the deepest shade of the forest. His face was covered with hair as most trappers seemed want to wear it, but his mouth was firm and his nose long and straight. But his eyes drew her again, mesmerized her. They were deep pools of soothing green.

"Who are you?" Her voice was a soft whisper.

The stranger stared into her eyes then his image grew smaller. He held out one arm. Long fringe swung back and forth and his fingers curled out and toward her.

"Help me."

Blaze stood absolutely still. She'd never heard voices in her visions. Often she heard the voices of spirits or gods when she called upon them for counsel or sought healing knowledge. But the deep voice of the trapper came to her as though he were standing beside her. It vibrated through her heart and soul.

She ran a finger over the side of the crystal. "How? Who are you?" An urge to go and find this man overcame her. She stared into his green eyes, saw the pain, the despair; then he began to fade.

"No, don't go!" But he was gone, locked deep inside the nearly translucent crystal. A wave of loneliness slammed against her hard, leaving her bereft as if he'd taken something from her. "I don't know where to find you." She ran her fingers along the sides of the crystal. "Come back," she whispered.

Nothing happened. Blaze dropped her hands to her sides and noticed that the wolves were gone, leaving her truly alone. She stared at the crystal sitting on her palm then dropped it back into the tiny pouch. For just a moment she'd felt a connection to someone. Now she was abandoned.

The sun was directly overhead as she made her way back to the spine of rock where she made her home. Blaze started up the narrow path that led up the slice of rock that separated stream from lake. There were two accessible paths to the top: this one from the west, which was not much more than a series of hand- and footholds that sloped upward, and a passage from the south, close to the main entrance of her cave.

Halfway up, she turned, balanced easily on a narrow shelf and stared out at the forest below, a river of sharp pointed treetops. Narrow trees, wide spreading canopies and everything in between for as far as she could see. Greens, all shades from light, dark and the blue-greens, all blended with the browns of trunks and branches and ripening cone-shaped fruit.

The stream followed the arm of stone as it wended its way out of sight. On the opposite bank stood a lone dead tree with a giant eagle nest. It rose high above the forest. Wider than the tallest warrior in her tribe and twice his depth, it was larger than the main room of her cave. It had been there as long as she could remember, with the same pair of eagles mating and raising eaglets year after year.

The gentle breeze played with her hair as she watched the female eagle return to the nest and drop a flopping fish down for the hungry eaglet that flapped its brownish black wings and danced around the fish as though trying to figure out the best way to tear into it.

Continuing her upward climb, Blaze used her hands to pull herself up the hard rock wall and steady her balance. After reaching the nearly flat top, she walked across to the other side. From this vantage point, the lake was a blue shimmer for as far as the eye could see. She heard the sound of the twin falls where some of the water from the stream found its way through the rock and fed the lake.

Inside the tree line, the tops of bark-covered lodges were just visible. Out farther, in a cleared part of the forest, a neat garden thrived, and from her height, the women and children tending the corn, squash and beans looked tiny.

Picking up a tiny pebble Blaze absently rubbed it between her fingers as she watched the small figures working in the distance. Every once in a while the wind carried to her the sound of laughter. Blaze sighed. She missed working in the gardens and often thought of defiantly returning to do her share. She loved digging in the warm, rich soil, feeling the primitive hum of life that came from mother earth. She yearned to be able to immerse herself in the circle of life. The planting of seeds, caring for them as they grew into mature plants. The harvesting of their fruits ending their life cycle but helping to sustain another.

In the end, all life returned to the soil to begin the cycle anew.

She sighed. Women nurtured life. They tended to their families, their gardens, their home. Blaze had no one to nurture, and no one to nurture her. She relied on herself, and the spirits.

Of all the things she missed or yearned for it was working in the gardens, being part of that cycle, sharing the laughter, the stories and companionship with other women in her village. But she no longer ventured down there, not since being blamed for the high winds of a summer storm that had flattened the corn and torn blossoms off the squash plants. She'd only meant to scare the girls who were being mean to her, but somehow, without meaning to, she'd called up the Wind Spirit. The wind had roared over her head and flattened the gardens and made everyone run.

Tossing a stone off the cliff, Blaze still felt ashamed. She'd never intended to destroy precious food or cause a major fright. She'd just wanted to get a bit of her own back by making those girls think she was going to do something to them.

She turned away from the gardens. The days following that wind storm had been nearly unbearable. No one talked to her, or even looked at her, and when they did, their eyes held fear. Her father had been furious as well. That was when he'd banished her from their lodge and sent her to this cave to live. Only the old shaman spoke to her. *Those with sacred gifts must learn to exercise them wisely.*

Blaze remembered telling the shaman that she didn't want her gifts, sacred or otherwise. She'd only ever wanted to be like everyone else. But he'd only shaken his head at her. *It is not for us to want but to accept and follow our paths. Learn to live with who you are and you will master your future.*

"Future!" Blaze continued to walk along the long spine of rock that snaked out, separating the fast moving stream from the calm body of water to her right. She'd come to accept, as much as one could, that she had no real future, but she'd also never forgotten the lesson learned that day: control your emotions. Not just anger, but everything. It was easier. Safer, for her as well as her people.

She didn't know why she was different, but since that day she'd tried hard to accept that she was unlike anyone else. A truce of sorts now existed. Blaze kept out of the gardens and village as much as possible, coming to aid the injured or sick whenever her father, the tribe's medicine man, asked for her assistance. In return, her people provided her with everything she needed. Food, furs, hides and other items needed for survival were left for her in the hollow roots of a giant pine at the base of the ridge of rock she called home. Once in a while she found a beautifully beaded pouch or a quilled pair of moccasins.

Turning from the sight of the village, Blaze wended her way down to the entrance to her home.

The main cavern was barely tall enough at the center for her to stand and move about comfortably. Tanned hides, fur robes and leather parfleches, some plain, some beaded, hung on the walls. A fire pit and altar took up the center flooring with her cooking utensils and other implements along the sides.

The cave narrowed at the back, the walls curving downward as though a fist had struck the molten rock. Large indentations like knuckle prints had been left in the nearly smooth back wall. Some of the natural shelves held her drying herbs, others held stones or feathers or rolls of hide.

To one side, in a natural dip, her neatly made pallet lay against the wall. She ignored her need for sleep and strode to the other side. Here, nature had stacked huge boulders from floor to ceiling.

Blaze slipped between two boulders into a tiny alcove. Beams of sunlight filtered in through a crack near the ceiling. A cool breeze entered. The tiny stone room was barely wide enough for one person to stand. It hummed with life and, needing to feel that surge of life, she rested her hand on a boulder. The ancient rock with its ancient energy made her palm tingle.

Some of the tension drained from her. On a natural ledge at eye level, several stones gleamed. Some were polished to a shine, others were raw hunks of rock. Blaze gave herself over to the need to touch her stones, and connect with the healing vibrations each held. She touched a smooth, red oval with a squiggly line etched deep into it. This rock represented the force of life.

A perfectly round, nearly flat and unpolished plain brown rock had a medicine wheel painted in red dots covering its surface. The dots formed the circle with a smaller circle of seven dots in the middle to represent the seven stars, or seven arrows. Blaze touched four dots: fear, courage, love and sorrow. The other three she had yet to name.

A sudden angry vibration swept through the cave, startling her. Blaze spun around, her hand going instinctively to the boulders, her body tuning in to the waves of sound. Raw emotion coursed through the rock into her.

She ran back to the entrance. The air crackled with the heavy sound of drumming and threw her momentarily back into her nightmares when the world around the child flared with the sound, with the lightning and thunder crashing into the world with spectacular and frightening intensity.

Blaze fought to separate dream and reality. This was no dream. This was real. The fierceness of the drums buckled the air and warned that something was wrong in her village. From where she stood, Blaze could not see what.

Calling upon the spirit of the wind, she sent her senses flaring out on the now briskly moving air. Seeking answers, she tipped her nose up and sniffed the air like a wolf or deer.

Sounds, smells and waves of emotions came at her, carried by *Tate*, the Wind Spirit. Blaze gripped her head. Too much, too fast. Her heart pounded as her mind struggled to separate the wealth of information in the air: the ominous drumming—a call to action; the wailing, chanting and weeping that rose to a high, desperate pitch. Inhaling a deep breath, she flared her nostrils. The air carried on it the sacred aroma of sage and cedar, and—

She bent over at the unexpected scent of blood mingled with putrid, festering flesh. The stench drove her to her knees. "Death." The wind carried death to her. She fought the sickness in her stomach. Then she heard the whistle, the pitch so high few could hear. But she heard it. This was her summons to come and heal.

"No. Can't do this." Her mind was filled with warring thoughts and fears. The child. The man with green eyes and this, all on top of no sleep for several nights. Her body felt weak with exhaustion and scattered in too many directions.

She wanted to run from death, run from demands made on her by human and spirit. Deep in the cool cavern beneath her feet was a place she could go and hide from others, but not from the calling deep in her soul. These people were not friends. She owed them nothing, but her very nature would not allow her to turn her back on anyone in need. Including a child surrounded by death, and a trapper with green eyes who begged her to help him.

Blaze got shakily to her feet and, with her hand on the stone entrance, she drew courage and strength from ancient rock, from the very essence of *Inyan*, ancestor of all gods and all things. Searching the sky above her head, she spotted a soaring eagle. Smaller than the female, she knew it was the male. Blaze lifted her hands, her fingers pointing sharply skyward.

"Hoye wa yelo." I am sending a voice.

"Spirit of anunkasan."

"Your vision I need. So I may see who calls for me."

"Mitakuye Oyasin." All my relations.

She sent out her plea, her need for assistance coming not just from her mind but from the heart. She imagined her prayer, her request for assistance, winging skyward on the soft breeze. The eagle dove toward her. Their gazes met and, in an instant, she felt his acceptance, his invitation. In less than half a heartbeat, her spirit merged with the spirit of the eagle. The two became as one within its body.

For just a moment, Blaze felt disoriented and breathless as the world dropped away below her. Her vision and hearing immediately sharpened. Leaves and blades of grass came into sharp focus, the song of life upon the earth below mingled with running water falling onto rock and stone. Even the calm summer breeze seemed to howl loudly in her head.

The lightning-quick change in sound, sight, smell was almost too much to bear. Merging her spirit with that of another always gave her a momentary panic. But as she circled high over the ridge of rock, the feeling of free flight calmed and soothed.

The wind now sang softly in her ears, slid silkily over her body, cushioning her from beneath, cupping her in its gentle breath as she flew over the glittering fall of water. The world from high above was a rainbow of color: greens, blues, browns and reds woven together to form a blanket of amazing beauty.

The temptation to just give herself over to the simple joy of free flight, to soar over the forest canopy and seek the tall mountains so far away was an overwhelming temptation. Whenever she mind-merged with a winged one, she had to be careful. It would be too easy to let herself go, to forget about the world below and just float free from the troubles and worries that plagued her daily.

Blaze dipped low over her earth-bound body. A wave of sadness engulfed her as she stared down at her silent and still flesh with arms outstretched, eyes closed, lips softly parted. She looked like a doll with her long hair streaming out behind her and the fringe on her skirt, sleeves and yoke swaying in the afternoon breeze.

Loneliness clung to her like moss to rock. An ache rose from deep inside. When had she not felt lonely? Or *different?* No one else she knew could merge spirits with hawk, eagle or owl and fly freely through the sky. She had no one to share how it felt to become as one with the sharp and cunning mind of a wolf, to run sure-footed through the woods or scamper high into the treetops merged with a chattering squirrel.

Once, as a young girl, she'd made the mistake of asking her father how to fly with the birds. Not just a mind merge, but to actually fly. In her heart she'd known it was possible, but her father had cut her off and forbidden her to ever speak of such things. Blaze never understood why he'd been so upset that day five winters past. She only knew that over the years, his indifference had given way to resentment and finally to hate. She'd always believed it was because her mother had died during childbirth.

A fist of raw grief hit her hard as she remembered the child in her dreams and the dead bodies of the girl's parents. Her vision blurred. She faltered, felt herself sliding from the bird's body like water over rocks.

His powers were his blood; his blood was blue. Inyan gave so much of himself to create life that all his blood flowed from his veins until he shrank, becoming hard and powerless.

CHAPTER THREE

Focus!

The voice came from nowhere and everywhere. Blaze obeyed now as she'd always obeyed that voice. It echoed not just in her mind but resonated through her heart and soul.

Focusing on keeping her spirit merged with that of the eagle, keeping her intent and need centered, she gave herself over to the spirit of the bird. Silently, she communicated her need. The bird flew close to the canopy of trees.

Individual leaves came into sharp focus and the immediate absence of all birdsong told Blaze that the smaller birds had spotted the eagle. In another tree she spotted a brown bear climbing toward a hive of bees. Then a group of longhouses came into view. Each wooden structure with bark walls and bark roofs formed the spoke of a great wheel and, in the center, the scene that met her eyes made concentration difficult.

Many of the warriors entering the village had injured men slung over their shoulders. Many more limped into the village center on their own where they were met by family members who led them to the various longhouses.

Women in their soft hide dresses and long black braids moved among the injured warriors. Voices were loud and shrill as they shouted orders. In contrast, the normally noisy children stood silent, hanging back, staying out of the way. Blaze circled the village, her sharp gaze focused on four warriors each bearing the weight of a pole on their shoulders. Strips of leather had been woven across the poles to form a litter for two who were dead.

The poles were lowered and the warriors walked away, their shoulders stiff, their faces grim with suppressed emotion. Screaming erupted behind them from a woman kneeling beside one of the dead men. She lifted her hands high then grabbed strands of hair, yanking it from her head. Her keening cry rose over the chorus of weeping and lamenting. It was a cry every mother understood and felt in the deepest reaches of her heart and soul.

Grief fused with anger, and fueled by the heavy heartbeat of the drums, choked the perfection of the summer day. Emotions rose like a cloud, coming at Blaze in huge, crashing waves. The pain hit her like a fist to her middle. She cried out. The eagle gave a loud shriek and shot straight up like an arrow aimed at the sun.

Blaze felt her mind sliding from the bird's as their

spirits were abruptly parted. She tumbled through a rushing stream of dark blues and violets then slammed back into her body. The uncontrolled return of mind and spirit caused pain and dizziness. Disoriented, she stumbled to her feet, swayed and lost her balance.

Crying out as she tumbled down the incline that led from forest up into her cave, she flung out her arms and grabbed the trunk of a stunted pine. Gasping, she lay there, breathing hard as pain shot through her back, arms and legs. Above her head, the eagle circled, as though concerned.

Staring up at the bird, pain wracked Blaze's mind and body. She hadn't lost control during a spirit merge in years, and had forgotten how painful and dangerous the return of spirit to body could be. "I am fine, my friend. Thank you for sharing your gift of flight and vision."

Cuts and bruises were a small price to pay for losing concentration. A spirit-mind merge required absolute concentration, and that was twice in one day that she'd failed to keep herself under rigid control.

Rubbing her eyes with her fingers, she knew it was more than lack of sleep. She felt restless, on edge. And unhappy, she admitted. She wanted acceptance, and not just from her people. She needed it from herself as well, but how could she accept herself when she had no idea what she was? Blaze brushed the dirt and leaves from her hair and arms then stood. Her legs felt weak and shaky as she concentrated on the calming beauty of the deep blue lake.

Precious moments were lost while she slowed the beat of her heart and the racing of her blood, but until she was calm, she'd be of no use to the injured. Of course, the injured didn't have time to wait, could not be held off until she was steady on her feet, so she rested one bloodied palm against the trunk of a tree.

"*Canpaza. Mitakuye oyasin*. We are relatives," she repeated. "Share with me the gift of life that runs beneath your bark. Impart to me your strength. Let my legs carry me to meet the needs of my people." Beneath her fingers, she felt the hum of life. The vibrations of the tree's essence traveled up her hand, arm, into her heart, mind and legs, sharing with her its towering strength.

Pausing for a moment, Blaze took a pinch of sacred sage from a tiny medicine pouch and sprinkled her heartfelt gift at the base of the tree, her thanks for the infusion of strength. Then, from the same leather bag, she removed a tiny gleaming river stone that she'd polished with her hands, using her deep connection to *Inyan*, ancestor of all gods and all things. This she tossed high into the air.

"From Earth I took you. To Earth you return."

The rays of the sun made the stone sparkle as it began its downward arc. The Spirits of Earth and Sky would see her show of appreciation, then one of her own people would find the rock and think it a powerful totem.

Blaze didn't return to her cave to gather her healing herbs, rocks or supplies. There was no time. She ran down the worn path to where rock met forest. There, a huge pine had fallen many winters before. A third of the dead tree lay in the water. She jumped down onto it and ran along its long length.

The huge, hollowed root ball lay exposed just inside the tree line. She climbed down; then, taking a deep breath, she brought forth the image of *mastinca* to her mind and called upon the Spirit of Rabbit to lend her speed and agility as she ran through the tangled and cool forest. She entered the village compound and, though she was prepared for the frenetic scene of death and injury, the force of primitive emotion brought her to an abrupt halt.

The drumming, the shrill wails and angry shouts increased with each warrior pronounced dead. Her heart pounded with each beat of taut leather drums. Moving quickly, she shoved her way past injured warriors being led or carried to their lodges by their relatives.

The two dead bodies had grown to four. The slain men were surrounded by grief-stricken women and grim-faced sons and brothers. Blaze stared around her. So many injured, so many who needed her healing skills. Focusing her mind, she sought the worst of the hurt. Turning in a slow circle, oblivious to the hush spreading among the grieving, she spotted a young warrior lying in the bright light of the overhead sun. A shield made from the shell of a turtle lay next to him.

Walks Like Turtle was cousin to their chief. She felt an urge to go to him. Obeying, she hurried over. Two warriors stepped in front of her, feet planted, arms crossed in front of their massively muscled chests. Their nearly black eyes radiated grief and fury. They were relatives standing guard over their brother.

"Let me pass." Blaze narrowed her eyes, unsurprised to see a flicker of fear enter each warrior's dark eyes. She shifted her attention to her father, who was kneeling beside Walks Like Turtle.

Red Thunder wore the skin of a bear, complete with head. Bear represented medicine, so her father always wore the pelt to help carry his medicine to those in need. Slashes of red paint streaked down the middle of the hide as well as on Red Thunder's face, hands and chest. He rose.

With each step, the circlets of bone around each of his ankles and each of his wrists, along with those layered around his neck, rattled. In one hand he held a gourd rattle, in the other he carried a carved stick with feathers attached by long leather thongs.

This imposing figure stepped between the warriors. Framed by two of the village's largest and strongest men, Blaze's father sent her a sharp glare and pulled his lips back into a snarl. "Leave. You were not summoned."

The fierceness of his pelt was enough to make most obey him instantly, but not Blaze. Around his neck, along with all his other tools of healing, was an eagle bone whistle that he used to summon her to his side when he needed her gifts.

Staring up into her father's cold and forbidding eyes, Blaze stood her ground. "I was summoned. If not by you then by the gods, the souls of the injured." She indicated the groaning men waiting to be tended. "It is their pain and grief that brought me here. Without me, many more will die."

"They would rather die than have you touch them," her father said.

Blaze ignored the pang of hurt his words caused. Without doubt what he said was true, but she was equally determined to do what she could to save lives. She shoved past her father and stared down at the bloodied body of the fallen warrior.

The sight that met her gaze made her suck in a breath. Gaping wounds in his abdomen, blood leaking from chest wounds, and numerous other injuries to his body made her step back with a cry.

"You can do nothing here. No one can. The spirits have taken his soul, and soon his body will leave this world. Not even your magic can save this one. He is dead."

Blaze shrugged her father's hand from her shoulder. Kneeling beside the warrior, she rubbed her palms together then held out her hands, palms down, one over his bloodied head, the other inches from the wounds over the warrior's heart. Closing her eyes, she concentrated on and sought the thread of life.

Her palms tingled lightly and grew warm. Opening her eyes, concentrating on the warrior's head, she made out the faint aura of his spirit still clinging to his body. Without taking her eyes off the warrior, she spoke: "His spirit remains."

Red Thunder strode to the warrior's other side. He reached down to shove Blaze aside, but when her eyes burned a hot blue, he backed away. "Do not give false hope. He cannot be healed." He lifted his hands. The bits of teeth and bone wrapped around his wrists and upper arms rattled, and his voice rose in a death chant.

The warrior's mother collapsed in a heap beside her son. Blaze glared at her father. "There is always hope. I can save him."

Though you could not and would not swallow your pride to even ask me to try. The words hung between father and daughter.

Red Thunder looked furious. "I forbid it! There are others who need my help. You are here, you will assist me with them." He motioned to the two warriors, who stepped toward Blaze.

Turning her eyes fully to the warriors, she let her anger fill her eyes. She'd been named Blaze because strong emotion caused her eyes to turn to blue fire. She lifted her hands and, without having to do anything else, the two warriors stumbled back and hurried away.

Blaze stood and faced her father. "It is not for you to choose whom I help. The spirits guided me to this man and I will do my best to save his life."

"You would defy me?" Angry color flooded Red Thunder's face.

"I do not wish to anger you, my father." Blaze wanted to cry. All she'd ever wanted was his love and support. She met his furious gaze. "*We* can heal this man." Her father should have been pleased and proud that his daughter had been gifted with a natural ability to heal, but her gift was just one more source of resentment that had grown into bitter hate.

Blaze swallowed her pain. Now was not the time to confront him. Soon she'd demand answers to the questions that plagued her. Questions like: Why did her own father hate her? And why did he seem afraid of her? To save this young warrior he would not swallow his pride and acknowledge her gift, yet when she'd been a child, he'd been pleased with her ability to help him heal. It had made him seem even more powerful in his people's eyes.

No, she knew the truth. It burned in her soul. Her father was not a healer like she was. He knew how to use plants to heal, and he always put on an impressive show of ritual, combining dance, chants and prayer; but he had no magic. The medicine from nature did the job. When it did not, he called Blaze in to assist.

"Father. He can be saved." Red Thunder feared being exposed. But even with so many eyes on them, Blaze knew that if he went into one of his showy dances she could quietly save this man and still keep the extent of her ability secret.

"No. If you will not help me, then leave." Red Thunder turned on his heel and stalked away, the sound of his bear jewelry clacking harshly together. The warrior's mother sobbed loudly as though in her mind she'd already lost her only son.

Blaze once again placed her hand over the warrior's heart. She felt the faint, erratic beat. The young man was near death, but he hadn't yet joined the others in the spirit world. Was it too late for even her abilities? It was close. The two other warriors stood nearby, not wanting her here but afraid to approach.

The mother reached out and grabbed Blaze's arm. "Save him, daughter of Red Thunder. Please save my son."

Staring into eyes nearly black with grief, Blaze whispered, "He is badly injured and is near death."

The woman's fingers dug into Blaze's arm. She boldly met Blaze's gaze, not shying away from the turbulent mix of colors there. "You can save him. I know you can." She leaned forward, her voice low. "It is you with the gift, not your father. Please, do not turn away from us."

Emotion lodged in her throat as Blaze stared into those pleading eyes. How could she say no to this mother? She risked exposing herself, but had no choice but to try and save this man. Fear made her mouth dry. She was afraid of failing and letting this woman down, but she was also afraid of succeeding. If she did this, and Walks Like Turtle lived, there'd be no hiding the truth that it was she who was the healer and not her father.

The woman dropped her hand from Blaze's

arm, leaving bloody prints. "I do not have the right to ask this of you. We do not." Her voice broke. "We are not deserving." She bowed her head. "But in my heart, I know you can help him. I've seen you heal. Many years ago. My husband. You drove the sickness from his lungs and he talked about walking down a golden path of stars and seeing you."

Tears gathering in her eyes, Blaze put her hand over the woman's. Her gift was meant to be used, not hidden. She had no choice but to try. "I cannot promise that it will work."

The woman nodded.

Blaze drew in a deep breath and wished for the comfort of her sage and sweetgrass and her stones; each part of a ritual that was a source of comfort as much as being a smoke screen to hide the truth. But she had no time to return to her cave. No time to seek the privacy of a lodge. Doing this meant she'd be opening herself for all to see just how different she truly was, but . . . "So be it," she whispered, and she drew her necklace out into the open.

The small white feathers fluttered in the breeze. Tiny claws were knotted beside odd-shaped beads and colored pebbles. But it was the large blue stone in the shape of an eagle that she sought. As she had the night before, she held it up over her head. Light sparked at the center, giving the stone a heart of blue fire.

Cupping between her palms her *wotai*—her personal stone, a gift from *Wakan Tanka* that she carried on her person always—she felt the stone grow warm then so hot that her palms burned. Blaze closed her eyes to shut out all sound and movement. She could not allow herself to think about the death cries around her or the feeling of being watched. Moving both hands over the warrior, she used her mind, her heart and the love in her very soul to enlarge her protective aura to encompass his. The light within her shimmered, grew brighter as her heart filled with love for even those who'd been cruel to her.

All doubt in her abilities fled. The certainty that she could heal this warrior came not just from her mind but from the very essence of her that was grounded in earth, wind, fire and water.

She had no idea how it was possible to do so, but she called upon the elements of her world, the core of primitive life deep inside her to aid her in healing this warrior. She was connected to ancient life, and that life surrounded her and came to her aid.

Around her, everything fell silent as though every living thing held its breath. Drawing her brows together, she focused not on the physical injuries of the body, but on the spirit of a man on the brink of shadow and light.

His spirit trail was faint, but she searched for and found him standing in the swirling darkness. Above their heads, the heavens beckoned and glowed with bright, vibrant hues. Blues, greens and violets swirled into a pool of soothing warmth. Beauty and light. There were choices to be made here. Peace and eternal rest or darkness and pain. The warrior moved toward the light.

No. Blaze expanded her personal shield of blue light to encompass him in a translucent bubble and stop his departure from the physical world. She walked toward him, unaware of the halo of light around her, beneath her, guiding her way. He shaded his eyes with his hands as though blinded.

"It is not your time," Blaze said. It was true; if it had been his time to leave, she wouldn't have been able to see him.

The warrior reached out to push his palm against the thin inner skin of the bubble. Then he lifted his hands high as he stared up at the kaleidoscope of colors above their heads. "I wish to roam the sky, to be free of pain and hunt without fear of our enemy attacking."

Blaze held his gaze. If he chose to leave his body for the spirit world, she'd have no choice but to let him go. She could not overcome free will. "Fear is no reason to leave the woman who gave birth to you."

The warrior closed his eyes. "The pain, it is too great. I die today a warrior. My mother will be proud of her son."

Blaze nodded. "She has reason to be proud, and her pride in her son will grow." Calling upon the spirits of the sky—the stars, the moon, the sun, all who lived in and with *Skan*, the most powerful of all gods, the Creator, the Four who were as One— she lifted her hands.

The air around her shimmered with bright pinpricks of light. Beneath her feet, a golden path formed from her to the wonder-stricken warrior. "The Gods offer the gift of life. Life is *Wakan Tanka*. Mysterious. Life is sacred and not to be taken or given up lightly. But it is your choice. Do you choose life? *Will* you choose life?" The tips of her fingers glowed and sparkled, the light that was in her and around her driving away the darkness.

"You are a god!" The warrior fell to his knees.

Blaze shook her head. "No. I am simply a woman sent to help you find your way back." Around them, the bubble of protectiveness grew thinner and more transparent.

"You must choose now," she warned softly. She felt the essence of his spirit ebbing. Respecting the free will that guided her own daily choices, Blaze simply held out her hand.

The warrior stood for a moment, then moved toward her, walking on the narrow golden path until he was able to touch her outstretched hand. Grasping his palm firmly, Blaze closed her eyes. The path of stardust she stood upon rolled outward until the warrior no longer stood on the brink of death.

"You choose to live," she said softly. "You walked the path one takes when death is upon him. You stood at the brink of the spirit world and beheld the power of all that is *Wakan Tanka*."

The warrior stared at her with wonder in his eyes. "You came after me. You gave me life."

Blaze met his awe-filled gaze. "Your life will

never be the same. You've gone full circle, from life to death, and now back to life. Live your life in honor of our people and hold close to your heart the spirits who give life to your heart and soul."

Blaze stepped back. The warrior followed the glittering path her healing spirit provided. His spirit, the soul of the man, merged back into his body.

With the warrior's spirit out of danger, Blaze called her totem animal—the large female eagle who accompanied her in all her spiritual travels. The bird was her protector. If any evil spirits got in her path, the mighty bird could fly her away safely. Directing her totem animal to seek the upper world, Blaze called upon the spirits to aid her in healing the warrior's wounds. She believed absolutely in herself, in her unselfish desire to help this man, and in the love and power of the gods and spirits that were one with her.

Bright white light surrounded Blaze and poured into her. It whirled behind her eyes, a pure white cloud that then flowed like water down the straight line of her spine to the internal gateways that controlled the functions of spirit and body.

Body, mind and soul, each perfectly balanced, fed her spirit and allowed her to surround the warrior with pure love. Her palms grew hot with the power of healing as she ran them over the deep, bleeding wounds and drove the chill of death from the man. Nothing mattered to Blaze. Not people, not time. She kept her focus on the mortally wounded warrior, conscious of her promise to give him life, confident in her ability to keep that promise even though she'd never before performed such extensive healing. She continued on faith, the faith that the gods who'd taught her all she knew would not let her down.

With her hands, she clamped together the ragged edges of his deeper wounds and fed his body with her essence, knowing that when it was mixed with his own desire to live it would speed the healing process.

Her life force sustained the warrior as he took from her the knowledge he needed to seal blood vessels and repair muscle and knit torn flesh. Blaze drew her hands over the warrior's wounds, pausing over his heart. The beat was growing stronger and steadier; air moved vigorously in his lungs and his blood pumped through his veins, the more serious of his wounds now closed.

Her strength ebbed until she finally pulled her hands away and gently brushed her hand over his closed eyes. Upon her silent command, he woke. Pain still filled his eyes. His body could finish the job of healing, but at a slower pace. He still had a long way to go. Nonetheless, he was alive.

"You have chosen to live. Know that you have been given a sacred gift. Use the time left to you wisely," she whispered.

The warrior's eyes were glazed, unfocused. "Who are you?" he asked. He reached up, his hand wavering as he reached out toward her. "Stars. We walked upon a golden path in the sky." He tried to rise but fell back weakly, his gaze roaming the gathered crowd.

Blaze tried to ignore the stares, the whispers and murmurings that were slowly growing louder. Her people formed a ring around her. She felt the gut-deep fear in their hearts. Their whispers grew to a loud buzz in her ears.

What had she done? For the second time in her life, she'd done something to stand out instead of blending in. While some like this warrior's mother knew or suspected that she had the gift of healing, all now knew the true extent of her abilities. There was also no longer any doubt that she was different, that she was not one of them.

Blaze stood, her knees weak, her body exhausted, the residual halo of healing light fading. Slowly, she glanced around.

Red Thunder pushed his way though the crowd and grabbed Blaze roughly by the arm. He pulled her through the crowd, anger radiating off him along with the scent of blood and sweat. "You fool!" He hissed the words so only she heard. "You've destroyed all that I have worked for. How am I going to explain this?"

So tired that she could barely stand, Blaze let the heat course through her and build until her father dropped her arm with a yelp, and he stepped back, a tinge of fear restraining his fury.

"I am a healer. The spirits led me to this man." Blaze kept her emotions tightly reined, but allowed her voice to rise. It infuriated her that her father only thought of himself and his position within the tribe. She'd get no thanks or praise for saving the life of this warrior.

Unable to endure the silence, or the hate in his eyes, Blaze turned away and fled. Behind her, the faint hum of the whispering crowd became a roar in her head.

Wise Owl entered her lodge ahead of her sister and Walks Like Turtle, her sister's son. The boy was weak yet and had to be carried. When Walks Like Turtle was settled on his pallet, she went to him, offering him water.

He drank. His eyes were wide as he looked into hers. "Tell me, my aunt. Was I dreaming?" His voice was hushed.

Smiling, Wise Owl took a wet cloth and began to wash the blood from his face, hands, arms and chest. The wounds were still serious, and would need care, but already she could see they were less raw, and looked to be healing right before her eyes. "No, my brave nephew. You were not dreaming. That girl healed you."

"I have pain," he said. "I can feel the wounds our enemy inflicted."

"But you are alive. You should have died this day, yet you did not. Your wounds are healing."

"Why? Why did she do this?"

"It was not your time."

Walks Like Turtle frowned. "She said that to me."

Wise Owl continued to bathe her nephew. When

she went to rise, he grabbed her arm and lifted his head and shoulders up off his pallet. His fingers trailed down over his healing wounds. "What magic did she use? How did she do this?"

Wise Owl stared at her nephew. "Is it for us to question the ways of the spirits and gods?"

"My uncle was a great shaman. He never healed in this manner."

"No, my nephew. My husband was not gifted in this way." Wise Owl pulled herself free and rose.

Walks Like Turtle sagged back onto his bed of furs. "No one is. It is not natural." His voice was growing fainter.

"Who is to say what is natural, my nephew? It is natural for birds to fly, yet we humans can only walk or run. Is the bird unnatural? A bear walks on two legs when he desires, but we do not ever walk on four. That is not our way."

She turned to go, but her nephew called her back. She turned.

"I was not afraid of her."

Wise Owl smiled. "And so you should not be." She left and went to her place at the back of the longhouse. Seeking the rack that held her personal belongings, she pulled down a wrapped bundle.

Opening it, she ran her fingers down the robe made from the fur of the fox with owl and eagle feathers lining its edges. It had belonged to her husband, and as she held it up to her face, she inhaled his scent and softly sighed. She missed him, and it hurt to know that his restless spirit roamed the land, unable to make the final journey to the spirit world. It was up to her to free him from his endless walk upon this world.

"My husband, you were right about the girl. She is special, and soon she will understand—as will all our people."

From outside came a long haunting cry of an owl. A single tear fell. It landed in a deep wrinkle on Wise Owl's face and slowly slid down a seamed path time had stamped onto her face.

Who are you?

The warrior's question hounded Blaze as she ran from the village. Reaching the stream, she hopped agilely across the stones, slipping only once into the white-capped water. Her moccasins left wet footprints across the trail of boulders, and the skirt of her pale yellow doeskin dress stuck to her legs. The stream deepened in the center where water from the twin falls swirled and collected before beginning its journey across the land.

Careful to keep from slipping again, what with the force of the falls nearly on top of her, Blaze ducked behind a curtain of water. The cavity beyond narrowed, forcing her to her hands and knees as she crawled toward the small sunny opening ahead. From there she climbed up the slick boulders until she reached a narrow nook with sheets of water streaming past on either side. There she sat, tucked into a comforting cradle of stone with the roar of the water loud enough to drown out all other sound.

But not the agony in her mind.

She sat with her legs crossed, the spray of water falling around her like a gentle mist. Down below, the force of the falls sent glittering droplets of water high. Across the stream, Blaze stared at a small meadow ringed by trees—another favorite place of hers—as she asked herself again and again, "Who am I? *What* am I?"

The breathtaking beauty, this portrait of the Earth Mother's power, did little to soothe her jagged nerves or ease the torment in her heart. She held up her hands, stared at her fingers. So small, yet so powerful. Turning them over she saw nothing unusual in them, yet her palms and fingertips tingled and burned and would for many hours yet. Holding her hands out to her sides, she let the water that drained from the lake cool and take away that heat.

Slowly the excess energy from healing left her body. Covering her face with her now cool palms, Blaze tried to calm her frantically racing heart and the buzzing in her head. She'd never brought a person back from the brink of death. Animals, yes. Many times. But never a person.

Today, for the first time, she'd stood on the brink of life and death with an injured warrior and used her gift and his will to bring him back from beyond. The sheer power still coursed through her. She'd never be quite the same, and she wasn't sure how she felt about that.

She didn't mind being a healer. Her gift came to

her naturally. In fact, she could do nothing *but* heal the sick or injured. Yet she'd learned at a young age that people were afraid of what could not be explained. And her existence could not be explained.

Blaze rested her arm over her face, blocking out the glare of the sun. She was tired and confused. What was she that she could heal like the gods? Over and over she thought of what she'd done, how she'd done it, and she remembered the shock and awe and fear on the faces of her people.

"*Toke!* Why!"

She did her best to not draw attention to herself, but after today she'd never be able to enter the village without seeing more fear in the eyes of her people. As natural as breathing was for all who lived, she used another of her powers: She sent her mind flaring outward, seeking solace. Far, far above, she saw the brown speck of an eagle.

Blaze yearned to call the bird to her, to merge with him and fly freely, without burden, without fear. Closing her eyes, she tried to form the words to call the bird to her, but she was just so tired, and the roar of the falls made thinking or forming words difficult.

The sun, a bright orange-red, seemed to burn with color through the closed lids of her eyes. Those colors swirled, and she felt herself spinning, drowning in a sea of it. Then the images came hard and fast.

"*Miye kinyan!*" I fly!

The high-pitched, childish voice echoed in her mind, the voice of the girl of her dreams, followed by a fleeting image of two people falling from a cliff with arms held out to their sides. She blinked, then saw two eagles soaring across the expansive sky. They had changed!

"I fly." The words echoed in her mind, and she saw herself standing on that cliff. She felt herself sway, saw the blue of the sky surrounding her, beckoning. She lifted one foot . . .

A loud screech snapped her eyes open, and with a cry of shock, Blaze saw that she truly was standing at the edge of the falls. The eagle rose up before her; his cry of warning ringing in her ears.

The shock of her vision tore through Blaze, and as her knees trembled and gave way, she sat down, scooting herself back into the shadows. Breathing rapidly, her heart pounding, Blaze put her head down on her knees. The child in her dreams had known that her parents were going to shift, had been thrilled to see it happen and had wanted with every bit of her young heart to join them. And she'd been filled with the certainty that one day she too would soar.

"How can I know this?" That image of the man and woman hadn't been part of her dreams. It was new—had to have come from the child.

She lifted her head and rubbed her hands up and down her arms as she stared into the twin curtains of water. The sudden certainty that she could actually step off the cliff and become an eagle frightened her; the fact that she was so tired and confused that she'd nearly done so made her afraid to even move.

Rubbing her forehead, she could not hold back a cry of raw grief. Denial. "Tell me what this means! I cannot sprout wings." Anger and fear grew inside her. But why? She might as well have sprouted wings and flown away in front of her people, for healing that warrior was no less amazing or frightening to those who didn't understand.

A cloud passed over the sun, making her shiver. Blaze concentrated on calming her racing heart. Anger was not only useless but for her had consequences, so she forced the darkness from her mind and tried to concentrate on something good. Like life. Saving life. Tears of exhaustion slipped from her eyes. She had no idea what to do and was very afraid, so she turned to the spirits and gods as she had all her life.

Standing, Blaze once again stood in the immense gushing falls and lifted her hands high, blinking water from her eyes as she glared up into the clouds gathering above.

"*Mahpiyah Ate.*"

"*Hoye wa yelo.*"

"*Unsimala ye.*"

She repeated the prayer, her voice rising to compete with the roaring falls.

"Father Sky."

"I am sending a voice."

"Have pity on me."

She stared up into the sky and added, "What do you want of me?"

She waited for the voice that always came to her, the voice that had comforted her as a child and guided her way as she discovered within herself things no one else knew. But this time, as last night, there were no answers.

Lifting her head, she called out, "If you will not speak with me, I will seek my own answers!" She made no apology for the defiance in her voice.

Closing her eyes, she sat and crossed her legs in front of her and concentrated on her heartbeat and the crashing of water hitting rock. It took total concentration to travel from this world to the one where spirits waited to guide their human counterparts.

Blocking out all thoughts but those of her need for answers, she brought to mind a large hollow in the base of a giant tree. She stood outside the dark doorway and silently voiced her intention, her question for the spirit guides of the world beyond.

Who am I? What am I? What do you want of me? She entered the darkness and traveled down a long tunnel that led deep underground. Bright light appeared at the end. She paused for a moment and again asked her questions.

Who am I? What am I? What do you want of me?

She needed those three questions answered. With her intent clear, she entered a world much like her own. Sometimes it was forest, other times it was a cavern. And sometimes, it was a place with no trees. Just hot dry land and strange plants. When she entered the alternate worlds where she went for guidance, she usually just strolled, allowing herself to be taken by whatever spirit or animal came to her to teach her what they wanted her to know. She had learned much from the animal guides.

This time, though, she stood in the open and shaded her eyes against the brilliant light. She took a deep breath and called out:

"Spirit of *Wanbli*. I seek counsel, I call upon you as one of my totem animals, my power animal, to come to me. I seek your wisdom. I beg you. Come to this cousin, for we are all related." In the ensuing silence, Blaze kept her focus on her reasons for journeying to the lower world. Around her and beneath her, the vibrations and essence of rock, water, and air flowed.

Time passed. How much, she didn't know; didn't care. Time had no meaning here. Finally, in the distance, she saw a brown speck. It grew larger until she could make out the outline of a bird. Moments later, a giant eagle with a white head landed on a thick branch of a tree. It folded its wings then perched on the ledge, blocking the glare of sunlight from her eyes.

I am here, came the voice of her power animal, that voice resonating in Blaze's mind.

Questions raged like a fire out of control in the forest. Blaze put a hand to her stomach to quell the nervousness. In her mind, she again asked the question, *Who am I?*

You are a child of the gods. This you know. The bird stretched its wings.

Blaze paced. *But what does that mean?*

The eagle shifted, wings tight against its body. The bird stood proud. *I cannot tell you what you already know. The answers are inside you, and only when you accept the truth will you find your direction.*

Blaze glared up at the eagle. *It is not that simple!*

No, it is not.

What do the gods want of me? Blaze felt like weeping with frustration.

The giant bird unfolded its wings. *Seek the truth and find your answers.*

Blaze held out her hand. *Stay with me. Please, stay with me.*

The bird flew toward her, growing smaller and smaller. It landed in her palm. *I am always with you. Seek the child. Learn her secrets. Only then can you help the others.*

Blaze held her hands to her heart as though pressing the spirit of the eagle deep inside her. "Others?" Panic raced through her. "What others?"

A sharp crack of thunder snapped Blaze out of the lower world. She was back on the ledge between the falls. Dark clouds slid across the sky, followed by a spear of light that slashed through the clouds, releasing a torrent of rain.

Already drenched from the falls, Blaze felt like shouting in anger. She'd gone in search of answers but was only left with more questions!

Frustrated, she left the falls the way she'd come, slipping more than once on the wet boulders. "Child of the gods?" She stared up into the rain clouds. Her father was no god. He wasn't even a true healer, so her gifts had to have come from her mother.

"Truth is within me." Blaze stared in the direction of her village. There had to be one person who knew the truth about her.

CHAPTER FOUR

Blaze entered the village and, as she rounded the side of one of the largest longhouses, a trio of warriors came to an abrupt halt. They quickly spun around and hurried away. Those women not tending to the injured or comforting grieving relatives or friends were busy preparing meals, and the women who lived in the lodge nearby were sitting outside, pounding pine nuts into fine meal. Spotting Blaze, they ran inside and pulled the flap over the door, leaving their tools and stone bowls outside.

Hurt speared through Blaze's heart like a lance. In the time it took for her to cross the compound, everyone who'd been outdoors had disappeared into forest or lodge. Wishing she could not care so she wouldn't be hurt, Blaze headed for her father's lodge. She entered without waiting for an invitation, but when her father whirled around and saw her, he turned his back.

"You were told to stay away. Leave," Red Thunder said, his voice low with fury that she'd disobeyed him once again.

Shoving the hurt of his cold reception aside, Blaze stood her ground. "I did no wrong today," she announced.

Red Thunder rounded on his daughter, his face red. "It is not for you to decide who is to live and who is to die."

"Nor is it yours," she replied.

"Had it not been for you, Walks Like Turtle would have journeyed to the spirit world. It is for the Creator to decide who lives and who dies. Walks Like Turtle would have died honorably."

Blaze stared at her father. "Healing is what we do—what *I* do. How could I turn my back on a man whose spirit was still strong? He had a choice, and he chose life. He is a brave warrior and will one day become a great leader."

The tribe's chiefs and holy men came from that family. She knew Walks Like Turtle's uncle; the holy man had been training his nephew to take his place. It had been that holy man who'd given her counsel, in secret, as her father had forbidden her to talk to anyone when she'd been younger. She missed his wise words.

Red Thunder's features turned ugly. "You play with life."

"No! I *save* life," Blaze replied. She stared at the man who, though he was her father, was every bit a stranger. "You hate me so much that you'd rather see our people die."

"You cheat death, but you will bring death to us all!"

The words cut deep, yet Blaze refused to show her pain. She'd once wanted to please this man above all else. Part of her still did. "You are bitter, Father. Once, there was a time when you found my gifts useful. Is that not how you gained the title of a great medicine man?"

Red Thunder flinched as though she'd struck him. His nostrils flared, and an ugly redness crept up his neck. "I have no need of a disrespectful daughter. Leave me," he growled.

Blaze shook her head sadly as she remembered how he had brought her into the lodges of the ill as his assistant, how he'd made her heal when his showy dances, dramatic chants and potions failed. No one had ever known that it had been his little girl who healed the sick and injured. Starved for love, she'd tried to win acceptance by pleasing this man. She'd healed when summoned, and had never questioned what her father asked of her or thought anything about his insistence that no one know the truth.

"I used to think my ability to heal came from you. All those years I thought we healed together, but you lied to me, to our people, and you continue to live a false life." She finally could admit to herself that besides not loving her, her father had used her. He'd betrayed her by using her for his own gain. And she could admit it to him. Could accuse him.

"And you helped create that lie," Red Thunder hissed. "You traded your power for acceptance."

The truth hurt horribly. Four years ago she'd first realized it; the death of a young boy had revealed the truth to her, but she'd kept quiet.

"I have healed out of love for our people," she said. She no longer sought her father's love or approval. But he was right that she'd known the truth, and by keeping silent, she'd become as guilty as he of the lie he lived.

"No more," she said. "I will help you no more." She had no desire to destroy the man who'd raised her, no desire for vengeance, but she could not live this way any longer.

"You will do as you are told," Red Thunder snarled.

Blaze shook her head. "All I ever wanted was for you to accept and love me. You, Father, cannot. And I will call you 'father' no more."

Red Thunder slashed both hands sharply down and across his body. "You are nothing more than a child, and as such you will do as told."

"I am no child to be—"

"Yes. You are a *foolish* child."

"A child," she repeated, thinking of the child in her dreams. "A foolish child." She spoke softly. *One who fills her head with dreams of flying*. Her father had used to taunt her with those words. A strange calmness came over her. *Truth. Seek the child*. The words echoed in her head.

"I used to believe I could fly. You told me I was foolish." She watched her father carefully. For the first time he looked uncomfortable, but he didn't back away; he came and stood close, trying to intimidate her.

"Go. Do not talk about his again." He pointed at the doorway.

Seek the truth. The words echoed in her head.

As he walked to the door, she followed. "I dream about this child. In the dream *I* am the child. I see what she sees, feels what she feels. Why? Who is this girl?" *Taya*. The name rose up in her without warning and released long-buried memories. For the first time, she let her walls of fear fall, and the name rang through her mind. Her heart and soul burned with the familiarity so much that it brought tears to her eyes.

Red Thunder's face whitened, and he took a step through the doorway.

Blaze touched his arm. "If you leave without telling me the truth, I will follow you. I will continue to ask you for the truth. I *will* have my answers. Now. Today."

Her father froze. "Your dreams do not interest me."

"Truth, father. Who am I? What am I? Am I this child named Taya?"

Red Thunder's lips twisted with hatred. "You destroyed my life once. I will not let you do so again!"

"It cannot be," she gasped, suddenly understanding, fighting to draw breath. Her voice shook. "Taya's life was destroyed. By you," she whispered. "You killed her parents—my parents. You took me from them. From my people." The shock of it nearly sent Blaze to her knees.

The truth brought blinding clarity. Her dream was real, as was her grief. Closing her eyes, tears streamed down her face.

Her mother and father—dead. Killed by a man who looked so angry that she was afraid. She shoved past him. He grabbed her roughly by the arm.

Red Thunder stood, his fists clenched tightly. "Tell no one. Nothing changes. Reveal the truth and be as damned as I. If not for me, these people would cast you out. They would *hurt* you." He grabbed his bearskin, put it on and shoved her to one side. The bear claws brushed against her as he strode out the door.

Blaze herself fled into the growing dusk. For so many years she'd tried to win her father's love and approval. Finally accepting that she'd receive neither, she'd sought to live in peace and harmony. It seemed those too were to be denied her.

"Luc! Luc!"

Luc bolted upright to find his father hunkered down beside him. He grabbed his rifle, which was always nearby. "What is it?"

"Get up. Now."

"What's going on?" Luc whispered as he glanced around. The embers from the fire had long ago died out; overhead the summer storm had passed, though a light gathering of clouds hid most of the moon and stars.

"We're leaving."

The urgency in his father's voice stopped him from asking questions. He bent down to gather his bedding. His father stopped him.

"No time. Let's go." Conrad hurried away.

Luc shrugged on a vest, grabbed his pack, shouldered it and joined his father and cousins who were helping Eagle Woman gather the girls.

Kangee ran up to her father. "We must hurry! They come!"

Luc tightened his grip on his rifle as he peered into the shadows. "Who?"

His father brushed past him. "Someone I thought I could trust with my life." He pushed the twins toward Luc and Kangee, and took Skye from her mother. He handed the little girl to Alex. "Head north," he told them. "Go to Old Man Rock. If anything happens to us, take the girls to their mother's people."

Tightening his grip on his rifle, Luc narrowed his eyes. "We all should stay together. We'll be safe together." He wanted to know what had happened, but judging from the fear in his mother's eyes, there was no time.

"Eagle Woman and I can save ourselves. The girls cannot."

"What about Kangee?" He'd never seen her shift, and didn't know the extent of her gifts—or even if she had any.

Kangee stepped forward. "I go with you."

Conrad gripped his son's shoulder, hard. "Whatever happens, you keep going. Take my daughters. Keep them safe. Promise me."

Luc nodded, then saw Travers. He motioned for his cousin to take the lead. He took Skye as Alex and Kangee each held the hand of one of the twins. He gave Skye a quick, reassuring hug. Her eyes were wide and full of fear. She clutched a small doll in her hands.

"We'll be fine, sweetheart," Luc said as he stroked one finger down his baby sister's cheek. Let's go. No noise." Heading down a faint deer trail, Luc herded the group to the stream. They followed the dark gleaming ribbon in silence. The near darkness made it difficult to find their way.

He kept his rifle ready in the crook of one arm, his mocassin-clad feet making no noise on the thick carpet of pine needles and fallen cones. Only the faint swish of clothing sounded in the night's unnatural quiet. A sudden howl broke the silence. It was followed by another, and another. Luc spun, his rifle raised.

"They come to help us," Skye whispered in his ear. "The enemy is near." Her voice trembled. She wrapped her hands tightly around his neck.

Luc quickened his pace. The Spiritwalkers had called for help? He wasn't sure if that was reassuring or not, as it made him wonder what was going on. "Keep moving," he said. The howls merged one into the next until the very air seemed to vibrate with keening cries. They hadn't traveled far when loud war whoops followed by the blast of gunfire shattered the night. Luc thrust Skye into Kangee's arms and spun around to face the sound. "Go," he commanded Travers. "Get the girls out of here. Head for Old Man Rock. The girls know the way."

"I remember how to get there." Travers's voice was tight. He gripped his rifle tightly as he herded the girls in front of him.

Above him, what little moonlight there was disappeared beneath clouds. Luc was torn between going with the children to keep his promise or going to the aid of his father and earth mother. Trouble was at their heels. He decided the best way to protect his sisters was to intercept the danger. That would give Travers and Alex time to get his sisters to safety.

Retracing his steps, he found the night filled with sound: rustling in the undergrowth, panicked flapping above from birds startled awake, and low, menacing growls. They grew closer and sent shivers up his spine.

Luc cursed himself and moved as fast as he dared. He had no idea who the enemy was or how many there were. He should never have left his father's side. Staying to the shadows, he moved through the night, careful to keep as silent as possible so he wouldn't alert anyone to his presence. But when he heard the menacing growls, howls of pain and screams, he broke into a run. All hell seemed to have broken loose, and nothing mattered except getting to his father and Eagle Woman.

He skidded to a stop behind a thick pine with low

overhanging branches that forced him to crouch. Shadows moved along the water. He had his rifle up, ready to fire. There were too many shadows. Some were low to the ground, others running from tree to tree. The loud retort of a shotgun not far from Luc made him hit the ground. Two more shots sounded. A bullet hit the tree above Luc.

"Alive. I want them alive," a low, muffled voice said.

Luc headed for the voice. There was too much noise to hear it clearly. As he tripped over a fallen body, he grabbed up the man's shotgun. The sound of gunfire had stopped but not the sounds of fighting. Luc tore through the trees, grateful that the clouds had passed over the moon, allowing him some much needed light.

He stopped as he saw two men fighting, and several others standing nearby. It was a ghostly scene. He focused on the men. One was his father. The other was short, stocky, and had a very familiar hat on his head.

Luc swallowed. "Uncle Al?" It couldn't be. But even in shadow, the hat his uncle treasured was recognizable. The men shifted and were hidden by shadows and dark phantom shapes merging in and out of the tree trunks.

Another shot from the far side of the action rang out. Luc heard a yelp and saw several wolves slink back into the cover of shrub and brush. A crash sounded, and one of the two fighting men went flying backward into a small clearing. It wasn't his father. Cordell had been knocked to the ground, but he jumped to his feet and pulled Eagle Woman out from behind a tree. He gave her a shove. "Go! Get out of here!" he cried.

The other man jumped back up and charged. Eagle Woman ran. Two men stepped out from behind the trees to block her path.

Wanting to help, Luc took aim and fired. He dropped his spent rifle and took aim with the shotgun, only to find it had been discharged. Luc's breath caught in his throat as his earth mother leaped high. One moment she was a desperate woman, the next she was a graceful owl soaring over his head, through the foliage above him.

A wolf flew at one of the attackers, but fell as a gunshot rang out. The attacked man ran into the shadows. Luc held his breath. *Go*, he silently ordered his mother as she soared through the sky.

Luc moved in to help his father, drawing his knife. But before he reached Cordell, he saw the glint of metal.

"No," he yelled as he charged forward. His father fell. The dark shadow that had to be his Uncle Albert jumped back. He held something high in his hands, and when his father struggled to grab for his ankle, he laughed and moved out of reach.

A loud shriek from overhead startled Luc. The owl had flown back, close enough that he felt the brush of wind on his face. Eagle Woman flew low, landed on her husband.

Suddenly she launched herself at the triumphant Al, using her talons and beak with deadly intent. She tumbled backward into the trees as his fist slammed into her. Luc ran forward to help his father, but he found his path blocked by two men, one of them bleeding from the wound obviously inflicted by a wolf.

One man held a knife, its long blade gleaming; the other held a war axe. Luc tossed himself sideways out of the way, then rolled back up onto the balls of his feet with his knife gripped in his hands. The two warriors circled him. Blades flashed, bodies moved, rolled, retreated and attacked. Luc slashed out at the warrior in front of him, felt the tip of his knife sink into flesh, then pulled back and retreated as the warrior behind him leapt forward.

The sting of a blade along his upper arm nearly brought him to his knees. He slashed out at his foe, went into a diving roll to avoid the return thrust. When he came up, he delivered a sharp kick to the second man's chest. The man went down, flipped up and stared at Luc, knife held high.

Staying light on the balls of his feet, Luc waited for one of the two to make the next move. The pair closed in, forcing Luc into the trees where he had less mobility.

Deciding it was better to attack than be trapped, he charged the warriors, his blood pumping, his voice lifted in a yell. At the last moment, he tossed his knife to his other hand, thrust it out and up hard just before going into another roll. The knife found one enemy's belly.

Getting to his feet, no time to draw his second knife, using only his wits and desperate need to live,

Luc spun around in time to see an axe flying toward him. Hitting the ground, he heard a thud as it struck a tree. The wind was knocked from him by the man who followed. The two rolled: Luc on top, then on the bottom as they rolled, fists flying. Slammed repeatedly into the hard ground, Luc felt the air rush out of his lungs. Glancing up, he saw a rock in his foe's fist and threw up his hands.

A flash of fur appeared and toppled his opponent. Luc got to his knees just as the snarling wolf swung around, but his foe was lying still. The wolf was an arm's length from him. Luc stared into the glitter of its eyes, but before he could move or even think, the animal whirled around, the fur on its back lifted. Before Luc could get to his feet, another shot rang out.

The wolf whimpered, but the bullet also hit Luc. It knocked him onto his back. Stunned, he stared up into the web of branches above his head. Pain radiated outward from his chest. Breathing hurt; thinking was impossible.

He lifted a hand to try to get up, but pain squeezed the air from his lungs. Luc cried out in agony. His chest was on fire, his vision blurred and narrowed as though he were staring out of a small hole or traveling through a tunnel. His last thought was of his sisters and how he'd failed to keep the promise he'd made to his father.

Sitting in front of her fire, huddled beneath a thick robe made of sewn-together rabbit fur, Blaze shivered with a cold that seeped deep into her heart. She'd long ago come to terms with her father's attitude toward her, though never truly understanding until today why he hated her. Never in all her wildest imaginings could she have guessed that truth.

He wasn't her father. She let the tears flow unchecked. Grief chewed her heart into tiny bits. So much had been lost to her. Though he'd never been loving, had rejected her love, the man had been family. Her family, even if he hadn't liked it. There had been some comfort in knowing he was there.

Now she had no one. She'd accepted that the dreams of the child were her past, which meant that her true parents were dead—killed by the man she'd tried so hard to love and please. Blaze pressed her hand into her stomach to try to ease the ache. She shivered from cold, and the shock of the revelations, the truth she had no choice but to accept. Still it explained everything except what she was.

A child of the gods?

Blaze let her eyes glaze, the colors of the fire blurring. So much made sense, yet nothing did. What was she? She was no god. She was human. Like the Sioux people she lived among. But where did she come from?

The question plagued her. She had no memories of her past. Did she have family? If so, where would she start her search? Her father had stolen her. Her lips firmed. No, not her father. Not ever her father.

He didn't deserve the title; the man she'd called father was nothing more than a *tusla*—a leech that sucked blood for life. He'd never cared about her, never loved her. He'd used her to gain respect and honor. And she'd let him.

Where did that leave her? What was she going to do? She could not—would not—allow him to continue to use her, yet if she refused, innocent people would suffer. "I can heal." She didn't need her father to heal. She was a *pejuta winan*—a powerful medicine woman in her own right.

No. The words of Wise Owl came back to her. Deep in her heart, she knew she was more than just a medicine woman or healer. She was a *winan wakan*. She'd been chosen by the gods to walk life as a holy woman, yet she knew her people would not accept her as such.

So what good was being a holy woman, possessing knowledge and a strong desire to help others, when her people feared her? A stab of pain to her heart reminded her that these were not her people—yet in her heart they were. She'd known them all her life.

She stared into the dying embers of the fire. Though the night was warm, she needed not only the warmth but the flare of life, the color, the connection to the earth. Fire and water, earth and air combined were the essence of primitive life and were gifts of the gods. She was a child of the gods but what did that really mean?

Standing, she dropped her fur and went to stand

at the entrance to her cave. The summer storm had passed and, high above, the stars glittered brilliantly. Her gaze swept across the sky as though answers floated high above her.

"The child is me and I am her." Wise Owl had been right. Dreams were messages from the spirits. The old woman had also told her to travel the wheel of the south. She'd discovered the child within and had accepted the bitter truth. She was truly alone, had no idea what she was or where she belonged.

Blaze lifted her head and allowed the cool breeze to sweep over her face. More than anything she needed answers, but to find them she had to leave. It was a frightening idea. If she stayed she knew what to expect, though her father—no, the man who'd stolen her—would be a problem. She had no idea what he'd do when she refused to participate in his deception.

She could reveal the truth, but then they'd both probably be outcast, and she had nowhere else to go. Did she have family out there, and if so, where would she even start her search? She fingered the tiny pouch the old woman had given her. She wished she dared go into the village and seek the old woman's advice. "What am I going to do?" She didn't expect an answer but a voice rumbled through her mind.

Listen. Follow your heart. There you will find your answers and more.

Many times over the last day she'd been told the answers lay to the south. Her fist tightened on the tiny pouch. She paused and pulled it out.

Use this on your journey.

Taking the crystal from the bag, she held it in her hand, her fingers closing over it. It grew warmer. Blaze drew in a deep breath, then held the stone up so that it caught and held beams of the heavens' light. Last night she'd seen a handsome, golden-haired trapper with green eyes. What would this special stone reveal to her this night? She waited, her mind strangely calm.

Suddenly she saw him. He moved in the swirl of mist as though lost. Something about this trapper tugged at her heart. From his clothing she had no doubt he was a white man who had come to the lands of her people to kill for fur. His dark, golden hair shimmered like a summer sunset. She wanted to go to him, to help him, but didn't even know if he was real.

"Who are you?" she whispered.

He turned to her, his bright green eyes boring deep into her soul. *Your destiny. Help me.*

In a blur of color, the trapper fell. A red stain blossomed on his chest and the earth beneath him turned red. Blaze cried out. "Where are you?" Her palms tingled with the need to help this man. Her heart cried out and, deep inside her, she felt her own life seeping from her soul as though she too were bleeding, as though she and this trapper were connected.

She felt his pain and despair. Everything in her said she had to find him before it was too late. Without conscious thought, Blaze hung the crystal pendent around her neck. It rested over her heart and the two stones together sent waves of vibration echoing through her body, mind and soul.

She ran into the cave, dropped the small bag that had contained the stone onto a shelf at the back of the cave then took down a large pearlescent shell and thick smudge stick. Kneeling beside the fire, she held one end of the stick into the fire and watched it flare briefly as the dried cedar, sage and grasses caught fire.

Blaze set the smudge stick on the shell and stood. Using a large, brown eagle feather to fan the glowing tip, she waited for soft tendrils of smoke to rise into the air. Blaze continued to fan the smudge stick with her feather. She inhaled the aromatic scent and, using the feather, swept the incense up and over her head then down her body to dispel any negative vibrations. She repeated the process facing each direction including above and below.

Then she faced south.

"Wakan Tanka."

"Pilamiya."

"Wakan Tanka."

"Wichoni hey."

Blaze closed her eyes and repeated the verse, using her power song, the rhythm in her heart and soul to carry her prayer to the gods.

"Great Spirit. I thank you. Great Spirit. For my life."

Her voice was low, melodic. When she was finished, she ended her prayer-song with the customary, *"Mitakuye Oyasin."* We are all related.

Once again she held up the smudge stick and offered it to each direction, starting with south, then east, west, north, back to south then up to Father Sky and then Mother Earth. The smoke traveled up in waves, thinning as it rose.

Setting the smoldering smudge stick on the shell, Blaze faced south once again. The old woman had told her to travel the wheel of the south, so it was to that direction she appealed as she held both hands high.

"*Itokagata ouye*, South power, and *Tate Topa*, four winds, four directions, I call upon you to guide me on your chosen path." She went through the well-known rituals, praying she'd be in time to save the trapper with green eyes. The spirits had to be guiding her to him, which meant she would find him. For what reason, she wasn't sure yet.

The rising smoke shifted and billowed around her. As she watched calmly, the head of a wolf appeared, lasting for only a moment before the subtly moving air swallowed the image. Blaze tipped her head back and put her heart into her prayer.

"*Wakan Tanka*." Great Spirit. Great Mystery.

"*Onsimala ye*." Have pity on me.

"*Tate Topa*." Four directions, four winds.

"*Onsimala ye*." Have pity on me.

"*Wamakaskan oyate*." Animal nation.

"*Onsimala ye. Hoye wa yelo*." Have pity on me. I am sending a voice.

"I have need of *sunkmanitu tanka*. I have need to find this man." She held up the crystal and, to her dismay, saw that it was a dark red, as though the trapper was bleeding to death inside the stone.

"Onsimala ye." Ho! She ended her prayer for help. She could not go to her people. They no longer traded with trappers or allowed them into their territory. They would not help her find this man. She nearly sobbed aloud. They would not help her because of what she was.

Then she heard it: off in the distance came the howling of wolves. The sounds traveled, a message passed from one pack to another. The keening howls spoke of danger and death and surrounded her. Blaze realized that the news, whatever it was, had reached the alpha pair who lived near her cave. Moving quickly, she snuffed out the smudge stick, grabbed a leather pouch and hurried outside. The howls grew around her. Closer. Louder.

Blaze ran down the path to the tree line where she spotted dark shapes slinking low to the ground. A pair of eyes glowed in the dark. Blaze looked at the alpha male. "You hear the messages carried by the wind," she told him. "You hear the song of your brothers. Will you help me? Will you lead me to this man?"

The alpha wolf didn't hesitate. The human had saved his mate, saved his children. He gave a low growl. Two more members of his pack slid out of the shadows. He turned, glanced back at the woman. When she followed, he turned and loped off into the dark.

Blaze kept pace with the wolves, ignoring her exhaustion. The ugly truth that her "father" had killed her parents—parents she still could not remember—and taken her from her own people snapped at her mind.

She tried to tamp down her grief. The rawness of it came not from memories, but from a deep pit inside of her. Anger rose from that long-forgotten grave with the fury of a fire that would not be denied. Around her, the wind gusted and blew with low keening cries.

The fire inside her leapt to life. Her dreams swept across her mind. She could no longer deny what had happened. She needed to cry, to scream, to grieve.

A low growl startled her. Blaze opened her eyes. Around her, the air vibrated with fury. The alpha male stood there, his eyes boring into hers. The other wolves surrounded him, pacing, clearly agitated.

"I'm sorry, my friend." Blaze put her hands to her head. "So tired." She just wanted to lie down and sleep and wake up to find that her life hadn't changed. Before the dreams, she'd at least been somewhat content with her life. She'd accepted what she had as all there was. Now she knew better, and the bitter truth was hard to accept.

Standing, she once again followed the wolves. By the time they came to a stop atop a grassy knoll, the swirling pink hues of the new day were blooming across the horizon. She sucked in a deep breath. And gagged.

Death rode the wind.

She gripped the trunk of a tree for support. The

wolves paced and whined, then turned and ran back the way they'd come. As Blaze ran down the hill, she understood that she was on her own.

Her heart nearly broke when she came upon the first lifeless bodies. Two wolves and one man lay with their blood darkening the earth. When Blaze came to the heart of the battle, she stopped with a cry. Death clouded the air. Her swiftly scanning gaze picked out two more bodies. Movement drew her attention. She spotted another wolf standing near some thick brush. She moved toward him but he turned to flee.

"Wait!" Blaze stopped and met the wolf's sorrowful gaze with her own. She reached out and tried to merge her mind with his to see what had happened, and what lay in wait for her beyond the trees, but she found it difficult to push past the images haunting the wolf. She sensed his deep loss, and when he turned once more she saw his raw, torn flesh and had to swallow her own cry of pain.

Again she sent images to the injured animal. She could help him. Could he help her? But as soon as the animal was within reach, the wolf bared his teeth. Yet he didn't run. He backed away then waited.

Blaze understood. The wolf had no desire for her to heal him, but he wanted her to follow. Entering the cool, aromatic stand of cedars, she heard the sound of running water. She followed the injured animal along the stream. Rounding a bend, the vibrations in the air changed.

The sound of a whine drew her attention. The

injured wolf limped into the tall, dried grass. He turned and gave a low cry in his throat. It took a moment for Blaze's overwhelmed mind to spot the booted foot poking out of the brush. When she did, she hurried over. Parting the grass, she cried out.

"Oh no!" she whispered as she stared down into open, sightless green eyes. These same eyes she'd seen in her crystals: those of the handsome trapper.

Blaze rushed to his side, tears sliding down her face. "I'm too late!" Staring down into the strong, rugged features, she pulled out her clear crystal and held it in one hand. It was completely blank. No green eyes, no red blood. Just the stars that seemed to pulse with life. Braced for the horror of death, she cupped her palm to one side of the young trapper's face, feeling as though she'd lost part of her soul.

Setting the crystal on his chest, she was startled when a tiny spark of green flickered in the heart of the stone. Stunned, she kept her palm on his face, and leaned close, her breath fanning over his face as she stretched out her other hand, holding it over him. She lowered her palm to his bloody chest.

There was no heartbeat, no sign of air going in and out of his lungs, yet she felt something, not physical but deeper. His body might have given up, but the spirit of the man remained.

"No!" She pressed her hand hard onto his chest and gripped the side of his face. Tears slipped from her eyes as she stared into his eyes. One dripped onto his cheek. "You cannot go."

Beneath her hand, she felt a sudden jolt. Hope flared in her soul.

"I'm not too late," she realized, and without thought to the danger of retrieving a soul that had already departed the body, Blaze merged with the stranger. He didn't feel like such a stranger to her heart.

In the instant before she connected, she heard a voice echo: *You play with life.* Her "father."

Staring down at the handsome stranger, Blaze shook her head. "No," she said softly. "I *save* life." And with that, she threw her protective aura up, and with the arrival of the first rays of dawn, she stared into the dying man's eyes and sought the life within.

Trapped by the consequence of his discontent and thirst for power, Inyan, the ancestor of all gods became part of Maka, *the earth, claiming the rocks, mountains and high hills as his domain. He was drab. Ugly. But he gave Earth depth and texture. Rocks and stones sang with the energy of his spirit.*

CHAPTER FIVE

So this was being near dead. Luc stood at the edge of life and death. Actually, he figured he was more dead than alive. Hell, maybe he was dead all the way. He felt nothing, saw nothing, heard nothing. Just a swirling gray mist that pulled him deeper into more shades of gray.

If this was dead, it wasn't so bad. He felt no pain, only an overwhelming sense of sadness. But why was he sad? Drifting, he stared into the smoky mists. He felt as though he'd forgotten something important or left something behind. But what? If he was truly dead—and he believed that he was— then what did it matter? But something did. He tried to go back, but where was back? Everything looked the same in this void of nothingness.

Trapper! Look for the light!

The sudden and unexpected sweet voice of a woman made Luc whirl around.

"Who's there? Show yourself."

Seek the light!

The voice came again, a low, husky command, the sound warming him from the inside, making him realize that he'd felt cold. He *felt*. The world of nothingness became more frightening. He struggled against the gray void that seemed to be pressing in around him, pushing him away from the voice of an angel.

"There is only darkness. Where are you?" He couldn't see anything. Where was that sweet voice coming from?

Follow my voice.

Luc shoved his way through the thickening mists. "Who are you?" He had to keep her talking so he could find her.

I am a friend. I have come to bring you back into the light of life.

Luc halted. "I'm dead." Speaking the words aloud made it sound final. Real. And he didn't want it to be real. He didn't want to die, he wanted to live.

It is not finished. You cannot leave this world.

Finished? Once again, Luc felt as though he'd left something or someone behind. The feeling nagged deep in his mind but he couldn't seem to think or even remember much. Like, how he had reached this place.

Where was he? Reaching out, he waved his hands, unable to even see them in the swirling gray. It dawned on him that he couldn't see his body, so what if he couldn't see his angel with the honey-sweet voice?

"Show yourself to me. I cannot see you," he said.

You must come to me.

The woman's soft voice mesmerized Luc. It washed over him, surrounded and filled him until all he could think about was doing what she asked. "Why can you not come to me?"

The more he heard the voice, the more desperate he became to find her. He didn't want to wander in this endless, colorless world. He wanted his angel. Needed to find his angel. More than anything, he wanted to see the face of his angel.

"How can I find you if I cannot see you?" He ran, but felt like he was moving through mud. Her voice stopped him.

Stop! You must choose life. Free will. I cannot make the choice for you. It must be yours. Choose now, Trapper.

Luc tried to move faster, but was hampered by the thickening mist. "Fine. I choose life."

Then you will find me. A soft, rhythmic chant swirled around him. When it grew fainter, he panicked and ran blindly. "Don't leave. Don't leave me alone in this place." The faster he ran to find her, the fainter her voice and the more sluggish his attempts to claw through the thick veil of nothingness.

Search for me with your heart.

Luc halted and forced himself to remain still. He concentrated on the soft voice, turned toward it and focused not just his mind but his heart. Moments before he'd accepted that he was dead; now he refused to accept it. The voice warmed his breast and gave him hope. That lightened the swirling gray.

"Keep talking. Let me hear your voice." Her sweet, sweet voice. Luc listened to her calm chanting, focused on her, yearned to see her, to touch her. Slowly, a small pinpoint of light grew in the center of the curtaining gray veil.

He walked toward the light, keeping her voice in his heart until it was all he knew or felt. The light blazed white-blue, a long, narrow bubble that came at him, then surrounded and encompassed him.

Warmth replaced the chill that had begun to invade his heart and soul, and the light inside the blue bubble filled and comforted him. He walked down the tunnel of brilliant light and saw her standing in the center of a blue cloud. No, blue flames. It was a blue fire with flames that shot out in all directions, blinding him to the woman's features.

Suddenly he stood before her, floating effortlessly inside the blue bubble. "This is a dream," he whispered. "Or heaven. You're an angel. I've gone to heaven." She came into focus and as he stared deep into her eyes he felt as though he were drowning. Her irises were a blue so brilliant it hurt to look into them.

Her hair, a sheen of blue-black, floated around her head, the strands long and endlessly flowing. She smiled gently and he felt as though he truly had died and gone to heaven. Her mouth was full, soft and alluring. Her cheeks were defined, her face a small oval. She was heavenly.

"My angel." If she was what awaited him in heaven, he'd go. He could look upon her forever and listen to that voice. Her beauty dropped him to his knees.

The woman came forward. She tipped her head to one side. "I know not of angels or this place you call heaven. The spirits led me to you and placed you in my care. We must return quickly." She turned.

Luc jumped to his feet and reached out to stop her. To his surprise, she felt warm. Soft. Real.

"Wait. Where are you going? Where are you taking me?"

Golden light burst around them in the form of tiny stars. "Home." She stepped onto the glittering golden path.

Luc stepped onto the path of stars, too, his eyes wide as they whirled downward. His angel faded. He reached out. Couldn't find her. He called out to her.

"Don't leave me!" But the air in front of him shimmered as the woman began fading.

Blaze kept one hand on the man's chest, felt the weak rise and fall of each shallow breath and the faint beat of his heart. Relief washed through her. She could now use her healing light to save him.

Her other hand was fisted around her sacred blue stone as she called upon the powers of healing gifted to her by *Wakan Tanka*. Twice in a two-day period she entered a higher realm, called forth what she needed for this man to start the healing process.

Closing her eyes, she allowed the heat to flow into her, through her, around her. Her stone grew warm and became a blue flame. Power could not be held fast. It was a gift to be honored and called upon when needed. It came to her from the gods. It demanded honor and respect.

But unlike Walks Like Turtle, she felt a connection to this man. She stared down at him, took in the rugged features, the thick beard on his chin. She couldn't see his jaw line but knew it was strong and firm.

His nose was long and straight, his brows a slash of golden brown, and his eyes . . . Those grass-green eyes had captivated her from the first moment the gods had revealed them to her.

Her destiny.

She wasn't sure what that meant. Her future was unknown, and she had no idea what role this man would play. He was a trapper, a white man, and he would not be welcomed or allowed into her village.

Yet it was clear that he was hers. She'd been led to him. He'd died, and somehow she'd been given the ability to call him back to life. The realization shook her to the core. How could she do such a wondrous thing and not be a holy woman?

She felt the hole in his chest start to close, and the wound in his back. The blood sealed and tissue began fusing together. His blood sang from her touch and surged powerfully through him.

She kept her hands on him until she knew for sure that he was well on the way to recovery. His body had taken from her the knowledge of how to heal and would do the job quickly while he slept.

When she was done, she sat there and stared down at him. His color was better, his breathing stronger, and the bleeding of his wounds had stopped. The wounds took on a dull sheen, showing that already they were scabbing over to heal from the outside in.

Taking some time to rest, Blaze stared at the trapper. He was handsome, with his golden hair the color of ripening grass. And his eyes—those deep, green eyes—reminded her of a rich meadow. She loved to run and twirl in the tall blades then fall and let its coolness surround her. It was like swimming in a lake of grass.

That was what his eyes felt like: a meadow. And the rest of him was also easy on the eyes. His bronzed skin, the firm chest and hard muscles—he not only looked good, he felt good to touch. Warm. Hard yet soft.

She ran a finger down the side of his face and studied the hard planes, the rugged valleys, but stopped at his mouth. It was relaxed in sleep, parting with each breath. Pulling her hand back, she continued to look her fill and to pretend for a short while that he was hers.

The sound of whining drew her attention to the wolf who'd remained close by. Once more she tried to merge with him. She offered her healing, though she was far too weak. As before, the wolf refused.

"Free will," she murmured as she watched the wolf saunter over to a boulder and plop down, his muzzle on his front paws. Weak, exhausted both in mind and body, she lay down next to her handsome trapper. Long after she'd poured heat, light and love into him, a faint glow remained, a bubble of protection as the sun rose above them.

Connie had ruined everything! Again! Pacing furiously along a narrow ribbon of water, the man kicked rocks that flew high then plopped down into the water. His selfish bastard of a brother had ruined all his plans, then he'd made things even worse by dying.

He'd stabbed his brother in the chest and had ripped the magical stone from around his neck. He wasn't sure what had happened to him after that, as he'd been attacked by that stupid owl.

Pacing, he tried to remember, but everything had happened so fast and it had been dark. But he had a sense that his brother had changed himself into a wolf—the same wolf that had come after him and fallen after it had been shot.

He'd sent Walt and Abe back to check the bodies, as he needed to know for sure if his brother was dead or alive. And the woman. The two trappers had come back with no information. They were now off to the side, muttering amongst themselves.

Idiots. They'd ruined everything by letting the squaw escape.

He stared down at the cold, flat stone he'd ripped from his brother's neck. It sat in the palm of his hand, a green and black magical disk. It was his now. As was the power it held. Problem was, he had no idea how to work it, and the fact that his brother had died before telling him now pissed him off royally.

He felt nothing for the loss of his brother. He'd always hated and resented Connie. Connie got everything. Connie was better than he was. Smarter and better looking, he hadn't had to work as hard to get what he needed.

He grinned, a twisted sneer. No matter. He'd always taken what he'd wanted from Connie. Food, toys, and later, girls. Not willing ones, but he'd taken them all the same. Hatred made his hands shake, and he swiped impatiently at a trickle of sweat running down his brow.

His hair was matted with dust and sweat. Flies swarmed around him, making him wish he hadn't lost his hat in the fight. It kept the flies off. Now what was he going to do? Nothing was going right. He hadn't meant to kill his baby brother, but it was Connie's fault for refusing to share his secrets.

All he'd meant to do was to scare him, to make that squaw give *him* a magical stone. Connie could have done that when he'd confronted him instead of telling him no. But as always, Connie wanted it all for himself. Holding the rock up into the bright light of the sun, he wondered how this tiny stone had transformed his brother into an owl. And all that stuff he'd overheard between Luc and Connie: shifting shapes, becoming wolves? It was true! He'd seen it with his own eyes. Twice.

It was stuff and nonsense. Old legends and stories mothers told their children. In all his years trapping, he'd never heard about any "SpiritWalkers." Didn't even know exactly what a SpiritWalker was. But he supposed he now knew enough. This little rock had power, and that power now belonged to him.

But unless he learned the magic words to make the stone work, it was useless. He studied the stone. One side was plain, the other had strange markings etched into the surface. Clutching it as his brother had done, he concentrated on turning into an owl. He even tried flapping his arms.

"Hey, gonna fly now?"

Whirling around, he glared at Walt. "Watch it," he growled, picking up his rifle.

Walt backed up. "Settle, mate. Jest havin' some fun."

"You find that woman?"

The man paled. "No sign of her. Boys and me went all over the area like you ordered." He glanced around, then spoke in a hushed voice. "I'm tellin' ya, I saw her turn into an owl and fly off."

"Drunk fool." He rubbed his face, winced at the stinging, then stared at the blood still seeping from his wounds. His face ached from the deep cuts and punctures made by the owl's talons, and the back of his arm was ripped to hell. He glared down at his shredded shirtsleeve.

Walt looked as well, but wisely didn't make any comments other than a muttered, "Wasn't *that* drunk." But Walt looked doubtful. "Leastways, didn't think so."

He didn't want Walt thinking too closely about what happened last night, so he said, "Your stupid pals probably disturbed that owl with all their damn shooting. Told you I wanted Connie and his whore alive." His plan had been good. Dress up his pals as natives and attack. But they'd been trigger-happy, and everything had gone wrong. He tucked the stone away.

"Saw the woman go down. She's out there." That was no lie. He'd struck the owl then saw the bird go down, then he'd seen the woman crawling away, but before he got to her, she'd vanished. Fools probably hadn't looked in all the brushes.

"We're going back." He had a choice: go after the girls, which was riskier, as Travers and Alex were with them, or go back to find the woman. If she'd crawled off somewhere hurt, she couldn't have gotten far. And if she'd gotten away, she'd return to look for Connie and Luc. His lips twisted. Luc had been killed. Too bad. But he had no use for the bastard son of a bastard.

So . . . if he couldn't find the woman, then hell, he'd go after the rest of them. They were all Spirit-Walkers, and no one knew he was behind the attack. Yeah, he had plenty of time to go after the girls. Especially the oldest one. She was a looker. He'd make her reveal the secret of what she was, and he could take his time. There were plenty of places in the wilderness to keep a woman hidden.

Watching Walt order the two remaining men to pack up, he slung his pack onto his back and prepared to go after everything he wanted.

* * *

Bright light pierced the cottony fog of Luc's mind, yanking him from his warm, safe cocoon. He rolled his head to the side to escape the painful light and forced himself to open his eyes. He winced, moaned, then struggled to bring his sight into focus. Everything seemed blurry. He concentrated on taking slow, deep, even breaths. He tried to move but felt stiff and sore.

And pinned down.

He froze, slowly taking stock of his surroundings. He lay on the ground. Couldn't see anything beyond the wall of ferns and the red-orange spotted lilies and some other orange-yellow flowers. Slowly he rolled his head.

And saw his angel.

The strange dream came back in a flash: the feeling of having died and gone to someplace where he was alone in a gray void. Then he'd heard a voice: her voice, he'd bet. She'd called to him, guided him and surrounded him with blue light and golden stars.

He rolled his eyes. Some dream, he thought. Yet as he stared at the woman, he knew her features. The full, soft mouth, the smooth-planed cheekbones that made her look like a princess; and the perfect oval of her face.

He tried to sit. His low curse and moan of pain woke the woman. She sat and blinked up at him. Her gentle hands firmly pushed him back down. "Do not move. Remain still," she said in Lakota, her voice husky from sleep.

Her touch calmed him as she wiped the sweat from his brow with a wet cloth. Luc allowed himself to just float for a moment. "Voice of an angel," he whispered in French.

"I must be dead." He felt his chest with his hand. His vest was open and stiff with blood. There was a bandage around his chest. He stared up at the woman. "Am I dead?" This time he used Lakota. He remembered being alone in a world of no color, no feeling, no warmth. Not until his angel with extraordinary eyes came to him. He remembered how they blazed with blue fire.

His angel shook her head. "No. You live."

Luc took shallow breaths. "If you say so," he rasped in French. He felt like hell. He tried to move, but found himself weak as a baby. Damn, but he hurt. He believed her: He was alive. No matter how much he hurt, it was better than that cold void where he felt nothing.

He rolled his head to the side, seeking relief from the sunlight. He lifted a hand and rested it over his eyes as he remembered how her beauty had overwhelmed him, but it had been her voice that had mesmerized him and led him onto a glittering path of stars.

He moved his hand and squinted, trying to see the woman's face, but the sun formed a halo around her, revealing a vibrant rainbow of color that seemed to pulse.

"Are you really an angel?" He lifted a hand, touched her, felt softness. "You saved my life." After remembering she didn't understand French, he reverted to Lakota.

She smiled sadly. "Ah, Trapper. You saved yourself. Free will. You had choice. You chose life. I gave you the ability to heal yourself, but had you chosen not to return to this world, I could have done nothing."

Luc remembered only the panic he'd felt at the thought of losing that voice, of never hearing it again. Blinking, his vision finally clear, he found himself staring up into the blazing, strangely colored eyes of the angel in his dream. He ran a finger down her cheek. "My angel."

Her tired eyes gazed down at him. "I do not know what an 'angel' is. I am called Blaze."

"Blaze . . ." He let the name roll off his tongue and found he liked it. He stared into her eyes. "I am Luc. Luc Cordell. You came to me. Saved my life." The thought of having been so close to death made his heart pound.

"You crossed over to the other side," she confirmed as she held her hand over his heart. Immediately, Luc felt his pulse slow.

"You brought me back. Why?" He ran his hand down his chest and felt the bandage made of strips of hide.

Sitting back on her heel, Blaze bowed her head again. "You chose to return," was all she replied.

Luc frowned but, when his angel stood, blocking the sun's rays, he sighed in relief. The color hovering around her seemed to fade, leaving Luc to believe that it had been caused by the sun in his eyes and his pain.

Angel or not, she was beautiful: a slim, dark-haired angel with the deepest blue eyes he'd ever seen. Her doeskin skirt was torn and short, revealing slim, bare legs. Luc knew where she'd gotten the strips to bandage his wounds.

She moved away. He cried out, "Don't leave!" The idea of losing her was painful.

"I am not leaving."

Luc lifted his head and watched as she picked up a fur-wrapped pouch. Moments later, she returned with a small wooden bowl. Water splashed over the side as she knelt beside him once again and held the cup to his lips.

"Drink, Trapper. You lost a lot of your life-giving blood. Your body will make more, but it needs time."

Luc drank, already feeling stronger. And much clearer in the head. When she took the water away, he sighed. He let out a gasp as his vision sharpened, the haze and blurriness clearing to allow him to see that the woman's eyes were a mixture of blues and browns that shaded into greens as they traveled around the black pupil. Blue and yellow webbing formed a second layer of color. It was . . . familiar.

"Your eyes." His mother's and sisters' eyes weren't quite so dramatic. They were more greens and brown, with hints of paler blue and yellows. But none of them had this second strange webbed ring of color.

Then the truth hit him. The angel who'd healed him was a SpiritWalker. Like his earth mother and sisters, and through marriage, his father. He'd never seen her before, knew she wasn't part of his earth mother's tribe, as her village was small, but who was she, and where had she come from? He'd never come across any other SpiritWalkers, and had never thought to ask if there were other tribes.

"Where are the others?" he asked. He didn't see anyone but the woman, which surprised him. The warriors in Eagle Woman's village guarded their women well.

"I am alone."

Luc eyed her with suspicion. "But . . . you're a woman."

She cocked her head. "The woman who saved your life," she said stiffly. Luc didn't have to hear the warning in her voice; he saw it in her eyes as blue flame ignited beneath the strange yellow webbing. Luc thought that he could stare into those fascinating eyes forever.

"Point taken," he conceded. "Why are you out here alone? It's too dangerous." He thought of his uncles. One of them had turned traitor and had betrayed Luc's family. Now he fully understood why his mother's people kept to themselves and guarded their secret from the rest of the world.

It hit Luc hard that he had been the one responsible for betraying his family's secret. Images of the night before slammed into his mind: his father waking him, their flight into the night, the attack. Denial made him shake his head back and forth. He welcomed the throbbing pain even as he tried to remember all the details. His memory of the battle was still hazy. He only remembered that he'd gone back to help his parents and had ended up in a fight for his life. He'd failed his father. Broken his promise.

"My family," he said hoarsely. "Where are they?" He struggled to his feet and glanced around. "Tell me what you know."

Blaze stood as well. "You are not well enough to get up."

The wind shifted, and for the first time since he'd awakened to find this angel sitting beside him, Luc became aware of the stench of death. The scent struck him hard.

"Merde!" He choked, and the scent dropped him to his knees. Fighting lightheadedness, he surveyed the area and spotted a dead body not far from where he sat. Forcing himself up, he stumbled over to it and froze.

"What the hell?" Though the man was dressed as a native, Luc knew him. He was part of Big Bart's outfit, one of the men who'd agreed to help Luc's family beat out Dan's outfit.

Clenching his fists, Luc searched the area. He found another dead trapper, also dressed as a native. Nearby, he came across a dead Chippewa scout. That made three men total. He also found the bodies of two dead wolves but no sign of his father or mother.

He stared down at the dead bodies of the wolves. They'd given their lives for his family. Standing, feeling weak, he reached out and put his hand on the strong trunk of a pine. A whisper of sound told him the woman was close. He whirled, his eyes hard, his mouth set in a firm line.

She looked sad as she stared around her. "You are the only one I found . . . alive." The word hung between them. He hadn't been alive. Somehow, she'd called him back from the dead.

Luc swayed as his gaze swept the area, settling on the stand of trees where he'd seen his earth mother shift into an owl. But what of his father? He tried to remember. Had his father managed to get away? It had been dark, and there'd been so many enemies. Luc started walking past the dead. His legs buckled and the ground rushed up at him.

Blaze reached out and kept him from eating dirt. She bore most of his weight. He breathed in her sweet scent—the pines, cedar and sunshine. Warmth radiated from her and as he held on to her and allowed her to lead him to a boulder, he found he liked the feel of her against him.

She sat beside him. A breeze swept over Luc, carrying away the stench of death.

"My family. My sisters, my cousins." There were no signs of Alex or Travers. Or Kangee and the girls. He prayed they'd made it to safety. A small movement made him brace his legs and pull the woman behind him.

A lone wolf crawled out of the brush. It stopped and stared at Luc. For just a moment, Luc wondered if it was his father. He quickly dismissed the idea. Had it been his father, he'd have changed back.

The animal lifted its head and gave a low whine, then sat weakly as its hind leg gave out.

Blaze moved closer. She glanced over her shoulder at Luc. "He led me to you."

Luc went to the animal and stared at the wounds. "Can you heal him?" What if it *was* his father? Or his earth mother? No, she had gotten away. He vaguely recalled her shifting into an owl and flying off. Still, the wolf looked badly injured. He had no idea if that could keep a SpiritWalker from shifting.

"The choice is his."

"Try." Luc knelt beside her.

"I will ask." Blaze looked deep into the animal's eyes then spoke. After a few moments, she held out her hands. A golden light surrounded the woman, and Luc felt the heat rising in her as she rested her palms against the wolf's torn flesh.

Staring at the wounds, Luc wondered if this was the same wolf who'd saved his life. He touched the bandaged wound on his chest where he'd been shot, but this wolf had more than one wound. It looked as though it had been in several battles.

The woman threw her head back, and a shimmer of pale blue light cocooned her and the wolf. Mesmerized, Luc stared at her smooth throat, the fine line of her jaw, the sweeping planes of her face and shape of her closed eyes. But it was her softly parted lips that held his gaze. They moved as though she was silently speaking.

He wanted to feel her mouth on his, to taste her, to feel her warmth seeping into him. Drawing a deep breath, he inhaled her sweet scent. A tug of desire slid through him, urging him to go to her, to hold her and mold his body to hers.

Unaware of him, Blaze arched her body, her head falling back, her throat taut, the pulse of her blood drawing Luc's gaze, tempting him to place his lips there to feel the beat of life.

His gaze followed the sheen of blue-black hair as it swept down her back, brushed the ground. His own hands tingled, his body cried out for hers. All he had to do was shift behind her and let her soft curves mold against his hard body. In his mind, he lifted his hands and twined his fingers with hers so that they were one.

The image was so strong, so compelling he had to fight it with all he had. When Blaze was done, he stood and backed away. His family was missing. He had no time for distractions—no matter how beautiful.

He stared hopefully down at the wolf and waited. But the animal just stared at him then put his head back down on his paws. Luc's shoulders sagged. Had the wolf been his father, he'd have changed back now that he was healed. For a brief minute he'd allowed himself to believe.

His earth mother had shifted into an owl. He'd seen her fly away. It stood to reason that his father had also escaped. If so, then his sisters would be safe. The question was, where were they?

Slowly, his memories were returning, and he remembered watching his father and one of his uncles fighting.

"My uncle." An image hit him hard. His uncle. The shape, the voice—both filled with hate. His Uncle Al was a mean son-of-a-bitch when he drank. But he'd raised his brothers. He'd never hurt any of them.

Still, his father had known their enemy. He'd said it was a man he trusted with his life. There were only two men that Luc knew his father had trusted with his life: his brothers. But as far as he knew, his father had told no one of his life as a SpiritWalker. Conrad Cordell would have died before exposing his wife or children to such danger.

"Someone saw," he whispered. It was the only thing that made sense, and if that were true, and if his family had escaped, they were still in danger. How was he going to find them? He turned to Blaze.

"You're a SpiritWalker. Help me find my family."

Blaze frowned. "What is a SpiritWalker?"

Staring into her confused eyes, Luc drew his brows together. Did she not understand him? He knew his Lakota was far from perfect, but so far she'd understood him well enough.

"What game are you playing? Lives are at stake!" When she just stared at him, he grabbed her by the shoulders and gave her a small shake. "Who really sent you?"

Blaze jerked out of his grip and glared. "You distrust me, Trapper?" She waved one hand to encompass the battle scene beyond them. "You think I had something to do with all those deaths?"

Luc saw the hurt in her eyes and heard it in her

voice. It stabbed at him, made him feel like a bully, but something was going on and she was his only hope of answers. He ignored the fact that she'd brought him back from the dead, unless he'd been totally out of his mind from the pain. He glanced down at his chest, saw the bandage, felt the pain and weakness that warned she had been right when she'd told him he was too weak yet.

"I don't know. You tell me."

As power cannot abide within the water or within any solid object, the powers of Inyan *separated from the water and rose to form the deep blue dome that surrounded earth and became* Skan, *the Sky God.*

CHAPTER SIX

Slowly, holding Luc's gaze, Blaze pulled from inside her dress two leather cords around her neck. One was knotted with small polished stones and beads between the knots. It hung down past her breasts.

His gaze fastened onto a blue stone in the shape of an eagle. Tiny, fluffy white feathers dangled from thin strands of sinew and brushed against the softly glowing blue stone.

She held it out. "This was given to me by the spirits. Touch it." Her voice held a challenge.

He did. "It's warm." He watched her drop the stone so that it swung against her fringed dress in a soft blur of color. He shrugged. "So? It was against your skin." Her soft, golden skin. He grew uncomfortable thinking about touching something that had rested against her bare skin; this was no time for *those* kind of thoughts. As he watched, she removed a second stone dangling around her neck. This one, a clear crystal pendent, she held out to him.

"Put out your hand."

He shoved his hands into his pockets. "I don't have time for games or to exchange gifts. I need answers."

Blaze waited for him to comply, her silence more compelling than a spoken command. Luc clenched his teeth in frustration. "Fine." He thrust out his right hand, palm up.

This crystal too was warm in his palm. From her, he thought. Warm and perfect like his angel. He tried to shake off the strange buzzing in his head, but found he couldn't take his eyes off her strangely glowing eyes. The colors were changing, turning as blue as the summer sky above their heads.

Keeping their gazes locked, Blaze closed his fingers around the crystal. She felt the tingle of power slide through his hand and into hers and up her arms. Her heart thudded.

She had no idea what was happening, but she felt as though she was being guided by the spirits in a ritual unknown to her. She traveled down a path never before revealed. She closed her right hand around her own stone, noting that it felt uncomfortably hot.

"Put your other hand around mine." She indicated her right hand.

Luc set his left hand on top of her right, his fingers sliding around hers so he totally enclosed her small hand in his own much larger one. His eyes were wide, his lips parted as though amazed.

Staring deep into his green eyes, she whispered,

"Accept this gift from the gods as you accepted the gift of life. Walk the path you were meant to walk." She brought their joined hands together. As soon as they touched, a faint light shimmered around them, growing larger, enclosing them in a translucent bubble of blues and greens.

Luc's stare was filled with awe.

Blaze felt the raw power flowing between them. Something important had just happened. Keeping them linked, she opened the hand holding her stone. Even before she saw it, she knew it was changed.

The center of her blue stone glowed with a green light. "The color of your eyes. A thread of your spirit now lives within me, Trapper. Within my soul stone." Her voice was hushed, filled with awe. She glanced at Luc, saw that he was pale and trembling.

"Look," she commanded softly, giving his right hand a soft squeeze.

Luc couldn't look away from Blaze. Her eyes were a soft, misty rainbow of heaven and earth. Light shone deep in her eyes reflecting wonder and awe. And something primitive made him lean forward to be closer, to feel what he saw on her face.

"Look," she said again. This time her long black lashes lowered as she stared at his closed fist. The stone seemed to burn and throb with life. Luc was afraid to look yet could not resist her gentle command. Tearing his gaze from hers, he took a deep breath and slowly opened his fingers.

"Impossible!"

The denial came out a harsh choking sound. He stared down at the green crystal in his hand, his mind rejecting what his eyes clearly saw. The clear six-sided pendant Blaze had given him moments before remained, but it was now the same green as his eyes . . . with a single, delicate thread of blue woven through.

"How—"

The truth of what she'd done blazed in his palm. She was a SpiritWalker, and unless he was very much mistaken, she'd just made him one. He stood in shocked and numb disbelief as the heat traveled up his arm and spread into every cell. A strange vibration hummed through him and that scared the hell out of him—more than any thought of dying had.

He thrust his hand out. "Take it."

Blaze shook her head. "It is yours, Trapper. A gift from the spirits." Her eyes were moist with tears as she ran a finger over the center glow of green. "I was just the caretaker. That crystal was meant to be yours."

"Luc. My name is Luc." He said it absently, as heat from the stone pulsed deep in his palm, hummed up his arm.

Spirits. SpiritWalkers.

He lifted his hand to toss the stone away, but seeing that thread of blue, the same blazing blue as Blaze's eyes, stopped him. He glanced from the stone to her then looked up into the sky and found that everything stood in sharp, clear focus, as though someone had wiped his eyes clean. While his sight had always been good, it was better now. Incredibly sharp.

High above his head, he saw a trail of ants crawling along pine needles. Lifting his gaze higher, he spotted a tiny bird nest nestled in a fork of branches. Three tiny beaks rested on the rim and he could hear their soft peeps. Carried to him by the wind, he heard an orchestra of bird song with animal chatter and the hum of bees mingled throughout.

His heart thudded and his lungs burned, as though someone was squeezing the air from him. "What have you done?" he asked, backing away from Blaze. The trunk of a tree stopped his retreat. A low vibrating hum ran down his back, and he could feel the sap running deep in the heart of the tree. He jumped away with a yell and his horror quickly turned to anger. He strode back to Blaze and towered over her.

"Tell me, damn you. Tell me that you didn't just turn me into a SpiritWalker!"

Blaze went still, her eyes locked onto his. "What is a SpiritWalker?" Her voice was low, hushed, her eyes wide as she brought her soul stone to her breast and held it there.

Luc tore his gaze from hers to keep from drowning in those soft misty depths. "What the hell game are you playing at, *Ange?*" His speech slid back and forth from Lakota to French, and he used the French word for angel. He paced in front of her.

"No game," she whispered.

Luc glared at her, his eyes hard, his lips tightly compressed. The muscles of his neck were so taut that an ache was growing at its base. "I know what you are, so tell me the truth! Tell me what you did! How did you turn me into a SpiritWalker? And why?"

"I don't know what a SpiritWalker is." She reached out to touch his arm.

Sparks from her fingers slid under his skin and flooded him with heat. And something else he didn't want to admit. Desire. Hot, strong, and primitive, it thundered through his body, pooling in his groin. He wanted her. Needed to touch her, to feel her hands sliding over his body, her breath mingling with his. She was his *ange*. His angel.

Luc wanted to gaze into her eyes and lose himself in the deep rainbow of color and be swallowed by the blue blaze. He wanted to walk along a golden path of stars with her. He wanted her. All of her. His body didn't care what she was, just that she would be his.

Feeling himself weakening fueled his indignant anger, his righteous fury. She'd changed him, made him into something he had no desire to become. He focused on that, used cold fury to put out the fire raging inside him from her innocent touch.

"How is this possible? I did not consent to become a SpiritWalker. And how can you not know?"

Luc took several deep breaths. He didn't want to be like his father. Or his sisters. He was happy being just plain human. It had been one of the factors in his decision to leave his family. He liked being normal, had wanted a normal life doing what normal people did.

In the back of his mind was the crazywoman who'd lived on the street where he'd grown up. She slept in the alleys and talked all the time, sometimes shouting at people. One day, while out playing, Luc's two friends decided to chase her off by throwing rocks and calling her names. When she started cursing them, the boys had called her a witch.

Then she'd looked right at Luc and pointed her finger at him, shouting that death would change his life. The look in her eyes had been frightening, and he and his friends had run off.

Luc had vowed to never to go near the old crazywoman again, but to his everlasting horror, his mother had died within a week and the curse came to pass: death changed his life. But it was only once he discovered his father's new abilities that he'd remembered the old woman and thought that perhaps she wasn't just an old crazy witch but a person with special abilities. Living so close to natives, he'd seen too many odd happenings to not believe in other forces.

Already his young sisters were growing in their strange abilities, and as much as he loved them, he did find the whole SpiritWalker thing uncomfortable. Whenever they visited Eagle Woman's people, Luc made excuses to go off on his own.

"I am sorry," Blaze said, hurt and devastated by what she'd done.

"You stole from me. You stole my free will."

GET UP TO
4 FREE BOOKS!

You can have the best romance delivered to your door for less than what you'd pay in a bookstore or online. Sign up for one of our book clubs today, and we'll send you **FREE* BOOKS** just for trying it out...**with no obligation to buy, ever!**

HISTORICAL ROMANCE BOOK CLUB

Travel from the Scottish Highlands to the American West, the decadent ballrooms of Regency England to Viking ships. Your shipments will include authors such as CONNIE MASON, CASSIE EDWARDS, LYNSAY SANDS, LEIGH GREENWOOD, and many, many more.

LOVE SPELL BOOK CLUB

Bring a little magic into your life with the romances of Love Spell—fun contemporaries, paranormals, time-travels, futuristics, and more. Your shipments will include authors such as KATIE MACALISTER, SUSAN GRANT, NINA BANGS, SANDRA HILL, and more.

As a book club member you also receive the following special benefits:

- **30% OFF** all orders through our website & telecenter!
  (Plus, you still get 1 book FREE for every 5 books you buy!)
- **Exclusive access to** special discounts!
- **Convenient** home delivery **and 10 days to return any books you don't want to keep.**

There is no minimum number of books to buy, and you may cancel membership at any time. See back to sign up!

*Please include $2.00 for shipping and handling.

YES! ☐

Sign me up for the **Historical Romance Book Club** and send my THREE FREE BOOKS! If I choose to stay in the club, I will pay only $13.50* each month, a savings of $6.47!

YES! ☐

Sign me up for the **Love Spell Book Club** and send my TWO FREE BOOKS! If I choose to stay in the club, I will pay only $8.50* each month, a savings of $5.48!

NAME: _____

ADDRESS: _____

_____

TELEPHONE: _____

E-MAIL: _____

☐ **I WANT TO PAY BY CREDIT CARD.**

☐ VISA ☐ MasterCard ☐ DISCOVER

ACCOUNT #: _____

EXPIRATION DATE: _____

SIGNATURE: _____

Send this card along with $2.00 shipping & handling for each club you wish to join, to:

Romance Book Clubs
1 Mechanic Street
Norwalk, CT 06850-3431

Or fax (must include credit card information!) to: 610.995.9274. You can also sign up online at www.dorchesterpub.com.

*Plus $2.00 for shipping. Offer open to residents of the U.S. and Canada only. Canadian residents please call 1.800.481.9191 for pricing information.
If under 18, a parent or guardian must sign. Terms, prices and conditions subject to change. Subscription subject to acceptance. Dorchester Publishing reserves the right to reject any order or cancel any subscription.

JOIN NOW!

Glaring at the woman, he saw she truly looked sorry. The irony of the situation struck Luc. Standing before him was a woman he found beautiful and mesmerizing, and for the first time he found himself wanting to have a woman at his side. Over the years, he'd met many beautiful women, but none that he'd wanted to settle down with.

Most native tribes and villages were friendly to trappers. They were eager for trade items, and Luc had heard stories of some tribes who'd traded their women for guns or whiskey. This woman was beautiful, and she'd saved his life. She was his angel, yet she was the very thing he'd avoided since learning the truth about his earth mother and father. Now he'd become one of them. How unfair.

He glared at her. Angel or not, Blaze would have to undo what she'd done. He was leaving. Now.

The thought of walking away, of leaving his angel sent pain slicing through his chest. He managed to stride away and, through sheer will, fight the pain, but the weakness of his injured body and the loss of blood made his knees buckle. Blaze caught him and with surprising strength led him away from the dead bodies to a clear area beside the stream where the air was clean.

She left him there, fighting waves of dizziness. When she returned, she had her leather pouch and his heavy pack.

"You have to rest, to allow your body to finish healing. I gave it what it needed, but you have to allow it to do the work."

Luc took shallow breaths and leaned on his pack, his eyes closed. He threw one arm over his face to block out the sun. Damn, his head hurt, though more from the raging thoughts than the nasty cut where he'd hit his head on a rock after he was shot.

No matter. He wouldn't be trapped. Wouldn't allow his heart to be stolen, or his life, and that was what his angel had done: she'd stolen from him what he was, what he wanted to be. "Take the damn rock back. I don't want it."

Silent tears streaked down Blaze's cheeks. "I cannot. It is your soul stone. I am sorry I've caused you pain, but I cannot undo what I did. I do not know what I did."

There it was again; her denial. Luc swung his arm off his face, his temper exploding. "How the hell can you not know what you did?"

Straightening her shoulders, Blaze stared down at him, her eyes beginning to spark with temper. "Spirits guided me." She held out her blue stone, letting the rays of the sun spark off the green center. "It just happened." Her voice was filled with both bewilderment and wonder.

"Well, figure out how to take it away. I . . . I don't want this." He bit out each word and slashed his hand down to punctuate his feelings on the matter. He felt frustrated, trapped, and he didn't like either feeling. He was a man who'd long been in charge of his destiny.

He glared at Blaze. "Look, *Ange*. I appreciate the honor, but the life of a SpiritWalker is not one for me. You had no right to do this to me." He folded his arms. "This was not of my free will, and I know that free will is the heart of what you people believe." His earth mother had drummed that into the girls daily, and Blaze had mentioned it herself. It was the SpiritWalkers' most important rule and one that could not be broken without severe consequences.

Blaze drew in a deep breath and lowered herself to the ground in front of him. He tore his gaze from the smooth expanse of thigh revealed by her short skirt. When she leaned forward, he had to close his eyes. The bewilderment in her look, the sorrow and pain tugged hard at his heart. She looked like she was ready to cry, and he couldn't bear the thought of hurting her. Angels didn't cry. But angels didn't change people into SpiritWalkers, either. He opened his eyes and held on to his anger.

"Please, tell me. What is a SpiritWalker?"

Luc didn't answer.

"You will not tell me? Why not?" She sounded completely confused. Deep in her eyes he saw hurt and desperation. "Did I not save your life?"

"You did more than save my life," Luc bit out, dragging his hand off his face.

"I did not know what I was doing." Anger was beginning to bubble inside her.

"Which means you cannot undo it." Luc let his head fall back. How could this woman not know what she was? "You saved my life, Angel. How can you not know?"

Blaze crossed her arms in front of her as though

warding off a chill. "I know only that I am different. I talk to the spirits, merge my spirit with those of my brothers and sisters . . ." She waved her hands to indicate all around her. "I can fly with the eagle or hawk, run with the wolf or be as still as a mouse hiding beneath a root or rock. I send my thoughts on the wind, listen to the voices that travel on the wind. I can also call up a storm or a breath of clean air to erase death."

She tipped her chin as though daring him to be afraid of her. "My greatest gift is healing, my greatest joy is taking a dull stone and giving it beauty, feeling the hum of ancient life bestowed by *Inyan*, ancestor of all, who is trapped in rocks and stones and mountains. But I do not know what you wish me to know." She fell silent.

Luc studied her, saw the eager hope in her eyes as she waited for him to speak. She held her hands in her lap but her fingers were twisted together. She was nervous. Looking deep in her eyes, he was shocked to see a glint of fear there as well.

"Is that all you have to say?" He leaned back. If she truly did not know what she was, he was in big trouble.

"Is that not enough?" This was not the reaction Blaze had expected. She'd expected to see the trapper's eyes change from further speculation to disbelief, distrust and even fear. But they didn't.

"You forgot to mention shifting shapes." Luc motioned to the still wolf lying several feet away, watching with intent but sad eyes. The animal seemed to be following Blaze wherever she went. Luc couldn't blame the animal for that. "Can you become a wolf?"

Blaze frowned. "I can merge my mind with one. I can see what he sees, feel what he feels, travel with his speed, but I cannot become other than what I am."

Luc eyed her with speculation. "My earth mother is a SpiritWalker. She once told me that she can call upon the spirits of earth's creations. She can become any shape just by calling upon the spirits. She can also merge with any spirit—not just her mind, but her body as well—by asking and receiving permission." He held up the crystal. "Eagle Woman gave my father a green stone and now he is one of them. He too has the ability to shift. To do all those things. A SpiritWalker is very powerful." He glanced at her. "But you know that, *Ange*. I can see that you do."

"Yes. But I never knew what I was. I've never met anyone who can do what I can do." Blaze felt a moment of disappointment. "And I still do not know that this is what I am. I cannot be one of these Spirit-Walkers, as I cannot merge my body. Just my mind."

She paused. The child in her dreams had believed with all her heart that someday she would fly like her parents. "Of course . . . as a child, I believed I could fly. The child within me knew the truth."

Luc watched her bite her lower lip. She looked young, confused. Vulnerable. Some of his anger faded.

"Seek the child within," she said. The words were soft as she stared at the blue stone and its new green center.

"What?"

Blaze looked Luc in the eyes. "Something I was told by the woman who gave me your soul stone.

Luc sat up. "Don't call it that."

Blaze stood and picked up her belongings. "I am sorry, Trapper, for what I've done. I will leave."

Luc was on his feet, though the sudden jolt had his entire body screaming in protest. His hand snaked around her waist. "You're not going anywhere. You're the only one who can undo this."

Blaze glared at him. "Let go of me, Trapper. The choice is mine, whether or not I stay with you." In her heart, she knew she had to stay with him—and not just for answers. Her fingers sought and touched the stone she'd dropped back beneath her dress. She was tied to this man as he was tied to her, and she had a feeling there was no way to undo that. How did one tear apart two spirits that had merged?

"No choice, sweetheart."

A blast of wind whipped around them. Luc's long, golden hair rose around his head and formed a halo of brightness. Hers formed a dark cloud.

Luc smiled grimly. "Gotta do better than that, sweetheart. Child's play. I got three young sisters who can call up the wind when they get mad."

Blaze froze. Forcing her raging emotions to calm and settle, she tipped her chin. "What if I cannot undo this?"

She'd been led to this man, had saved his life and then somehow had merged them together. There was no doubt that this man was important to her future. She just didn't know how or why. She'd connected their spirits, maybe even their hearts and souls. She didn't dare tell Luc that she didn't think anything but death could sever the connection.

She felt it that deep, and the fact that the color of his stone was now in the heart of her soul stone was all the proof she needed.

"You better hope you can," Luc said.

The whine of the wolf drew their attention. He was pacing restlessly, limping.

Blaze stared at the animal. Lifting her head, she sent her senses flaring outward, searching, seeking for whatever was making the animal uneasy. She smelled them, long before she heard: unwashed bodies slick with sweat and dust and a coating of death.

"Someone comes." She grabbed her things and ran into the forest, past the bloating bodies.

Luc grabbed two knives from the dead. He too had caught the scent of someone approaching. He didn't recognize them, and didn't even know how he knew there were two. But his senses were so sharp now, he didn't question his instincts.

He hurried past the scene of death, past the scattering ravens and buzzards, grateful that it wasn't his body about to be picked clean by vultures and opportunistic animals. When they reached a dark thicket, he stopped Blaze.

"Get down. Gotta see who this is," he said. He wiped his knives clean.

Blaze's eyes were wide. "We cannot stay."

"Have to." He calmly slid one knife into his empty sheath; the other he held in his hand. "My family is out there somewhere. Don't know who betrayed them or what happened to them or where they are."

He almost choked. He wasn't even sure they were still alive. He had to find out. "Someone knows that my parents are SpiritWalkers. They attacked, and I need to see who was responsible."

The voices were growing louder. Beside Luc, Blaze held herself still so not even a leaf rustled. Two men drifted out of the shadows, each holding a rifle.

Luc recognized them immediately. Abe and Walt, from Bart's outfit. Two of the man's best trackers. Damn. They were close friends of his Uncle Albert.

Walt stopped in the middle of the scene of death. "Cordell *est fou!*" Crazy. He spat the word as he stared at the dead bodies and the flapping vultures high in the trees above.

Luc's heart sank. This confirmed his knowledge that one of his uncles was involved. He'd had a hard time accepting it. They were a family. To Albert, there was nothing more important. And William— he'd always kept the peace between brothers. How could one of them have betrayed his father like this?

Walt checked every body to be sure it was dead,

and poked into each bush surrounding the area. The stench of death was so bad both men tied cloths over their faces.

"Ain't no one here. Jest a bunch of damn stinkin' bodies. Let's go." Abe's eyes were streaming as he wandered into the trees. "Hey, got me a hat!" He came back holding a hat made of fox fur.

"That's Cordell's." Walt stared around him. "Wait. We're missin' one body. Cordell's nephew. Saw it earlier. No way he got up and walked outta here. He was dead. Or close to it."

Abe joined Walt. "Not here now. Boss ain't gonna be happy if the kid got up and walked off."

Walt got down onto his knees and searched the area. When he found where Luc had bled into the earth, he sat back on his heels. "Didn't walk off alone." He crawled on his hands and knees then picked up a thin strip of fringe.

"Get Cordell and them Chippewa scouts. A woman was here. Got pieces of her dress, and her footprints are all over this place. Gotta be Conrad's woman. The boss is right. She's alive. That'll make him happy. I'll stay and pick up their trail."

Luc felt Blaze stiffen beside him as Abe ran off. He tightened his hand on the handle of his knife. Walt and Abe were both good trackers, and the Chippewa were the best he'd ever worked with. Luc knew no matter how careful he was, the scouts would be on his trail and stick like moss to a tree.

Moving slowly, Luc moved into a low crouch and lifted his hand. He'd buy some time to get a good head start. But Blaze's hand stopped him from throwing the knife.

Looking deep into her eyes, he shook his head. "No choice," he whispered. When she closed her eyes, he drew his arm back and let the knife fly.

Magnificent and majestic to behold, Inyan's mountains rose high, took on the sharpness of peaks, the flatness of bluffs. He became rock and stone. Life flowed around him, and through him.

CHAPTER SEVEN

Red Thunder paced in his lodge. He glared at the eagle whistle. He'd called Blaze many times. Was she making good on her word that she wasn't going to help him? If so, what was he going to do? How was he going to keep the girl quiet? If she refused to help him heal, it would ruin everything he'd worked so hard to achieve.

Standing in his doorway he stared out into the village. As was his due as a medicine man, his lodge was placed near the center. Across from him, the chief and his family had their lodge. On either side were the clans of the Wolf and Turtle.

He liked his position in the village, the high regard and importance that until yesterday he'd accepted as his due. If the girl exposed him, he'd be forced to leave.

Years ago, when he'd first wandered into the village, he'd found it easy to convince the elders and chief that his tribe was gone, that he and his young daughter had no home. He'd been welcomed, and over the years he'd earned their trust.

He'd had an extensive knowledge of healing plants, but it was the girl who'd given him the opportunity to become known as a great healer. He hadn't been able to totally hide her gift, but these people believed she'd gotten that from him.

Healing that warrior yesterday had ruined everything. It was clear that her gift was much more powerful than his. He chewed on the inside of his cheeks while pondering a way to use that to his benefit.

Since the early dawn, he'd heard snatches of conversation outside lodge. Everyone was talking about how Blaze had brought Walks Like Turtle back to life after he, their medicine man, had refused to help. He'd even heard whispers suggesting his daughter was a holy woman.

Red Thunder turned and paced angrily. It was he who should be shaman, should have been appointed shaman after that old fool died. He glared across at the longhouse of the chief and his family.

For years he'd been trying to gain that status. Had the girl confided in him the true extent of her abilities, he'd have already had the title and all that went with it. What other powers did she have that she'd hidden from him?

Pulling a stone from around his neck, he stared down at it. It was red and as cold as the man he'd stolen it from. It held power, great power. He just didn't know how to access it. But as he'd taken it from the man-eagle he'd shot from the sky so many years ago, he knew it was more than just a *wotawe*, a personal stone. This had to be a *wotai*, a stone gift from *Wakan Tanka*.

He fisted his hand around it and shoved it back beneath his shirt just as he shoved the memories of that day back deep into his mind. What was done was done. He ran a hand over his jaw. How long was he to pay for that day when he'd been a young warrior?

How was he to have known that those two eagles were humans? The legend of SpiritWalkers was a myth, a story! At least, he'd believed that at the time. He knew better now.

He ignored the voice reminding him that while he couldn't have known, he should have followed the ways of his people, known that eagles were not for him to shoot. He hadn't engaged in the hunting ceremony where he asked permission to take life. He'd left his tribe to seek visions, and had wandered far from his village when he'd come across the lake where he'd seen that little girl playing on the shore. He'd been amazed to see an eagle soar in low enough to touch her. In the excitement of the moment, all he'd thought about was how the feathers from an eagle would make him a fine headdress. And returning home with a prize of not one but two eagles would make all believe that he was indeed a great medicine man and powerful warrior. He'd wanted that title above all else, for medicine men and shamans were revered. Their power was greater than even that of a chief.

No, he'd not thought of anything else but his own greed as he'd taken aim. He hadn't taken the time for any of the hunting rituals or prayers that a warrior must engage in before taking any form of life. He'd killed not for need, but out of greed. He'd never forget that day, staring down at the dead bodies and being afraid that the gods would strike him dead.

When the Thunder Being started throwing bolts of light down at him, hitting the trees, he'd grabbed the girl and using her as a shield, run. For many years he hadn't fully understood what he'd seen, or what the little girl truly was. It was only over time that he'd unearthed the full legend of SpiritWalkers, and realized that the myth was in fact real, and that child he'd stolen was a child of the gods.

A thrill of fear always snaked through him when he allowed himself to think of what the girl truly was. She had no idea, even now, and he planned to keep it that way. He wanted the power that flowed in her veins, but if he couldn't figure out how to get it, at least he'd have her.

Yes, she would provide the means to his having the life he'd always wanted—had already provided it—and he wasn't going to allow her to ruin what he'd worked so hard to gain. He gathered his bow and arrow, pulled his bearskin over his body and adjusted it to hide the weapons he carried. Then he gathered two gourd rattles and left his lodge.

The bands of claws, teeth, stone, shell and bits of wood all rattled and jingled with every movement.

More rattles covered his chest. To any watching, he looked as though he were going to heal or comfort the injured and dying.

But he planned to go to the girl's cave. He'd wait for her to return, and if she didn't agree to keep their secret . . . ? Then he had no further use for her. He couldn't risk anyone else learning the truth about what she was.

Passing the lodge that belonged to the Turtle clan, he ignored the wailing that came from inside, but when a woman rushed out and ran toward him, he was forced to pause. She bore cuts on her hands and arms, and her hair had been cut to her chin. She pointed a bloodied finger at him. "Your daughter never came during the night. She saved the son of my sister. Why did she not come and save my husband?"

Red Thunder kept his features stoic. "I do not know. I called for her."

The woman began screaming and pulling at her shorn hair. The cut hair and wounds on her body— even to the degree of cutting off fingers—showed the depth of one's grief. Two men rushed out of the lodge, too, but the women refused to let them lead her back inside. Wailing, she threw herself to the ground at Red Thunder's feet.

Red Thunder looked at the men, then at the sobbing woman. He held out the hand that held his staff. "Take her inside. I will prepare a broth for her to ease her pain." He'd been awakened during the night and had spent time trying to heal her husband, but nothing had worked. The man had died.

The woman fought, then gave in and sagged as she was hauled to her feet. "You let my husband die," she accused.

As though being led by spirits, Red Thunder lifted his head proudly and tipped his head back, then drew in a deep breath. Opening his eyes, he stared directly at the woman and her sons.

"Life is for our Creator to give or take. If the Creator, the mysterious *Wakan Tanka*, had wished for the husband of Yellow Bird to live, he would have sent my daughter to him. He would not have allowed such a great warrior to leave us. It was his choice to take that great warrior to the spirit world. A great honor."

The warriors gently led their mother back into the lodge. Relieved, Red Thunder turned, then froze when he saw his chief standing there. Immediately he donned an expression of grief.

Two Arrows looked at him thoughtfully. "What you say is true. A warrior who falls in battle is honored." Chief Two Arrows's voice was low, soft, a direct contrast to his impressive size and stature. "Where is your daughter now? Why did she not come when you summoned her?"

"I do not know." Red Thunder fingered the eagle bone whistle on his chest. "I sent for her. I even went to fetch her myself, but she was not in her cave." He had summoned her as asked, and when she hadn't come he'd gone to fetch her, but the sounds of a wolf pack on the prowl had stopped him. He knew the girl had a gift with animals—

many times he'd caught her running or playing with wild wolves or young deer or bears. For all he knew, they guarded her at night. So he'd turned around and had not left the safety of the woods.

"I have not seen her since she left after healing Walks Like Turtle." Had she run off? Would she be foolish enough or angry enough to leave for good? He thought not. But also knew he had to find her, to talk to her and somehow convince her to keep quiet and do as she was told.

At the very least, if the truth was discovered he'd be outcast; but he had an even darker secret, and for that he'd forfeit his life. Red Thunder would do whatever it took to keep uncovered what he'd done.

Two Arrows crossed his arms on his chest. "Where would she go?"

Furious but knowing he had to hide it beneath sorrow and shame, Red Thunder lowered his head. "I do not know. Healing Walks Like Turtle was hard on her. She needed time to recover."

"Find her. I wish to speak with her. Bring her to me."

The great chief watched his medicine man move stiffly away, angrily off through the trees. A soft sound from behind made him glance over his shoulder. He saw his mother standing in the doorway, a look of worry in her dark eyes. "You may be right about him, my mother."

Wise Owl nodded. "She is a SpiritWalker. She proved that when she healed Walks Like Turtle."

"But, that is legend." He remembered hearing his father speak of SpiritWalkers over the fire on stormy nights.

"Truth comes from legend." Wise Owl moved to stand beside her son.

"What of her father? What of Red Thunder?" Two Arrows believed his mother. The question was, what to do about Blaze.

"Red Thunder is not what he pretends to be. He has fooled us all these years. My husband was right when he warned us of him." She took a deep breath. "The girl needs our protection."

Seeing the worry in his mother's eyes, Two Arrows folded his arms on his chest. "Then we will protect her. We will watch Red Thunder and keep the girl from harm."

He motioned to two of his warriors standing in the shadows to follow the medicine man. Entering his lodge, he grabbed weapons. He'd seen the outline of the bow and quiver beneath the bear fur. Going back out, he put a hand on his mother's shoulder.

"We will follow him and find the girl. We will bring her back to the village where she will be safe."

As he strode out of the village, a large owl passed over his head.

Dusk was settling over the land. Shadows lengthened and deepened, providing concealment for small creatures, some of whom were snuggling down for the night, others who were just stirring.

A small mouse, her whiskers twitching, traveled beneath broad fern leaves, around exposed tree roots and over rotting branches. Her cheeks were already full of seeds and tiny fruits. She was on her way back to her burrow beneath a rotting log. Nearly there, she froze when a shadow swept over her. Fear froze the tiny creature, and when the large owl kept going, she didn't move. Not for a long time.

The owl knew she was there; he'd spotted her from high above long before she'd become aware of his presence. But he had no interest in her. His interest lay in the couple moving along a dry bed of rocks. They'd crossed it many times, veered off into the forest, always following the faint animal trails. Behind them, the enemy had stopped to rest.

The dark was his world. Not just as an owl, but all the time. He flew low. So much depended on this girl. He was tired. He longed to move on. To leave this earthly world for his place in the spirit world, but he could not. Not until the man who'd murdered him was brought to justice. The girl was the key. So he followed, sweeping low over the couple.

Luc watched the owl soar into the trees. Each step he took grew slower and shorter; his chest was on fire and his legs were so weak that they trembled. He locked his knees and stood a moment as though studying the land. In truth, he had to give his body time for the cresting pain to abate before moving forward.

He needed to stop and rest but didn't dare. Not

yet, not with skilled trackers following. He and Blaze had stuck to faint animal trails and followed dry creek beds and streams, stopping only to drink.

Abe by himself was a good tracker, but his Uncle Albert was better and Luc was very much afraid that was who was behind them. And then there were the Indian scouts. Luc had no idea how many had survived the battle. If there were Chippewa warriors on his tail, that made his circumstances so much the worse.

His legs buckled. From behind, Blaze caught him around the waist and led him past a tree split into two by lightning. Reaching a large, gray boulder beneath a stand of cedars, she helped him sit. "Rest, Trapper."

Luc sighed heavily. "We can't stop. Not yet." Running a hand through his sweat-soaked hair he glanced at Blaze.

"Sorry, *Ange*, but your life is in as much danger as mine now." His uncle thought that Blaze was his earth mother. They were after not so much Luc as Eagle Woman. If they found Blaze instead, she'd be in danger, for it was clear from her eyes that she was like Eagle Woman. His uncle would see and wonder and know. So no matter how angry he was at what she'd done, he'd never deliberately put her in danger.

"Why do you call me '*ange*'?"

"Why do you call me 'trapper'?"

Blaze smiled. "The name fits," she said, and she carefully lowered herself to the ground and closed her eyes.

"And you are an *ange*. Or, as my mother would have said, an angel. My mother used to tell me that I had an angel who looked after only me."

"That sounds nice," Blaze said wistfully. "Tell me about this angel. I do not look after children. They run from me."

The sadness in her voice softened Luc's resentment. "Angels live in heaven. They have soft feathery wings and long, flowing gowns. They fly through the clouds and walk on a path of gold." He leaned his head back. "They come down here to help us humans." His voice trailed off as exhaustion overtook him.

"Sleep, Trapper. We are safe. For now. There is no scent on the wind."

"*Ange*, there is no wind," he agreed. Sighing, Luc slid off the boulder. His chest ached so much that he needed to rest against something. He eyed the soft woman beside him. Her scent surrounded him, and he wanted to hold her close, to breathe her deep into his lungs.

She leaned her head back against the tree. "*Tate*. Spirit of the wind is here." She flicked her wrist and a breeze swept over them. "You just have to ask. And believe."

Luc frowned. "And want, *Ange*. Do not forget, I do not *want* to be a SpiritWalker."

"You have made that clear, but heed this, Trapper: what we want is not always what we get."

She sounded lost and forlorn. Luc didn't have the heart or energy to fight, so he left it alone. For now.

He had bigger worries: his family. He wanted to believe that his parents had escaped. The lack of their corpses left hope, and if it were true, then the girls would be safe.

"We need to eat." He pulled his pack over and untied the flap. It was dark enough that he couldn't see inside, but when his hands closed over something small and very familiar he froze. "What the hell?"

He pulled a tiny, fist-sized doll from his pack and held it out. Skye's doll. "How did this get in here?" Last he remembered, Skye had it in her hands when they fled the enemy. Pain immediately swamped him as he suffered from worry and guilt. He remembered when his earth mother had finished the detailed dress for this doll, which was as detailed as any young girl's fancy dress. Even the teeny moccasins were beaded. This was Skye's most prized possession, and she never went anywhere without it.

She must have stuck it in his pack before he handed her to Kangee. But why? He fingered the two braids made from a lock of Skye's own hair. Would he ever see her again?

"Why did I do it?" He should never have brought up the subject of SpiritWalkers when talking to his father. It was his fault that someone had overheard them. And if they'd been close enough to overhear, that person, one of his uncles, had most likely seen his father shift shape.

As if that wasn't enough, he'd broken his promise to his father. He'd failed to protect his sisters. He'd gone back to help his parents and ended up good as dead. Until this angel had shown up.

He glanced over at her. A strand of her hair was caught in the corner of her mouth. He reached over, his finger brushing her lips as he tucked a stray strand of hair behind her ear. "I never thanked you for saving my life."

Blaze narrowed her eyes. "No. You did not."

"I don't like what you did, *Ange*, but I believe that you didn't know what you were doing."

Sighing, Blaze wrapped her hands around her knees. "Yet you cannot accept that it is meant to be? Your family are SpiritWalkers. Does it not seem possible that you too were meant to be a Spirit-Walker? It was a SpiritWalker who gave you back the gift of life!"

"No. I did not agree to this. You offered life, I accepted. You stole my free will, and as soon as I find my family, we'll figure out how to undo what you did."

Blaze fell silent. Luc brooded and stared at the doll.

After several long heartbeats, Blaze sighed. "You'll find them, Luc."

"Damn right! *We* will find them. They are out there. Safe." He had to believe that.

"You are fortunate to have a family," Blaze said, her voice low and husky.

"Don't you have family?" Luc studied her. She was staring at the doll in his hands.

"No. I have no one."

The finality of her statement made him frown. In

SUSAN EDWARDS

the growing dark he saw the glimmer of tears in her
eyes. He wanted to pull her into his arms and comfort her, but he didn't. He couldn't let her vulnerable, haunting beauty sway him, and the last thing he
wanted to talk about was family.

The doll in his hands was a reminder that things
would never be the same. He brought the doll to his
face and inhaled. A fresh wave of pain swept through
Luc, and he closed his eyes. Greed and secrets had
destroyed them. He'd been left for dead, and one of
his uncles was tracking him like an animal.

A whisper of sound told him Blaze was standing
beside him. He felt the fringe of her skirt brush his
arm as she knelt on the ground. Her touch, warm
and gentle on his arm, tugged at something deep inside him. He tried to ignore it but her very presence
cloaked him, warmed him, and eased some of his
exhaustion and the pain in his heart.

One hand covered his. Her fingers touched the
doll. The other hand stroked down one side of his
face. "She is alive. The doll is a sign. She left this
doll with you. On purpose. To help you."

"*Ange*, if you are trying to make me feel better,
you're not succeeding."

"Trapper, for someone who says he knows about
SpiritWalkers, you do not seem to know much.
Sometimes when I touch something, I can see its
past. More a feeling, a sense." She put her other
hand over his, sandwiching the doll between them.

Up close, Luc noticed the lines of exhaustion
around her lips, the creases in her forehead and the

pallor of her skin. "Concentrate. Bring your sister's image into focus. See her. Feel her. She is connected to this doll."

Luc grimaced and would have pulled his hands away, but both of hers trapped his between them. He sighed but couldn't help but think of Skye, her beautiful face, her happy smile or the way she giggled when he tickled her belly.

Immediately, a burst of happiness swept through him, and he remembered the day Skye ran up to him, eager to show her big brother her new doll. His cousins had laughed as Luc helped her choose a name.

He glanced at Blaze in wonder. "I feel her. I can really feel her!"

"Focus on what you feel. Feel with not just your mind, but your heart. Let your love of your sister connect you with her."

Luc frowned. It was strange, but he actually felt the presence of his young sister as though she were standing right beside him. But that was it. There was nothing more than memories of her, nothing of the here and now.

Shaking his head, he looked over at Blaze. "I just feel her." Which in his mind was pretty amazing, as that had never happened before.

"Your stone. Hold it and the doll together." Blaze moved closer.

Mention of the stone reminded Luc of what she'd done. He shook his head. "No. I want no part of this." Anger edged his voice and deepened it.

"It is a part of you already. The ability to see and feel your sister is within you. You just do not know how to use it." She reached over and pulled the stone from beneath his shirt and lifted it from around his neck.

Vibrations hummed from her fingertips, up her arm and into her heart. "This stone is a symbol of what we are, what we share, but it is also ancient and therefore holds its own powers. Once connected to a human soul, its purpose changes as it tries to connect with not only you, but the higher power. You can use the knowledge of the stone to seek answers." She put it into his reluctant hand beside the doll then covered his hands with her own.

The heat of the stone made Luc's palm tingle. "Blaze," he began in a low warning tone, unaware that he'd used her name for the first time. Her hands squeezed his and he stopped trying to pull away.

"Luc. Your sisters could be in danger. Would you not use everything in your power to find them and keep them safe?"

Luc's green eyes were dark with anger. "Fine. But when they are safe, you are going to find a way to undo what you did."

"You cannot run from your destiny and, like it or not, *I* am your destiny. If as you say I am a Spirit-Walker, and your family are SpiritWalkers, then this too is part of your destiny. Close your eyes. Let the essence of your sister flow into your mind. See her. Hear her."

Luc tamped down his anger and resentment.

Dammit. His angel was right. If he had the power within him to find his sisters and keep them safe, he had no choice but to use it. But she was wrong about this being his destiny. He'd do what he had to for now; and he'd do whatever it took later, when this whole nightmare was over, to undo what she'd done.

Taking a deep breath, he brought an image of Skye into his mind and waited. Nothing happened. He was ready to quit, to tell Blaze he couldn't do it when everything started twirling. Greens and blues swirled together as though mixed by an invisible hand. An image slowly took form.

"*Skye.*" He saw her clearly, clutching the doll in her hands, her beautiful blue, green and brown eyes wide yet strangely calm. Her mouth moved but he couldn't hear her. "Louder, baby. Speak louder." When she began to fade, he grew frantic. *Help me.*

Focus. See what you cannot hear. The voice entered his head smooth as oil.

Luc narrowed his eyes onto Skye's mouth and read the words he could not hear. "Old Man Rock." He opened his eyes. "They are at Old Man Rock. They made it safely."

Relief poured through him. He swallowed his pride and stared into Blaze's eyes. "Thank you for helping me. She is safe."

Blaze shook her head. "That was not my voice speaking to you. The spirits answered your need."

Dumbfounded, Luc shook his head. "You heard the voice?"

She shrugged. "We are connected. I gave you strength, but the voice came from the spirits."

"Impossible," he said. Yet he knew his earth mother spoke to the spirits and gods and often said they spoke to her. Even his sisters talked the same way. It was one of the reasons he'd decided to leave. Sometimes it made him uncomfortable, and his family always seemed to know it, no matter how hard he tried to keep his feelings from them.

They stayed silent for a long time. Blaze moved to pick up her pouch and removed a smaller one from the belt around her waist. She held it up to the sky.

"All my relations. Thank you, Father Sky." Then she held the pouch toward the earth. "All my relations," she repeated. "Thank you, Mother Earth."

She poured a small amount of seed into the palm of her hand. Lifting it, she allowed a strong gust of wind to scatter her gift.

"What is that for?" Luc knew about offering the spirits gifts to show appreciation. Even bits of every meal were left as a way of honoring and thanking the animal or plant that gave its life to feed them. It was becoming second nature to him to not eat every morsel of food when they ate.

Blaze brushed her hand down her skirt. "I am thanking the spirits."

Luc grimaced. "I know. What are you thanking them for?"

She pointed to the doll. "For connecting you to your sister. For letting you know that they are safe. For now." She sat back down across from him. Luc stared up into the dark sky. Stars twinkled and the moon had risen.

Somewhere out there, his sisters were running for their lives. Time passed as thoughts and images played out in his head. He finally accepted that Blaze was right. "I'll do whatever I have to do to find my family, be whatever I have to be." His voice was soft, so soft he wasn't sure if she heard.

"I will give whatever I can give you as well, Trapper." Her voice sounded faint, as though she were falling asleep. Giving in to the need to hold her, he crawled over and took her into his arms as he leaned against the tree and tucked her beneath his arm. "Sleep. I'll watch over you."

Blaze snuggled in close. "You mean, guard me. Make sure I don't leave."

Luc smiled grimly. "You won't leave. I have the answers you need."

She sighed. "You are right, Trapper. I won't leave. Not because I cannot. I can call the spirit of brother wolf to me and ask him to share with me his strength and agility." She lifted one hand and snapped her fingers. "That fast. I could be gone."

"That fast, huh?" He leaned his head back. "Then I'd be right behind you, sweetheart."

Tipping her chin at him, Blaze said, "I am a child of the gods. But I will not leave. We are meant to be together."

Luc glanced down at her. Her breathing slowed and her hands relaxed and fell to his lap. In the pale wash of moonlight she looked young and vulnerable. And incredibly beautiful. He reached down and fingered a strand of her silky hair. *His destiny*.

Luc shook his head. Part of him yearned to accept her as his. But another part of him wanted nothing to do with what she was. Free will. It was something his earth mother spoke of often in using her gifts and abilities. Everything had free will, and as a SpiritWalker, respecting free will was the most important rule.

Would he have agreed had she asked? Luc wasn't sure. But that didn't matter. She hadn't asked, he hadn't given permission, so they were at an impasse. Luc dropped the strand of hair, then gently brushed it off her face.

Her warmth soothed his aches and pains. He fought the exhaustion attacking his body. He needed to watch over his angel as she'd watched over him. Her lashes fluttered and her lips parted on a soft sigh as her body snuggled as close to him as she could get.

Sliding a hand beneath her head, the soft silky strands were more than he could resist. He stroked and rubbed her hair between his fingers. Twisting his fingers in her long hair, he pulled her tighter against him. Her head was pillowed on his shoulder and as he rubbed his cheek against the top of her head, he sighed.

His last thought before sliding into sleep was that his angel was pretty special. She was everything he'd want in a woman.

Maka, ancestress of all growing things, loved the water that flowed over her and was part of her. She separated the water into lakes, oceans and streams, wearing them as her ornaments.

CHAPTER EIGHT

Kangee paced in the dark, going from one cedar to another, her steps muffled by the thick padding of composted leaves. Tips of ferns brushed against her bare legs, her plain, unadorned skirt hitting her just below the knee.

"Will you give it a rest?"

She glared at Travers. They'd arrived at Old Man Rock after running through the night. They were all tired, hungry and worried sick. She felt too edgy to sit. "We need to keep going." She rubbed her arms. Night in the deep forest tended to be cool even in the summer and being tired didn't help.

"No. Your father said to wait here. We are not moving. Besides, your sisters need to rest." Travers straddled an old rotting log. Huddled together behind him, three young girls watched silently, their eyes glittering.

"We sleep here. I'll take watch and tomorrow I'll scout around."

"No. Not stopping. Not yet." Kangee couldn't rest. Her family should be here by now. Unless something had happened. She faced the dark void of Old Man Rock. Morning wasn't far off, yet it felt like forever.

If only she could go into her mind and see what was happening like her mother could. Frustrated and feeling as though she was letting everyone down, Kangee tried to concentrate, to communicate with the spirits. But as always, there was nothing to see. No answers. No reassurance.

She glared out into the darkness. Why couldn't she see things that were happening like her mother, or shape-shift to go find out what was going on? She couldn't even mind merge, yet she was a Spirit-walker. She had the eyes of her people but no special abilities or gifts. Her gaze latched onto her sisters. They were scared and counting on her. She couldn't fail. She had to get them all to her mother's people.

She addressed Alex. "Can you keep going?"

"We make camp here, and tomorrow I'll scout around."

Alex sighed. "Travers is right. We need to wait."

Frustrated, Kangee knelt in front of her sisters. She brushed the hair from Skye's face. "I know you're all tired and hungry. What do you think?"

Skye reached out and wrapped her arms around Kangee. "I'm not tired." But her voice broke on a huge yawn and she scrubbed her eyes with her fist.

The twins each stood, ready to side with their big sister. "We're not tired either."

"We continue," Kangee told Travers. She spoke in French, as his Lakota was worse than Luc's. "You two can stay here. We're going on." She turned and, using her excellent night vision, moved off through the forest.

The night closed in around them. The sounds of rustling in the brush and through the trees overhead normally calmed her, but not tonight. She had no fear of winged creatures, or the four-legs, but she was afraid of running into them. Anyone not of her tribe was a potential enemy, and a strange white trapper could be even more of a danger. She knew that because her father never left her or her sisters or mother alone. If he had to go off trapping, he always took them back home.

The crunch of twigs behind her made her smile. Travers would never dare let her go off on her own. Her father would skin him alive if he did.

"Stubborn woman," the young man muttered as he caught up and grabbed her arm. He pulled Skye away from her and handed the little girl to Alex, then glanced down at the twins.

"Your father said to meet at Old Man Rock. He'll come. If we leave now, we might miss him and Luc. Uncle Conrad will come. We are staying here. Go back with Alex. Get some sleep. If your parents do not show up tomorrow, then we will take you to your mother's people. But we need to give the others time to get here."

Furious that the girls did leave with Alex, Kangee stalked over to Travers. "You have no right!"

"I have every right. Luc put me in charge. Your father put him in charge."

"I wish Luc was with us. He wouldn't have stopped." Kangee was not happy to be stuck with Travers. He should have gone back, leaving Luc to guard them and see them to their safety. But in her heart, she knew she wasn't being fair; Luc would have done no different. She was just worried sick, and Travers made a good target.

"Me too. You're a pain in the butt."

Weariness overcame her. She turned, and the fight went out of her. "We should have all stayed together." Kangee couldn't help the quaver in her voice.

Travers moved close. "I'm sure Uncle Connie and your mother and Luc are safe, Kangee."

"But you do not *know*." She whirled around, found him way too close and stepped back. As much as she disliked Travers, he was the only one for her to vent her fear on. "I can't *feel* them," she said, her stomach twisted into a knot.

Travers pulled off his fur cap. "Don't go getting all weird on me, Ka. You're tired. We all are."

Ready to unleash her anger and frustration, Kangee was stopped by Skye as the little girl ran back. Kangee bent down and picked her up. "I have you, little one. Don't be afraid. Everything will be fine."

Skye leaned back in her arms. "I know. I'm not afraid. But you are. I can feel it." She took her big sister's face into her small hands. "Luc was gone, but he's back—and there is a pretty woman with him. She has eyes like us."

Kangee held Skye close. Skye knew. She always knew. It had been her cry of warning that had alerted her father and mother to the danger. She drew in a deep breath. "Mother and Father! What about them?"

Skye wrapped her hands around Kangee's neck. "I do not know. I feel them, but not like before." She sighed and slumped back onto her big sister's shoulder.

Kangee held Skye tightly. "Thank you little sister." Kangee hated the fact that she had the least ability, and often grew weary of waiting for her powers to be revealed to her. She *was* a SpiritWalker, for all the good it did her. Or the rest of them.

"See? Your parents are still alive. They'll be here. Can we go back and get some rest now?"

Kangee gave a loud sniff as she shoved branches out of her way, then smirked with satisfaction when she heard the snap of a branch, the sting of wood on flesh and Travers's muffled curse.

Night in the forest created its own beauty: The ghostly canopy of leaves and branches high above, the deeper black patches where no moon or starlight penetrated. The forest hummed with life.

Insects in the undergrowth, small animals darting from shadow to shadow and in the trees, night birds, their sharp vision seeking prey. A pack of wolves moved silently, and a small wildcat leaped from the branch to the ground.

Soaring silently through the night, the owl moved as one with the wind. He was a spirit, a restless spirit trapped in the form of an owl, cursed to fly the land until he found freedom.

He twisted and glided through a canopy of branches and thick trunks until he came to a tight knot of trees. He landed without sound high above the man and woman. His golden eyes blinked slowly, and the weary old bird drooped slightly. He longed to leave this world and move on, but his work here was not finished. He stared down at Blaze, saw the child she'd once been and knew he hadn't done right by her. That, as much as the way he'd died, kept him from the great lodge awaiting him in the sky.

So much he could have done. So much he should have done. He could only hope that she would one day forgive him, and discover within herself her true purpose in life—a purpose he'd not realized until it was too late.

He let out a soft sound of regret, then fluttered his wings and settled on a branch high above the couple. So much depended on their strength, courage and the faith that they put in who and what they were.

Below the owl, Luc stared up into the dark void of night. His mind was so jumbled and confused that sleep was impossible. So much had happened, in such a short time. His announcement to leave seemed to have triggered everything that had gone terribly wrong.

This time yesterday he and his family had been running from an unknown enemy, and Luc had been fighting not just for his life but for the lives of a family he'd thought he could just up and leave forever. Heart-sore and filled with guilt, Luc vowed to find them. It was his fault that someone had learned the truth of what his father had become.

Someone I'd trust with my life.

His father had trusted his brothers. The Cordell men stuck together no matter what. Whoever had led the attack had been one of his uncles. Walt had called the man in charge Cordell, which only confirmed Luc's suspicions, and of the two men, Luc was sure that it was Albert. He just didn't want to believe it.

Uncle Albert had raised both William and Conrad. The man was nearly fanatical in keeping the brothers together, and he'd been furious the night Luc announced his intention to leave. He'd gone beyond fury when Luc's father also decided to leave. But would he go so far as to kill his own brother, and Luc?

Could this have nothing to do with the others being SpiritWalkers? Maybe his Uncle Albert had been drunk and had attacked out of rage? Luc didn't know. He felt betrayed, yet he knew he was also the betrayer.

The guilt of that sat like a hot, heavy stone in his belly. He rolled his head to the side where Blaze slept soundly. Why had she saved his life? He didn't deserve it. Had it not been for her he'd have stayed dead. There was no doubt that he'd died during that battle—the battle that his thoughtlessness caused.

Stars peeped down through leaves and the wind found its way from sky to ground. In the deep forest, the night was cool but he welcomed the slight discomfort, finding the quiet lull of a world at rest soothing. Night had always been his thinking time, even when his mother had been alive. He sighed with sadness as he recalled how she'd always teased him about being a night owl.

Kept me up all night when I carried you, kept me from sleep when you were a baby. My little night owl.

Thoughts of his mother tripped through his mind. He'd give almost anything to see her now, to talk to her. His mother had been an intelligent and strong-willed woman who'd chosen to live most of her life with her son while Luc's father spent most of his time in the wilderness. He remembered how happy she'd been when his father had announced that he was staying for good during that last winter she'd had been alive. But Luc had had reservations about living with a man he barely knew. Still, if it made his mother happy, he'd have been willing to give his father a chance. Then his mother had been killed in that coach accident, and the life he'd imagined and wished for all of his life was gone forever.

Taking a deep breath, Luc knew his life had again changed—he'd changed—and he wasn't sure things would ever be the same, even if his angel could undo whatever she'd done to connect them. He frowned and turned his head to look at Blaze. She slept soundly, curled onto her side facing him. His angel. Without conscious thought, his fingers found the crystal stone around his neck that had made him a SpiritWalker.

Drawing in a deep breath, he fisted his hand over the green stone and took it off. Though he'd resisted looking at it all day, he now held it up and found himself mesmerized by the bright glow that shone in the stone's heart, as though the stars and moon were captured and held deep inside.

"This cannot be real," he whispered, but in his heart and soul he knew it was. He was different; he felt it. His sight was sharper, his hearing more acute. He drew in another deep breath. Everything seemed crisper, cleaner and clearer, and there was a feeling of oneness with his surroundings that he'd never experienced in all his years in the wilderness.

Oh, he'd learned to blend when needed, to trap and track with easy skill, but he'd never felt as though he were a part of the land he walked. He was a stranger, an outsider who came into the woods to take what he needed. That was another of the reasons he'd decided to leave and return to the world of his birth. He'd wanted to make something of his life, to be someone with an innate purpose and do something that helped people. Trapping only helped the rich buy their coveted furs. He'd been so sure a day ago that leaving was the right thing to do. But now? Staring into the stone, he was afraid things had changed.

What *was* he going to do if Blaze could not undo

what she'd done? Not once in the last eight years had he ever wanted what his earth mother, father or sisters had. And now he supposed he could do all those things. But he didn't try. He had no desire to be more than he'd been. Not in this way, at least. "Should just toss it." That would take care of things.

Would you truly not use whatever is in your power to save your family?

Startled at the voice flowing like water through his mind, Luc sat up and glanced around. It was the same thing Blaze had asked, but she was asleep. A soft, sad cry above his head drew his attention. Scanning the deep dark, he sucked in his breath as he saw a huge dark shape swooping down toward him. It flew over his head and landed on a low branch of the pine in front of him.

Luc's gaze connected with the round, deep orange eyes of the owl. While he'd seen many of the night birds during his years in the wilderness, he'd never seen one so close.

Awe filled him. And something else, a connection to a wild animal that he'd never before felt, even though his earth mother taught all her children that animals were part of the whole circle of life and that they often intentionally crossed paths with their human cousins carrying messages from the spirit world. She'd called them spirit guides or animal helpers, and he knew the wolf was one of her animal totems.

Holding his breath, he waited. For what he wasn't sure, but never in all his time trapping had an owl come so close. Nor had one ever just sat and stared at him so intently.

In his palm, the green crystal stone grew warm, and though he wanted to deny any feelings of power, it hummed in his hand and rose into his arm and shimmered through and around him.

His mind reached out almost as though he'd split himself into two people—one who knew how to use his new gifts and the other who didn't and who wanted nothing to do with being a SpiritWalker.

But then he thought of what the voice had said, and knew he'd do and become anything to find and bring his family back together. Safely. Alive. And that included suspending disbelief in order to embrace hope.

"Where are they?" His voice was a mere whisper. "Can you help me find them?" In the ensuring silence he felt a bit silly, but he desperately needed to believe that he had the ability to help those he loved and that they were alive.

Then he heard it. A voice yet not a voice. A vibration that took the form of words sweeping through not just his mind but echoing deep into his heart and soul.

Secrets destroy life. Welcome truth and have the courage to embrace it. The woman is the key. The revelations to many secrets lies within her.

"Secrets."

His father certainly had a secret, and it was a sure bet that someone knew that secret now—all because of his carelessness when he thought he and his father had been alone. Before he could ask for more detail, the owl blinked, spread out its wings and, with a strong flap of wings, it was gone as silently as it had come.

Luc blinked. "Dreaming. Must have fallen asleep." He rubbed his face with his hand then looked back at the branch where the owl had sat—or the owl in his dream. Wrapping his fist around his stone he decided that for the time being, he was stuck with it, with her, and with being a SpiritWalker.

Later, if his angel could not undo what she'd done, and none in his mother's tribe could, then he'd simply return the stone and leave. The thought of losing the woman sleeping at his side made his heart squeeze painfully, but he ignored it. He'd do what needed to be done and that was that.

A small moan drew his attention. His angel was twisting and turning. A small fur blanket that he'd had in his pack slipped from her shoulders and she flung out both arms as though warding off an attack.

"*Hiya!*"

She twisted and turned, and when he put his hands on her shoulders to wake her, she started screaming. "Killed them! Killed them!" A low howl of wind came out of nowhere, and over their heads a branch snapped and fell, landing beside Luc.

"Blaze! Wake up." He held her still, his voice lifting as the howling wind increased.

She struggled. "My mother. My father. You killed them. *You killed them*." Her voice rose to a shriek.

"Not me, baby. Not me. Wake up now. You're

safe." He continued to murmur softly and gently, but she didn't seem able to hear. Her fists balled and struck out at him.

Grabbing her hands, he slid his fingers through hers. The crystal rested between their palms, and the heat it generated seemed to pulse. But she didn't calm. Her eyes were wide open, seeing something only she could see. She continued to cry, sob and scream, her voice thick with grief.

"Come on, sweetheart. Wake up. Nothing can hurt you. I'm here. Come on *petit ange*." He continued to murmur softly until he heard the snap of more branches. One fell and hit Luc on the back. He ducked, shielding her. Leaves torn from branches rained down on him as painful sobs shook her body. Her cry grew to a low keening wail that sent the wind shrieking in protest. Luc lifted his head. He had to get them out of there, away from the trees, but it was still dark, and they were deep in the forest.

Wake her. Do not let her lose control!

The voice in his head made him shout out, "Think I'm not trying?" A low tearing sound had his heart lodging in his throat. He felt the tremble in the earth, the cry in his ears as life was pulled up by the roots.

"Damn, who is going to protect me from you?" He knew, somehow he knew, that his angel was causing this destruction. He felt her pain, the raw fury mingled with bone-deep grief that trapped her and kept her from responding to his voice. The crashing and tearing of wood continued. Desperate, Luc bent his head and swallowed her next scream. He ignored everything. All that mattered was reaching his angel, helping her as she'd helped him.

The moment his lips touched hers, he felt a well of heat rise inside him—a spark of flame fanned by his attraction to her. Urging that spark to flare and reach into her, to warm her and bring her back to him, he gently moved his mouth over hers, swallowing each rapid breath, breathing in calm, gentle bursts of air.

"Wake, my beautiful angel, my *ange de lumiere*." His angel of light had come to him. He had to help her.

"Wake. You're safe. Feel me." His lips played over hers and as she slowly relaxed beneath him, her mouth softened and parted. He released her hands and ran his fingers through her hair, gripping her head between his hands.

Silence fell around them. "That's it. Kiss me, *Ange*," he said. "Kiss me." His voice quavered, his body trembled and his heart tumbled at the sweet taste of her, and when her arms rose to wrap around his shoulders, he melted into her.

Her soft moan fanned the flame until he thought it would burst and consume them both. Unable to hold back, he deepened the kiss but kept it slow and gentle until he felt another storm gathering, this one deep inside him that he couldn't fight. He took from her all that she shyly offered.

He drank from her. She was sweet, moist, soft.

She was his. His heart and soul were one with hers. When she sank into him, teased his lips with hers, dipped her tongue into his mouth, copying his every move, he moaned. Her fingers slid into his hair and gripped him hard.

Luc moaned and lifted his head. He stared down into her dark, glittering eyes. "Damn, who is going to protect you from me?" He needed her and wanted her. All of her, no matter what the sacrifice to his own heart and soul.

She lifted her hands and cupped his face between her palms, her fingers combing through the thick beard. Her voice trembled. "I am sorry." She reached up and brushed leaves from his hair. Her troubled gaze latched onto a tree that lay directly above them, its trunk caught in the fork of another tree.

"What happened?" She asked the question, but she knew. She'd felt the rage inside her but had been helpless to stop it or to wake from the gripping night dream. But it was no dream and she knew it. Knew the truth now.

Luc reached down to wipe the tears from her face. "Had yourself one hell of a nightmare, *Ange*." He glanced around them then grimaced as he stared at the fallen tree. "That was pretty damn close, sweetheart."

Blaze closed her eyes. "Not a dream. It was real." Tears slid down her cheeks. She tried not to think about what the man she'd believed to be her father had done to her. All his lies. His secrets.

Luc pulled her close, curving her into his arms so

he could see her as he held her. He rubbed her hands with his to warm her. "Tell me about it." Right then, nothing mattered but soothing the tears from his angel's face. Judging by the storm she'd created, he suspected she had dark, deep demons nipping at her heels.

Blaze could not stop the tears. She clung to Luc, afraid to let go, afraid he'd put her aside. She needed his touch, the gently rhythmic stroking of his palm circling her back and the sound of his soft, soothing voice. She'd tried to put the grief from her but the truth and the betrayal were too strong. Grief held her in its greedy grip. She didn't remember her parents, but her heart still needed to grieve.

"I saw them die." The words came out stark and painful. It would be so easy for her to turn her anger, pain and the sheer rage of her past onto the man who'd stolen her not just from her people but stolen her very life. No one knew better that anger was a wasted emotion. And for her, a dangerous one, as evidenced by the destruction around her. "My father killed them."

"Who, sweetheart? Who did your father kill?"

"My parents. My *birth* parents." It had been so much easier for her to think of the death of her parents as a bad dream, or something that had happened to that child; but it had happened to *her*, and she had no choice to a deal with the pain and anger of it.

She recounted the dream, leaving nothing out. She found her inner child, or the child she'd once been. Her innocence and joy had been ripped from her soul that day and, though she'd lived, she knew now that an important part of her had been lost. Perhaps forever.

She closed her eyes when she came to next part—even now the pain was nearly unbearable. That child had known the truth, but somehow, she'd buried it. "I am that child. That is why I do not know what I am."

"You could not be expected to know if no one has ever told you or taught you." Luc's fingers caressed the back of her neck.

Sighing, Blaze fingered his crystal, which he'd dropped into her palm. "I never lose control. Not even in sleep." She felt ashamed. She'd nearly gotten them killed.

"He stole me from my family." Tears ran down her face, a waterfall of sadness and grief. Luc's vest was soaking wet and still she couldn't stop. She'd lost more than her family that day. She'd lost who and what she was; and though she might one day get that back, she'd never know the man and woman who'd given her life. All she had were her memories, and even that happy time of running along the lake was shadowed by pain and grief.

Luc continued to hold and stroke Blaze and rock her gently in his arms. His heart bled for her and, deep inside, his anger grew at the man who'd caused her such pain. His angel had been tormented for years, and still she was filled with a goodness he feared he'd never live up to.

"Do you remember any of your family?" She'd fallen silent.

"I can't remember names or even remember clearly what they looked like, but I think I have two brothers." She frowned. "And a sister. A baby sister, but she would be an adult now." She let out a long shuddering breath. "He took them from me as well."

"I'm sorry, *Ange.*" Luc brushed his lips across her forehead.

Blaze felt drained. Exhausted. Her mind felt numb, yet she hurt so bad she just wanted to curl up and find a safe, quiet peaceful place where she wouldn't have to think or feel. So much had happened over the last few days.

"Everything makes so much sense now: his trying to keep me from making friends, from being a part of our village. He was training me—that was what he said. Said I had more important things to learn than stretching hides, and I believed him.

She stared at her hands. "I believed it all. He's lied to me from the beginning, and has been using me to gain respect and status from our people. His life is a lie and I helped him create it. I never questioned him. I only wanted to help our people. I had a gift I needed to use."

Angry at the guilt in her voice, Luc gripped her chin and made her look at him. "You were a child trying to please her father."

"What I did was wrong."

"You were but a child. A better question to ask is why this man went to great lengths to hide the truth. It doesn't sound like he meant to kill your parents. If they had taken the form of eagles, would he have known? Could he have been held responsible?"

Blaze sniffled and shook her head, her eyes closed. "He was afraid. I remember that. I was afraid, too."

"Of him?"

She frowned. "I don't know. I don't think so. I remember fire, trees exploding with flame. Everywhere. And the sky. It was angry. It shouted with a loud voice and the water in the lake churned and crashed around me. I remember thinking that the gods were angry."

She sighed. "For many years whenever there was a storm I cried. I was afraid. I thought the gods were angry and that they were going to kill us. I never understood why, and my father never told me." Her voice broke. "He told me if they were angry at me then it was because I did not honor or respect them."

Holding Blaze tight, Luc ran his hands through her wet hair, his fingers gently untangling the long strands. "He lied." He tipped her face up to his. "He lied because he was afraid. Of you."

Luc held up his hand, pointing to the gray sky. "Last night the wind. Today a storm that topples trees. I have no trouble believing that you, as a frightened young child, caused the fire and those storms."

Blaze stared pensively at the sky. "Your sisters. Do they also do this?"

She looked so worried, so scared and so hurt, he was tempted to lie. But he didn't. "No. Not like this." He bent his head and kissed her gently. "They know what they are and have been taught since birth the consequences of their actions. Like your father knew. He stole not just a child, but a child of the gods."

"Child of the gods." Blazes voice held wonder. "I've been told that. By spirits." She grabbed Luc's vest, her fingers curling around the softened buckskin. "I can talk to them, can hear them, but they never told me what I was. Only that I was their child. I never understood. We are all children of the gods."

To Luc, the whole thing seemed incredible—a child's fanciful story or fantasy, but faced with his father shifting shape and the things his young sisters could do, he had no choice but to believe in the legend of SpiritWalkers.

"I don't know it—never cared enough to learn it all—but there is a legend of a race of people descended from the gods. I wish I'd paid more attention to the stories my earth mother told, but in truth I found the whole business a bit unnerving." He bunched his fingers in her hair. "I mean, who expects that there are people who can do the impossible? After all, a mere mortal cannot wield the power of the nature. "But you called up a windstorm and, when you were crying, it rained. Hard."

Both times that the weather was affected, she'd been overwrought.

He glanced around. The rain was still falling, though not as hard or fast. It was a soft gentle rain, but the ground was running from so much water so fast hitting the dry, hard earth.

"Think you could stop crying now? I'm not in the mood to swim."

Blaze gave a weak laugh. "Maybe." She stared at his mouth, just inches from her own. "Maybe I need help."

"How?" His body thrummed with desire.

"Like this." Blaze reached up and sealed their lips.

By the time he drew back, Luc was breathing hard. He stared down at Blaze. Her eyes were a molten blue with golden sparks shining bright. Her lips were full, a woman well-kissed.

She lifted a hand to his face. Her eyes traveled from his eyes to his wet hair and wet shirt. She glanced up at the sky and sighed. "I think I lost control again."

Luc laughed and cupped her face between his hands. "That you did, *Ange*. That you did. I'm so sorry that I've put you in danger.

"It's not your fault." She reached up and ran the tips of her fingers along the strong column of his throat.

"Yeah, *Ange*, it is."

"I'm the one who nearly got us both killed." She was staring at the fallen trees and broken branches.

"Rest for a little bit longer. Though . . . you

wouldn't have a way to dry us, would you?" He took back his crystal and hung it around his neck.

Smiling, Blaze shook her head. "Not even I can call forth the sun."

Maka's world was dark. She could not see how beautiful she was, so she complained to Skan who then created Wi, the Sun.

CHAPTER NINE

The sky was just beginning to lighten when Red Thunder crept into the trees. He flapped his bearskin-clad arms and frightened off scavengers, both four-footed and winged. When the last of the scavengers squawked and fluttered out of reach, he walked through the battle scene. He stared at what remained of the bodies of white men, Chippewa and wolves.

Eyeing the ground, he searched for signs of Blaze. Her tracks led here. Her trail had been easy to spot. Only his daughter ran with wolves at her side, and she hadn't bothered to cover her tracks.

Few knew that about her, and no matter how many times he'd forbidden her to do so, it was something she'd always done. The wolf tracks had ended up on a small hill. The smell of death had led him here and, after careful search, he found her small, moccasin-clad footprints were all over. Carefully he pushed his way through the undergrowth and spotted more bodies, the flesh eaten by scavengers. He edged away, giving no sign of emotion when he viewed an enemy warrior with his throat turn out by the dead wolf close by. There wasn't much of either left.

His nostrils flared and he stayed alert. When he came to an area where the grass was flattened, he bent down. The ground bore a dark stain. Blood. He glanced around for a body but found nothing. He frowned and parted the matted grass and crushed plant life.

His patience paid off and he smiled grimly when he found a thin piece of buckskin: fringe from his daughter's dress. She had been here. He found more, as though she'd torn them from her skirt.

There was only one reason he could think of for her to have ripped her skirt—to make a dressing. His fingernail scraped the hard dirt and he saw bits of crushed leaves. He sniffed. Sage. A powder to help stop bleeding. Standing, he fisted his hands. She had not only been here, she'd healed. Again.

She hadn't answered his call during the night. The presence of the wolves proved that she'd ignored his summons then had left with the animals. Judging from the number of dead, this had been a battle to the death, and one person—at least one— had survived. Helped by the girl.

Furious, he stared around, taking it all in: the positions of the bodies, the means of death, and the account of the battle etched into the ground. So where had she gone? Had she healed an enemy, and would she offer her gifts to another tribe?

He spotted her tracks near the stream. Had she crossed? Something shiny drew his attention. He bent down and picked up the gleaming stone. He gripped it in his fist then threw it as far from him as he could.

"Foolish girl!" She never even realized what she did with stones half the time. It was as unconscious an act for her as playing with hair was to others. A weakness. Her leaving proved she was going to be true to her word: She was going to ruin everything.

He glanced around, eyed the birds fluttering through the trees to be sure he was alone. Chief Two Arrows had wanted to speak to the girl, and that was something Red Thunder couldn't allow. She wanted to leave; he'd make sure she never returned.

There was only one person he knew who had knowledge of the legend of SpiritWalkers, and he was dead. But right now, that didn't reassure him, for the old shaman was the chief's father, and Chief Two Arrows was acting strangely. No matter. He vowed to find the girl and take care of her before she could return to ruin his life.

Finding five sets of tracks leading away from the battle, he set off at a run. He'd run long throughout the day. He might be a medicine man, but he'd never let his body go soft. His body was in prime condition. Condition to kill.

* * *

"Ange!"

Blaze woke instantly. "What is it?"

Luc's breath warmed her face, and the closeness of his lips teased her. She tried to sit, but he was leaning so close that if she moved, she'd bring their mouths together.

"We have company. Be quiet. I'll be right back." He'd just started to fall asleep when something in the wind brought him to full alertness. He'd sensed them, knew they were coming. He didn't question how he knew or even the why of it. He took one last look into Blaze's eyes to be sure she was awake, then he slid from her, moving with a quiet grace he'd learned from eight years of being a part of this land.

Blaze didn't have a chance to say anything before he was gone. She got to her knees, her heart thudding against her ribs. His scent and warmth faded as the chill of the night seeped into her. She knew it was the absence of his touch that made her shiver in the dark. Already he was a part of her heart and soul. She no longer felt lost or alone. She had someone.

But he was someone who didn't want her or what she was. He'd rejected what she'd unknowingly given him. Yet he'd also kissed her. She'd felt his desire, knew he wanted *her*. She knew enough of the ways between a man and woman to know he was attracted to her. She sighed. For now, that had to be enough.

Her gaze pierced the shadows. The darkness of night pressed in around her, but high above, she saw a faint lightening of the sky. Dawn would soon be upon them. She tried to find Luc among the shadows then gave up and sent her senses flaring out on the wind. Closing her eyes, she focused on the scents in the air.

Luc was off somewhere behind her, a family of mice were burrowed beneath a rotting log, a bat flew among the trees and beneath a brush so close she could reach out and touch it, was a pair of *wiciteglega*, the masked animals that often got into the food stores in their longhouses. Then she caught another scent that had her heart leaping into her throat.

Men. Closing her eyes she concentrated, drawing in deep breaths of air through her nose. She heard the quiet tread of their feet, scented the sweat on their bodies and the lingering coating of death. There were two of them creeping toward where she hid, and another two off in the trees further back. She held her breath, not daring to move.

A hand snaked out and covered her mouth. Her eyes went wide. "Just me, *Ange*. Don't make a sound. We've got to move. Now." Luc's voice was pitched low so that only she heard him.

Blaze nodded, and when Luc eased away, she followed, walking lightly on her feet so as not to break any twigs to give away their presence. Luc led her to a group of boulders. "Wait here. I'm going back."

She reached out. "No. It's too dangerous."

"No choice, *Ange*. They are too close for comfort, and neither of us can outrun a gun or arrow, and I don't think we are in good enough shape to try. I'm going to lead them away, plant a false trail then double back to get you. I'll buy us some time." Luc turned away, but Blaze put a hand on his arm.

"Too late, Luc." Her eyes were wide, the colors deepening with fear.

Luc froze, for the sound of two men breathing reached his ears. Damn, she was right. They were almost at the spot where they'd slept. "Can't stay here. It's the first place they'll look." Now he wished he knew how to do the shifting-shape thing; it would have come in handy right then. The sky was lightening, the inky blackness giving way to a pale gray.

"We can." Blaze was feeling up the rock for hand and footholds. "Come on. Up."

"It's not high enough to hide us, sweetheart. They'll spot us."

Blaze shook her head. "Not if we use what we are to hide ourselves."

Luc frowned. "I may be a SpiritWalker now *Ange*, but I have no idea how to do *any* of the things you do. Hell, I barely speak Lakota, and only because my one sister beats me over the head until I get it right. Guess I have to thank her when I find her."

She sensed his sorrow. "You'll find her, Luc."

"Yeah, but that doesn't help us now. I'm not fluent enough to be doing chants or other rituals. Should have paid more attention to Eagle Woman's lessons to her daughters."

"Don't need to." She put her hand on his arm. "All you need is intent. Words are not as important as what comes out of your heart. Let your need speak for you, and show that you mean no harm. Respect and honor all things. Come on. We will be safe up here."

Luc watched Blaze climb nimbly up the boulder. She squeezed herself into a long, narrow crevice in the center of the jagged grouping of granite, but her body was still visible. He shook his head. "It's not going to work," he muttered, torn between his need to stay close to her, to protect her, and the need to go deal with the threat. Fight, or stay and protect? Her eyes remained on him, her features calm but set in determination. Luc sighed. He had no choice. He could not leave his beautiful angel.

He climbed up and tucked himself into the crevice in front of her, pulling her close, as tight to him as he could in order to shield her. She was so close he could feel her breath on his throat and see the pulsing blue of her wide eyes. Glancing around, his heart sank. They were still visible.

He pulled her closer, trying to cover her body with his. "Now what? Are you going to turn us into birds?"

Blaze shook her head. "I have never done that. We are going to merge our spirits with those of the rocks."

"What?" The word came out a disbelieving hiss. If that was her plan, he'd be better off going after the trackers with a heavy branch.

"Listen! And believe." Her eyes flashed with warning.

"All right. Tell me what to do." Just in case, his

hand slid down to make sure he could grab his knife if needed. He'd stashed their belongings beneath a low, dense shrub.

Blaze sent him a dark look, as though she felt his doubt. "Everything that has a shadow has a spirit, and spirits can be called upon in times of need." She took his hands with hers.

"*Inyan*. Ancestor of all gods and all things, you are the rocks, the mountains."

"*Cewakiay. I beseech. I pray.*" She paused.

"*Omakiya. Help me.*"

Blaze looked at Luc. "We are two, but we send you one voice. Our prayers come from joined hearts. Blend us and hide us from the enemy. Let our spirits merge with yours until trouble has passed. *Mitakuye oyasin.*"

Luc repeated her words in his mind. He didn't have time to argue or even doubt her. He had to trust, and to believe in her and what she was doing. Concentrating as she repeated the prayer three more times, he wasn't sure what to expect but fisted one hand around his crystal and waited.

He was ready to tell her he didn't feel anything when waves of vibrations swept through him. It was unlike anything he'd ever felt. It felt old. Powerful. Like a blast of wind inside his body. The power she'd called upon hummed through him. He felt an acceptance, a sense of belonging, as though he was a part of the very rock he sat upon.

His eyes went wide. Surely they weren't going to turn into rocks? "What's happening?"

"Let your mind join with the spirit of the rock. He has accepted our request. He is willing to hide us. Concentrate on the colors around us. See yourself becoming part of this rock, blending your spirit with his spirit. He is old. Very old and very powerful. Ancient life," she murmured as she closed her eyes. "Feel him. Feel me. We are three joined as one."

Luc had no choice but to do as she said. He closed his eyes, imagined how he'd look as a rock, the gray, white and black speckles covering his body. He let his warmth flow into Blaze and hers into him.

And then he felt it: the blending of man, woman and rock. Blaze became a part of him. Her warmth, her unique scent and the essence of her life joined with his and around them; as though cupped in a giant hand of granite, he felt the hum of earth. It was unlike anything he'd ever felt. It made him nervous, yet his angel's presence soothed him.

Opening his eyes, he carefully peered around him. He no longer felt exposed. Glancing at Blaze, he was surprised that he could see her. "Shouldn't you be blending in with the rock?" Was he as exposed as she was?

Blaze smiled. "We are safe." She held up a hand. They come. "You must remain very still. Keep your mind focused."

Luc froze. From below, he saw a crouching figure slide out of the woods. Another followed. Both warriors wore breechcloths and moccasins. One had a feather tied in his hair; the other had paint splashed over his face and cheeks. Each warrior carried a lance and bow. Their hoarse and nasal voices drifted to him. Keeping the image of the rock in his head and Blaze's hand in his, he watched the Chippewa scouts.

It didn't take the warriors long to find the place they'd slept. Luc frowned. It wouldn't take them long to realize the trail stopped here. They'd search. And then they'd come to the rocks and climb them, searching for a trail. He couldn't allow them— wouldn't allow them—to find Blaze or to hurt her. Everything in him demanded he destroy the threat to his woman.

His woman? The thought made him narrow his eyes. She wasn't his woman. Yet he'd kissed her and had wanted her with the same primitive need as to breathe. From the moment he'd first seen her, he'd been captivated by her quiet beauty, and he'd gone to her, trusted her, needed her—and in return, she'd stolen his heart and soul.

He fought the feeling. She'd taken away his free will. What he felt was not of his choosing; she left him no choice but to want her. His body and his heart didn't care, but his mind rejected the idea. He didn't like being tricked or forced.

A loud shout startled him. He glanced down. One of the warriors was staring right at him—as if he could see his head.

Blaze gave Luc a sharp squeeze. Her eyes flashed with warning. *Luc! Focus!* she ordered, her voice a mere thread of sound in his head.

Startled to hear her, Luc looked at her. She had her eyes closed, her brows drawn as she concentrated. He realized he'd let his mind wander and had broken the connection, and that *she* was now keeping his spirit merged with hers and that of the rock.

Repeating the words she'd used in her prayer in his head, he concentrated until he felt the vibrations wrap around him once again. But it was too late. The warriors were moving cautiously toward the boulders.

A swish of sound made him curse and duck, pushing Blaze's head beneath his. Two arrows flew over his head, close enough the feathered shaft scraped against his head.

"Damn it! I'm not cut out for this," Luc ground out. In front of him, he felt Blaze trembling. Now what? He needed a distraction, something he could use for cover so they could get out of here.

An idea came to mind and he smiled grimly. A tantrum right about now should do. He'd have to thank his sisters for the idea when he found them. He gathered his anger, his fury. Someone close to him had betrayed his family, and he now had a use for that anger. He was a SpritWalker, which just added fuel to his anger. Now he planned to use what he was to protect his angel.

Blaze felt Luc shift behind her, felt a growing rage in him. She kept her head down, struggled to keep them merged, but she too knew it was too late. Even if they remained shielded, the warriors knew where they hid. Blaze fought to keep Luc's anger from her, afraid of losing control. She concentrated on keeping them merged with the rock.

"Blaze, call up the wind!" The command was filled with urgency, and then his intent slammed into her. Merged with him, she saw what he planned to do. Immediately she let her own emotions flow from her. Normally she kept them under tight rein, but she let her mind merge with his, let his anger fuel hers. She thought of the dead bodies, the dead wolves, and his pain rolled through her.

She thought of her "father" and his betrayal, and finally, she let grief wash into her. Greed had stolen her from her family and killed her true parents, and greed had nearly taken the life of the man beside her.

He was her spirit mate. She felt it—the rightness of it in the blending of their thoughts and in the rhythmic beating of their hearts—and someone was after both of them. Blaze would protect what was hers; and this trapper with his meadow-green eyes was hers.

The storm when it hit, hit hard. A bolt of lightning struck the ground and rumbled deep in the earth. The warriors pulled up short and stared at the sky. Dark, massive clouds came out of nowhere with sparks of flame jumping from one to another. The wind howled through the trees, throwing the warriors back.

Blaze tried to keep her anger under control. She used it for protection, not destruction. But wrapped around her, Luc's fury continued to grow, the anger and rage rolling off him in great sheets so that she could barely control her own anger. She wanted to merge hers with his and let loose.

Above their heads, a cloud swirled and dropped to the ground, twisting in the grass, throwing rocks, twigs and leaves high into the air. Blaze gasped, tamped down her own anger, released it and called upon the control she'd used all her life. It had little effect. Luc's fury alone was massive, and he was out of control. Sweat dripped from his skin and deep lines of pain lined his face. He shook, and she felt everything he felt.

Gasping, fighting the pull, she shook his arm. "Stop! Stop, Luc." His eyes were closed, his lips pressed hard together. She shook him again. Harder. He opened his eyes. They were a dark, menacing green. She felt the heat radiating from him.

"Too much," she said. And as he had done last night, she stopped him the only way she knew: with a kiss.

He cowered beneath the bushes, his fisted hands around the stone. "I'm not giving up!" he shouted. He heard a gunshot but had no idea what was going on. He'd stayed back, giving the scouts plenty of room to work. And if there was an ambush, he'd know in time to avoid it.

The show of power ahead *was* an ambush, and it kept him from moving forward—but it also deepened his greed. He wanted more than anything to be able to call up the wind and send lightning striking the ground. He could rule the world with a storm like this one.

He grinned, and even when the wind hit him, showering him with leaves and twigs and tugging at the stone in his hand, he held on. It was his now. Beside him, Abe pulled on his arm.

"Something's behind us."

Turning quickly, his gun pointing into the bushes, he peered into the thick shrubs. "Nothing there. Luc and the woman are ahead. He adjusted the fox-fur cap on his head to keep the wind from whipping it from his head.

"Something's there. I saw red glowing eyes." Abe licked his lips nervously.

"Don't be stupid. It's just an animal. You got the gun. It don't." He kept his eye on the eye of the storm. Movement drew his attention. The two scouts came running, their eyes round and white. The wind whipped their backsides as they ran for their lives, running past him and Abe. Beside him, Abe was jabbering incoherently.

"Nothing's worth dying for," the man stammered. He turned and ran back the way they'd come.

"Cowards!" But he didn't care. Better this way. Now it was just him. Only he'd known about Connie's woman. *SpiritWalkers*. Yeah, he liked the sound of that. He just had to figure out how to get her to make *him* into one.

It was clear he couldn't go after the woman and his nephew now. If he tried, he'd get sucked into this wind tunnel that grew while seeming to stand still. If the woman could do this, he probably couldn't get close enough to get her at all. He thought about that. This show of power did nothing to dim the desire growing in him. He wanted that power; but how was he going to get it?

A grin spread across his face. "There is a way," he said with a low laugh. He'd make the woman give him what he wanted. A trade. He giggled with glee. After all, he was a trapper. He'd just go trap him a couple of pretty little girls.

Luc heard his name through the haze of fury, Blaze's calm, angelic voice. Protect her. He had to protect her. At all cost. There was an anger in him unlike anything he'd ever experienced. The world had gone dark, cold as the storm of anger consuming him.

A beacon of light pierced the darkness, and then he felt *her*. She surrounded him with her beauty, her goodness. His angel was there, with him in the darkness that seemed to have swallowed him.

"Trapper, come back to me. Feel me."

The desperation in her voice penetrated the swirling anger of his mind, and as before when he'd wandered aimlessly in the gray void of death, he turned to his angel of light. Slowly the tide ebbed, replacing anger with another emotion.

Need. He opened his eyelids and stared down into eyes that had gone dark like the midnight sky. Blaze had her arms wrapped around his neck, and he held her tightly, the softness of her breasts pressed against his chest.

She was kissing him, claiming his mouth with hers. Passion swept through him and replaced anger. With a groan, he responded. He needed her, the touch of her, the scent of her, the feel of her.

He took control of the kiss, demanding from her the same need that exploded inside him. His blood surged with primitive need, and even as he fought it, wanting to be gentle, tender, the remnants of power were too strong; they needed an equally strong outlet.

Blaze gave it to him. There was no gentleness in her response. Her fire equaled his, making demands of him as he did of her. Their mouths mated, lips and teeth nipping, tongues dueling. Blaze gave, he took. And then she took from him.

His hands splayed across her back, roamed down, cupped her buttocks through her soft deerskin dress. He pulled it up, needing to touch her, to feel her warmth slide into him.

Her fingers dug into his hair, scraped over his head as she moaned and tried to get closer. Lifting one arm, he ran a hand over the strong line of her jaw then pulled back to allow them both to breathe. Her moist, full lips were made for kissing. Made for him.

In her eyes, he saw intense emotion. Need . . . and something else he wasn't ready to acknowledge. She rose up and shifted closer, her knees on either side of his hips. His hand dropped down to her knee and trailed up, his fingers sliding beneath her skirt.

"I want you, *Ange*. All of you. Here. Now." With

the storm still swirling around them. He had no idea if the enemy was still out there. The storm protected them, shielded them. He waited for her to protest or stop him, but she just stared, the blue in her eyes sparking flames in his.

"You are mine, Trapper," she whispered. Then she dropped her weight onto him as she clung, her lips finding his. Her need was as wild as the wind, and hot as the flashing lights playing over their heads. Nothing mattered. Not the storm. Not the warriors, not her father. Just him and how he made her feel.

Luc pulled her tight and shoved her dress up and cupped a softly rounded buttock in each palm. His fingers dug in and his hips moved forward, and with excruciating slowness he pressed her heated mound to his bulging hardness.

They were chest to breast, softness to hardness as he stroked up and down her spine. Slowly, his fingers retraced the path beneath her dress. One hand slid around to the front, and he eased some space between them so he could reach up and cup one small, soft breast.

She moaned and pressed herself against him, unconsciously seeking release from the building desire that held them both in its wondrous grip. She trembled as he touched her hardened nipple, then dropped her head back when he used both hands to lift her dress and cup the full ripeness of her breasts. Bending his head, he ran the tip of his tongue around each dusky pink tip.

Luc needed his angel in a way he'd never needed anyone else. With a quick upward pull, he removed her dress, shrugged out of his vest. He needed her flesh against his. Her softness and warmth merging into him.

He pulled her close until they were chest to breast, her arms wrapped tight around his neck. He was stroking her back, one hand trailing down over the curve of her buttocks along the line of her thigh.

His cheek slid against hers and he used his mouth to follow the strong line of her jaw and the sweet hollow of her throat. Her head fell back, her long silky hair forming a soft cloud around them. She was soft. Smooth. Sweet.

"Beautiful. My beautiful *ange*," he murmured, lifting his head and taking in the magnificence of her breasts, the dark pink nipples that begged to be kissed and suckled. He couldn't resist. His lips closed over one pert tip.

Blaze cried out. He was hard, hot, and he made her feel things she never before had. She wanted more, sensed that there *was* so much more. Her hands touched him everywhere. She couldn't stay still.

Her mouth found his and, when he laid her back, using her dress and his vest to cushion them from the stone, Blaze couldn't bear to let him go. She needed to keep him close, to let his scent blend with hers.

When he lifted his head, she moaned in frustration, her hips moving restlessly, needing to feel him between her legs. She sighed as he pressed a knee to the junction of her thighs and when he pushed, she thought she would explode with need.

"Luc!"

"I know, sweetheart. Not yet." Once again he lowered his head to her breasts. This time, as he suckled, his hand reached down and replaced his hard thigh. Her fingers dug into his sides, holding him to her. It wasn't enough. The feel of his fingers over the soft downy curls made her lift her hips.

She groaned as he moved his fingers in a brief stroke. "I need you, Luc. Touch me." She felt a wildness inside her that she'd never felt, that she'd never allowed.

Sitting, Luc untied his breeches and slid them down. Blaze's eyes widened as his maleness sprang out. "Touch me, *Ange*. All of me." He took her hesitant hand and showed her how to stroke him.

Blaze let out a gasp of sheer pleasure. He was hard yet feather soft at his tip. A bead of moisture dewed there. She stroked it away, pleased as he let out a long moan of pleasure.

She knew enough of the mating ritual to know she wasn't hurting him any more than he was hurting her. Filled with heat and her own storm that made her feel like she was losing control, she lay back and held out her arms.

Luc fell gently atop her. Above their heads, the wind whirled, yet nothing touched them. They were safe. But she didn't want safe, not from this man. Not now.

"Make me yours. Make us one. One heart, one soul, one spirit."

"God help me, I cannot say no, *Ange*." Luc settled himself between her legs and held her head tenderly in his hands. "Watch me. See what you do to me. Let me see what I do to you."

With that he began to slowly stroke her. Blaze's breath came out in gasps as he rubbed the heart of her womanhood over and over with his manhood. Stroke after stroke sent her higher and higher until she felt the gathering of something wondrous deep in her belly.

Her hips thrust up to meet his every stroke until her body lifted, her hips slamming against his pelvis. Her fingers were clenched in his tight buttocks to hold him to her as she shattered into tiny pieces.

Tremors wracked her body and she cried out. Luc reached down and thrust one finger inside her, felt her spasms. His own body tightened, and the pain made him gasp for breath.

"Can't wait, *Ange*. I can't wait any longer." Removing his hand, he entered her. He wanted to go slow, to ease into her, but the storm around him, in him and in her, was too much. He breached her innocence in one hard thrust.

Blaze cried out. Luc swallowed her cry, and kissed her hard and deep. He needed her to want him as he wanted her. He needed to feel her passion, her need. As if she knew what he wanted, she lifted her legs and wrapped them around his hips. He groaned as she tightened her grip, pulling him deeper.

Her heat sheathed him, and as he pulsed deep inside her, he felt her begin to move. That was all it took. His body began a rhythm that once begun would shatter what control he retained. He gave in. Let it come. She matched him thrust for thrust, kiss for kiss. He closed his eyes and arched his back and, with one final plunge, the darkness around him shattered. Golden stars floated above and below him. Blue light surrounded them as they flew to the heavens together.

Skan commanded Wi to give light and heat to the new world, and Maka was content for a time. Then she grew unhappy, for now it was bright all the time and hot so she once again complained to Skan.

CHAPTER TEN

Standing on a tower of stone rising into the air like a finger pointing into the sky, Storm Warrior watched the horizon as he had all during the night. With the arrival of dawn the spectacular storm grew fainter.

It had been a storm that had assaulted air and land, and even now traces of vibrations continued to spark across the sky and roll toward him. It had been no ordinary storm and not the first one during the night.

The first burst of elements slamming into Earth had come while he slept. The force of the thunder strikes and the fury of the wind had jerked him awake. Something about the vibrations had driven him to climb the Peak of the Gods, but by the time he got up there, it was gone. But a thread of awareness deep inside his mind and heart had flickered to life and kept his gaze focused on the night sky until dawn had lightened the sky from black to gray.

When the second storm slashed the new day, the shock of recognition had stunned him. He hadn't felt her for more than twelve winters.

Taya.

His baby sister Taya, who'd been stolen from his family when she'd been a small child. With a small seed of hope swelling in his heart, he'd watched the strength of the storm grow. And when the clouds and wind grew until it swirled into a twisting funnel, the hope in his heart blossomed, for there was no doubt in his mind that this was not a display from Mother Earth but an emotional display wielded by a child of the gods.

It came from the power of a SpiritWalker.

Taya.

It came from Taya. The spirit of wind had carried her essence, her scent, her power to him. Taya's spirit had brushed his. Even now he was afraid to believe. This was the first time since she'd disappeared that he'd sensed her presence. He'd never given up, but life had a way of pushing forward.

He remembered the storm she'd called when he was but a boy. People of his race left impressions behind when they used their gifts in such a powerful fashion. The very air he breathed was alive with Taya's spirit. A thrill of excitement and sheer joy brought tears to his hardened, warrior's eyes. Happiness slid through his heart and soul.

As he watched the horizon, he noted that the storm had slowed and seemed to have frozen, a circle of wind whirling to a point in the sky. It was a storm unlike anything he'd ever witnessed. Behind him, he heard noise and immediately felt the presence of his younger brother and sister. They joined him on the narrow tip of the tower. They stood, one on either side of him.

"Why did you call us?" Thunder Hawk asked.

Storm Warrior stood with his arms crossed. He was the eldest of the three siblings, four including Taya. As siblings they were connected by more than blood and birthright. Their spirits were intertwined not only with those who'd given them life but with the very gods who'd gifted them with their powers, and it was an easy thing to just send his thoughts on the wings of the spirit that was his very essence.

"What is wrong, my brother?" Raven Mist put her hand on his arm.

Pointing to what was left of the storm, Storm Warrior drew in a deep breath. "Taya. That came from her."

"Are you sure?" Raven Mist tipped her head back. "I barely remember her. I was so young."

"I am sure. She is alive. This is what remains of the second storm."

"We tried to find her...." Raven Mist's voice was soft.

Storm Warrior remembered the day she'd disappeared. He'd just turned thirteen summers, and had gone on a hunt with a group of warriors when he'd felt the death of his parents. He and the other warriors and young braves had returned quickly, but it had been too late; Taya was gone and his parents were dead. A torrent of wind, rain and fire had struck the land and kept them from being able to follow.

Many times he'd sought her. He'd gone on long journeys but had never found any sign of her. Yet in his heart, he knew she lived. He glanced below to where the land was still barren from the fire and the death of his parents.

"What are we going to do?" Raven Mist asked.

Storm Warrior stepped to the edge. "Find her." Closing his eyes, he lifted his hands slowly, turning them outward as he let himself fall. Behind him, Raven Mist and Thunder Hawk followed.

Luc held Blaze tight against him. She surrounded him with her heat, her softness, and the pulse of her desire throbbed around and into him. They were one, truly merged in mind and body. Long strands of her dark hair streamed across his chest as the wind continued to circle them protectively.

His hands trailed up and down her spine and down the curve of her buttocks. She was soft, smooth and incredibly beautiful. His fingers slid over the curve of her waist and up to cup one soft breast that filled his palm.

Opening his eyes, he stared down into her serene features. She lay with her eyes closed, her lips parted. He'd never experienced anything like this wild lovemaking with his angel.

"That was some storm, sweetheart." Twice now he'd seen stars, traveled their golden, wondrous path with this woman, and twice in the space of hours he'd found himself caught in the midst of a storm—one of his own making.

He'd never forget the cold panic of realizing he'd lost his focus and had exposed Blaze to danger or the surge of power that had gripped him when he realized he'd do anything to protect her. Whatever he had, he'd use.

Power sang through his veins. It was unlike anything he'd ever experienced. It had been wild and more than a bit frightening. He had an idea now how Blaze felt when she lost control.

As he shifted, he found himself automatically sending his senses flaring outward, seeking the wind, listening to the heartbeat of the woods around them. Scents assailed him. Aromatic pines, sweet and spicy wildflowers, composting leaves and rotted wood mingled with the rich soil, fresh air and the husky scent of a woman he'd just made love to.

Blaze snuggled deeper into his arms. He felt her lips curve into a smile against his throat. Her breath sweeping against his skin sent a fresh wave of need surging through him.

"Remind me not to ever make you mad," she said, her breath sliding over his skin.

Blaze's comment made Luc frown. Anger? He'd been filled with it, and as he stared down at Blaze, the glow of loving was snuffed out like a candle. A fresh thread of anger rose like smoke. To protect the woman in his arms, he'd sought the anger deep inside him and unleashed it.

He didn't remember all of it. Just the rage, the primitive need to protect his woman.

His woman. He sat up abruptly.

Above them, the wind which had nearly died gave a low howl. Horrified, he realized what he'd done. He'd created that windstorm then taken his angel while fueled with anger. He glanced around. The rock was hard, bits of stone and dirt clung to them, and he could see the evidence of her innocence in the streaks of blood on her thighs.

What have I done? He'd never lost control like this. How could he call up a storm like that and then take a woman in such a primitive, rough fashion? What had he become?

SpiritWalker.

The word snapped through his mind like the breaking of a branch. He glared down at Blaze. "What did you do?"

Blaze looked confused. "I kissed you. You were out of control and I couldn't reach you." She looked wary.

"You did more. Much more." He needed no other proof of the impact of what she'd done to him. He'd created a storm. One hell of a storm. He'd used powers that he hadn't wanted: from sensing the enemy to helping shield himself and Blaze from the warriors. He'd taken what he needed from what was available to him. Without thought to the consequences. And that scared him witless. Calling up that storm had come easily. Anger had not just filled him but consumed him. He'd lost control. What would have happened had Blaze not stopped him?

To make matters worse, he'd taken something precious from his angel.

He needed to lash out at something. Anything. "Damn. What are you doing to me? What else will you make me do?"

Blaze narrowed her eyes and grabbed her dress. She held it in front of her like a shield. "I made you do nothing." She tipped her quivering chin up at him. "You mated with me of your own free will."

"Free will! I didn't choose this—any of this!" he shouted, waving to indicate the fading storm and the two of them sitting out in the open after being attacked by his uncle's warriors. "I took you on a bunch of damn rocks in the middle of a storm that should have destroyed the whole damn area. And *in the middle of an attack*. You could have been killed!"

It didn't matter that neither of them bore a single scratch. Glancing down at the wooded area where they'd spent several hours resting, he stared in horrified silence. Everything was gone. Blown to hell and beyond. The area looked as though a giant hand had flattened it. He clenched his jaw when he saw the blackened ground where the bolt of lightning struck. He was furious—not with her, but with himself.

The blame lay squarely on him. He was the one who'd betrayed his father; it was his fault one of his uncles knew that his father and mother and sisters were SpiritWalkers. But what hurt the most was that it was his fault that Blaze was here, in danger. If he hadn't unwittingly betrayed his father, none of this would have happened. She'd never have left her home in search of him. Then, if that wasn't enough for any one man, he'd embraced wholeheartedly the nature and gifts and powers of a SpiritWalker, the very thing he'd rejected.

He'd done it to protect Blaze, though. Maybe he'd do so again. But that didn't excuse his taking a woman while consumed by anger.

Grabbing his clothes, he climbed down from the boulders, went to the stream and waded in. He stayed in the cold until the anger and shame had cooled. Then he dressed.

Sensing Blaze behind him, he turned and saw the hurt and pain in her eyes. Anger had seeped out of him, leaving him feeling as though he'd kicked a helpless puppy. He wanted to run. Just to run and keep going, to run from himself and from the mess he'd created.

So many innocent people were suffering because of him. And he kept hurting those around him. He held up one hand as she started to speak.

"You can't hate me more than I hate myself, *Ange.*"

Dressed, with her hair swinging down her back in a fall of gleaming blue-black, Blaze moved to stand in front of Luc. Reaching out, she grabbed his arm. "You did nothing wrong."

Her soft voice, her comforting touch and the break in her voice infuriated Luc. "Don't! Just don't. You might have taken my free will, made me into something I want no part of, but my actions now are my own. What I did to you was unforgivable." He'd be damned if he'd let her take his guilt and self-loathing from him.

"I don't understand." She looked bewildered. "What you did was wonderful. I've never felt like that. We were connected—I wasn't alone. I felt . . ." She broke off, a look of utter sadness in her eyes.

"Felt what? What did you feel, Blaze?" He wanted her to say that she hated him. Maybe then he'd feel better, but he knew deep in his heart that if she were to denounce him right then he'd want to die. He felt raw, ragged, confused.

Blaze stared at Luc. If was one of the rare times he'd used her name. Longing filled her. She wanted this man. No, she *needed* him. He was the air she drew into her lungs, the life that flowed in her blood. This green-eyed trapper made her feel whole. But he didn't love her. He hated what she'd done to him.

She turned away. No one had ever loved her— not that she remembered—and in truth, she couldn't blame her people. She could be scary even to herself. But Luc knew what she was, he wasn't afraid of her. He just didn't want her. Not any part.

The truth was bitter in her mouth. She could only shake her head and blink back tears. She felt vulnerable. And scared. He was her spirit-mate; her heart cried out for him to accept and love her. His warm hands on her shoulders released a single tear. She didn't fight him when he turned her to face him.

For a long moment they stared at one another, her eyes swimming with tears, his filled with pain and regret. "I'm sorry, *Ange*. I didn't mean to hurt you."

"You didn't." Her chin trembled.

"I did. Up there, and just now. Just tell me one thing. Did you take away my free will up there? Did you make me . . . ?" What could he say? Had she made him take her with roughness and violence? All he could remember was a need that rivaled that of the storm taking hold of him. Never had he felt that wild, primitive desire to make love to a woman— no, *mate*. He'd acted like a horny, rutting bull.

Blaze stared down at her hands. One part of her readied to fight for what she wanted. Another wanted to just give up and find a place to be alone. But in her heart, she knew she couldn't abandon this man. If she wanted him, she knew she'd have to fight.

"No. Our hearts, minds and souls connected. Our spirits merged. We were as one. In every sense." She reached up and stroked his face. "Fight it if you must, but the truth cannot be denied. I was led to you. I offered you life. You chose that gift."

"I did not choose to become a SpiritWalker."

Blaze smiled sadly and stepped away. She gazed at her golden-haired trapper, felt the impact of his blazing green eyes and the pain radiating from inside him as he struggled with the truth.

"There is always choice. Always free will. Your choice now, Trapper: do you accept what's happened, or do you run from it?"

* * *

233

The sun rolled across the sky as Blaze followed Luc through the thick woods. He hadn't spoken a word since they set off. She sighed as she stared at his stiff, unyielding shoulders. They were so wide, his arms so strong. The vest he wore was molded to his back revealing the thick cords of muscle.

Her gaze drifted down, and she couldn't help another soft sigh. His breeches were tight, revealing his mounded buttocks. Nice to look at, nice to touch. She longed to reach out and just rest her hands on his narrow hips and lean close and let his male scent envelope her. As before.

Warm, a bit spicy with the scent of the land clinging to him, he had a unique smell, and it bonded him to her even more. Her body reacted to him—sight, feel, and scent. He was hers and she was his.

She frowned. When would he realize the truth? Tired of his silence, Blaze quickened her pace to match his. He was actually slowing, and he kept rubbing his chest wound with his hand. She knew he was still weak: She felt the pain that he bore in silence.

Her hair brushed against his arm, and he flinched and moved away. Determined to make him understand, she tried to find a way to reach him. "Do your people not believe in gods?" He was a trapper from a world that she knew nothing about. He spoke a different tongue, yet he was also very Sioux. He was of the earth in his heart, even before she'd made him into a SpiritWalker.

Luc didn't answer, but his lips tightened. He took a sudden turn through a stand of pines, some rising so tall she couldn't see their tops. She followed as he wound his way through this forest that he seemed to know well.

Frustrated as he turned sideways to go between two thick trunks, forcing her to step back, she stopped and called out, "Trapper!"

Luc stopped abruptly and turned to glare at her. He hated when she called him that, and she likely did so to make him react.

He stalked back to her. "You know my name, dammit. Use it."

Blaze shrugged, folded her arms across her hips and stuck out one hip. "Luc is a nice-sounding name. You are not being nice. You are being stubborn and difficult."

"With reason, *Ange*."

"Perhaps that is so. Will you not accept that I did not know what I was doing?" She held up one hand. "We each walk our path. It is often not of our choosing. Do you think I would have chosen to witness the death of my parents, or to live with a man who hates me? Do you think I would choose to live among people who are afraid of me and have rejected me just because I am different?"

"It's not the same thing. You were born a Spirit-Walker. I was not." Luc turned on his heel and continued. By the time she caught up to him, his breathing was labored.

Blaze knew he was pushing himself. It had been

hours since they'd begun their trek through the forest. A sheen of sweat covered his brow. She was just as tired and just as frustrated and angry over the events of the last few days. She had been badly hurt and betrayed by her "father." Luc wasn't the only one who endured.

"Your parents and sisters are SpiritWalkers. Is it so hard to believe that you too were meant to become one?" The more time they spent together, the stronger their connection. She was pretty sure it was far too late to break this. Especially after they'd joined mind, body, and spirit.

Throwing up her hands, Blaze gave up for the moment. "Where are we going?" If she was stuck with him, she'd at least know his plan.

"To Old Man Rock. My sisters will go there. We have to get there before the enemy. Before my uncle."

"Your body has not fully healed, Luc. You need to rest. We can reach my village by nightfall." Blaze had checked his wounds, and while they were healing nicely, they had a long way to go. He was still pale from loss of blood, and neither of them had eaten in a day except for some berries on the run yesterday. They had only one knife for a weapon.

Luc shook his head. "No. If the storm scared off those warriors, Abe and my uncle, we need to keep going. He might go after the girls if he can't have me. I won't let anyone hurt them."

Blaze took the time to check the wind for signs that they were being followed. Reassured that no one followed, she put a hand on his arm. "I touched

Skye's doll. I will know if anything happens to her. And as her brother, *so will you.*"

Luc narrowed his eyes, the green going dark. "Now that I'm a SpiritWalker, you mean?"

Sighing, Blaze held tight when he would have continued through the woods to avoid talking. "Yes. You are connected. All of you are. First by blood, then by becoming as they are." She hesitated. "And through you, *I* am connected." That amazed Blaze. For the first time in her life she felt a connection to others. She belonged. More than anything, it had been the strong connection to Luc's sister that made Blaze believe that Luc was right, that she was indeed a SpiritWalker.

She had tried to remember her parents, but the memories were buried or long forgotten. Still, as though recalled by learning the secret of her past, memories were starting to come back. Nothing specific; just vague images. Her siblings. Her brother. An older brother who bossed her around.

It felt right. As though a dam had broken, her mind was starting to remember more of her childhood. But if she met her brother tomorrow, would she know him? How would she find her family? Her people?

She put it from her as she focused on Luc. Stubbornness warred with pride, which conflicted with physical pain and exhaustion. She saw and felt his fear and worry. She felt the overwhelming emotions tearing him into pieces, and knew she had to put her past aside and help him find his family.

"You need to regain your strength. At least rest."

Luc stubbornly shook his head. "Can't."

Blaze herself had a choice. She could go with him or go home. There was nothing he could do to stop her. Sighing, she realized she didn't have much of a choice. Luc had her heart.

Silence fell between them. Finally, Luc spoke. "Your people do not know you are a SpiritWalker." It was a statement, not a question.

She shrugged. "No. Only my "father" knows, and he kept that a secret from even me."

"Secrets destroy life." Luc's voice was bitter. "My father's secret has destroyed our family."

She stared at him. "Some secrets are necessary. They protect."

Luc came to a halt, and she stumbled and nearly tripped over an exposed root. He pulled her to him. "Did your father's secret protect you, or did it protect him?" His voice was harsh.

Blaze sucked in a deep breath. Pain sliced through her heart at the insensitivity of his question. Her sight blurred. "My father sought only to protect himself," she said harshly. "He hid the truth and used me to make himself into a great medicine man. He was wrong to do so." She tossed her hair back and pulled anger to her like a thick fur robe. She glared at Luc. "But your father kept his secret to protect his family."

"And that very secret might cost them their lives." Luc jerked on the medicine bag around his neck. "Him becoming a SpiritWalker is what has destroyed my family. I want no part of it."

Blaze tried not to be hurt, but she was. He was rejecting her, just like her "father." Just like her people. She hugged her arms close to her body and marched past him, ducking beneath a web of tangled branches. Luc went around.

He caught up with her. "I am grateful you came to me," he said at last. "It's just too much to take in. To accept."

Blaze didn't know what to say, so she said nothing. As they walked, the warmth of the air washed his scent over her. Her body responded with the need to lean into him, to merge completely and know that rush of power that had overtaken them earlier, during their mating.

His spirit, his essence ran in her blood now, and she wanted and needed this man, this trapper, more than she'd ever needed or wanted anything. She forced herself to push away from Luc to keep her mind clear.

"You believe in animal totems." It was another clear statement of fact from Luc.

"Yes. Of course."

"So, if an owl came to you and said that secrets destroy life, would you believe him?"

Blaze glanced over at Luc. "What?"

He shrugged. "Forget it. It was just a dream, likely. I thought I was awake, but it was just a dream." He could swear he'd been awake, but to believe that would mean accepting the world of the SpiritWalker. He preferred denial at the moment.

"You dreamed of an owl?"

"Yeah. A talking owl." He sent her an amused look, but found her staring at him with wide serious eyes.

"*Hinyan* is a symbol of darkness, and darkness hides many secrets." Blaze trailed off, and when she continued, her voice was low, husky and a bit shaky. "Secrets live in all of us." She glanced at Luc. "Secrets surround us. Now tell me about your dream."

Luc actually found that he wanted to share what had happened. In his heart, he knew he hadn't been asleep and his angel was the one person who'd understand, better than he, the meaning behind the visit of an owl. Telling her might also clear up some of the tension surrounding them.

"You were sleeping. I was awake—at least I thought I was—when I saw an owl high in the tree. It flew down and sat in the branches so close that I could see into its eyes. It sat there and just stared at me." He didn't tell her he'd been debating whether to toss the crystal from him when the owl showed up.

Blaze stopped, her eyes moist with tears. "The spirit of *Hinyan* honors you! Not all people get a visit from the animal world. Owl is your totem animal, your protector and your travel mate. Listen to him. Take his words to heart."

Luc frowned. "If he wants me to understand and heed his words, then he needs to speak clearly and not in riddles."

Blaze didn't comment. She waited. The silence between them stretched, broken only by the occasional burst of birdsong or the faint crackle of leaves and twigs on the forest floor. They pushed forward through a dense pocket of trees and shrubs.

Recognizing that her silence was not a way of ignoring him but that she was giving him whatever time he needed to find the right words to speak, Luc sighed. His earth mother was very good at being silent while her children talked, and had taught they often found their own answers without her having to say much at all.

"'Welcome truth and have the courage to embrace it. The child holds the key. The answers to so many secrets lies within the child.'" Luc stared straight ahead, yet his ears strained to hear what Blaze had to say about the words from the owl.

Her eyes went wide. "An old woman said that to me. Wise Owl. She was wife to the old shaman. *She* told me to seek the child."

Luc stopped to rest a moment. They were walking uphill. "Did you?"

Blaze nodded. "I am the child." She stared into Luc's green eyes. They were dark, like the boughs of pine above their heads.

After a moment she added, "I too have seen an owl. He did not speak to me, but the night I saw him was the night I spoke with Wise Owl. She told me to travel the wheel of the south." Blaze stopped to lean against a thick trunk and let the essence of life seep into her.

"'Discover the child. The innocence. Find in you the trust and faith of the innocence. Remember, in innocence are we born, in faith do we grow.'" She paused after repeating the words of Wise Owl.

Luc didn't know what to say. He sure wished he'd paid more attention to his earth mother during her impromptu lessons and stories. They'd always carried a seed of wisdom to be used in their daily walks upon the earth, but he'd never really felt part of his father's new life. He'd never truly accepted her fully.

"I never had an owl come that close and just stare," he remarked.

Blaze tipped her head and smiled. "Have you ever looked? Have you ever *asked* for the spirit of the owl to come to you?"

Luc stared up into the bright glare of sunlight piercing the canopy of leaves above. "No. I can't say that I have. But then, I've never been a SpiritWalker."

"You do not have to be a SpiritWalker to communicate with the animals of our world. You need only pay attention and listen to the messages they carry. The birds, the four-legs, the creeping-crawlers, the swimmers, the fish and winged ones—all show themselves to us every day that we walk upon Mother Earth. Each carries a special message.

"Your people do not listen to Mother Earth or hear Father Sky. They have gone far from their earth-roots." Blaze walked to some rocks and waited. Luc joined her.

"Give me your hand." She waited until he complied, then placed his palm on a large boulder. "Your people do not feel the ancient power in stones or feel the flow of life in a tree trunk." She took his other hand and held it to the tree, connecting them, human, rock and plant. "Feel life."

Frowning, Luc tried to pull his hands away. "I don't feel anything."

Blaze released him. "Your mind is like that of a child. It must be taught how to listen. Owl warns of secrets. Our fathers each carried a secret. My father used his to cover his crimes, your father to protect those he loved. One out of selfish greed, the other out of love."

Luc grew thoughtful. "One of my uncles was responsible for the attack on my family and on us. The question is, which one?"

"Some answers are only revealed by time."

"Time is running out, *Ange*." He started walking, cutting across the hillside toward a gully.

To her right, the hill crested. High above the trees on the hill, a lone eagle flew in lazy circles over the forest canopy, as though sweeping the area from above. Images from what Blaze now knew was her childhood slid through her.

Eagles flying. People shifting into eagles. According to Luc, she should be able to call upon the spirit of an animal and not just merge minds but shift to become that animal. She didn't know how to do that, but in her heart she knew one day she'd learn.

It was a burning desire now. She remembered it from childhood, when her "father" had scoffed at her and gotten so angry that she'd never talked about it again. No, she'd never wanted to be different or feared. She'd wanted to be normal—accepted and loved. Yet, she'd known that there was so much good that she could do with her abilities.

Her people had rejected her. Just as Luc would when this was over. Unless she could prove to him that being a SpiritWalker was meant to be—for both of them. If she could use her abilities to find his sisters, wouldn't that prove something? Wouldn't it prove the change worthwhile?

Watching the bird, her longing to join it in flight was just as strong as it had been in her dreams. An idea came to her. Perhaps there was something she could give Luc now, something to ease his worry.

"Luc. Wait."

"No. We keep moving." His voice was low and tense.

She climbed up the steep side of the hill, grabbing hold of tree trunks to keep herself from back-sliding. Finally, she reached the top.

Forests of dense wood and thick undergrowth spread out on two sides. An eroded hillside was on the third, and land blackened by fire on the fourth. Behind her, she heard the crunch of branches.

"What the hell are you up to, *Ange?*"

Blaze stared around her, then looked at Luc. "You believe I am a SpiritWalker?"

"Of course, *Ange*. What's your point?"

"There is something I can do. From the air I might be able to see your sisters."

"You said you couldn't shift shape . . ." Luc stared out into the distance as though seeking his siblings.

"Not yet. But I can mind merge. If the eagle is willing, he might show me where your sisters are, let me see that they are safe."

Nodding, Luc set his pack down. "Okay."

Blaze glanced up and closed her eyes. She lifted her hands high and focused on her need, her intent. One of her greatest joys came from this, soaring in the arms of the wind, but today she had a mission. She needed to help Luc find his family, even if he'd leave when this was all done. He was her heart and soul. Her spirit mate. She had to do what she could to ease his fear and worry.

Hoye wa yelo.
Spirit of Wambli.
Your vision I need.
So I may see those who need me.
Mitakuye Oyasin.

She opened her eyes and sent out her request to merge with the eagle. For just a moment, Blaze felt disoriented and breathless, then something happened that had never before happened: she slammed into a wall, some sort of invisible blockage. Pain struck Blaze between the eyes, the shock so great, she felt as though she'd been shot. Above her head, the eagle bolted out of his lazy circle. A loud cry rent the air as the bird went into a dive.

Immediately she was thrown back into her nightmare, saw the two eagles plummeting to earth. Her eyes went wide with horror.

"Not again," she moaned, but the bird fell from the sky. Her eyes rolled back in her head, and everything went black.

*Skan decreed that Wi would rise in the east each
morning then set in the west. Darkness and light would
now share the day.*

CHAPTER ELEVEN

"*Ange!* Come on, mon *petit ange*. Wake up!" Luc
held Blaze in his arms. "Blaze. Sweetheart, come
back to me."

In his arms, Blaze was pale and her skin clammy.
Luc's heart was racing and his mind screamed with
fear.

One moment she'd been fine, standing like a god-
dess on the hill, hands uplifted, the fringe on her
dress blowing, her hair a dark smooth river down
her back. He'd been enthralled, his heart and mind
caught up in her angelic beauty.

His mother had liked to talk about angels, and
he'd always imagined them to be blond-haired,
blue-eyed beauties. But Blaze was his little angel,
his angel of light. At least she had the blue eyes.

When she stirred, he sighed with relief. He'd never
felt more afraid than while seeing her faint and the
eagle go into its dive. It had shaken him to his core.

He patted her cheeks and rubbed her cold hands,

and when she finally opened her eyes, he gave a huge sigh of relief, even though their color was pale compared to normal.

"Come on, sweetheart. Snap out of it." She shuddered and shook in his arms and didn't make a sound. He somehow knew she was remembering her nightmare of the night of her parents' murder.

"No more tricks, sweetheart. I don't think my heart could stand it. Even if you could heal me again." He smiled, forcing it. Damn, but she'd given him a fright. He didn't think he could survive any more surprises, shocks or scares.

"It's all right. *You're* all right." He was reassuring himself every bit as much as her.

"No." Tears slipped down her face and she huddled into him. "I killed it. I killed the eagle."

Luc held her tight, his lips on her hair. "Not on purpose, baby. Not on purpose." He rocked her gently, unable to find the words to ease the pain of what she'd done. His own shock and disbelief when the bird fell had driven him to his knees.

"I wanted to help you." Tears ran down the sides of her face. Her eyes were blank. "I didn't wait for it to give me permission. I tried to merge without consideration. I took the bird's free will—and now it is dead."

Sighing, Luc saw this was his fault. "I'm sorry, *Ange*." He'd been hurting her with his rejection of what she was, what she'd shared with him; but he couldn't help it. He should take her back to her people, see her safe, then go on to find his sisters alone.

Something deep inside him violently rejected the idea of leaving his angel behind. He felt like an animal who scented bait and had one foot moving toward the trap. The longer he stayed with his angel, the more surely the steel jaws of the trap were sprung.

She'd said repeatedly that they were forever connected, and he was beginning to fear that they were. Since making love to her, the threads of that connection seemed to be getting shorter, tighter, as their hearts and spirits were woven nearer together.

"I'm so sorry for all I've done." Blaze's voice trembled. It broke.

"We'll deal with this." Somehow. He stared out at the horizon as she continued to shake in his arms. Control was the issue. He'd lost control of his life the moment he'd decided to make a change. His decision to return home had not just affected him but everyone around him. Including this woman.

Yes, she'd been drawn into this mess and was in danger just by being with him. Yet he didn't dare leave her alone to go to Old Man Rock and find his sisters. He had no idea where his uncle was, or the warriors he and Blaze had frightened off that morning. The fact that she was a SpiritWalker, easily identified by her eyes, meant he was stuck with her. He would never allow her to be hurt.

Can you accept what you now are?

The voice snaked through his mind. He shook his head. *No.* Not for good he couldn't. He'd felt and seen firsthand how dangerous he could be like this.

And together, he and his angel with their combined emotions had created one hell of a storm. That alone was enough to make him reject what he'd become. He didn't have much of a temper; it took a lot for him to lose control, but as he'd witnessed earlier, when he lost it, he really lost control. What if he got angry and ended up killing someone?

Had it not been for Blaze, he might have done more damage. And even with that release of fury, more anger waited deep inside. He'd never forget how he'd felt when he'd lost his focus and exposed both of them to danger. Power corrupted. How many times had he seen it even out here?

Greed. Money. Power. All were corruptors. And power had sung through his veins. It was unlike anything he'd ever experienced. It had been wild and more than a bit frightening. He had an idea now how Blaze felt when she'd lost control.

His anger was caged for the moment, but the lock was fragile and he was very much afraid of what he'd do when he found his uncles. And if his father was dead? He shook his head. God help whomever was responsible.

Shifting Blaze in his arms, he stared down into her face then gently wiped the tears that streaked her cheeks. She was pale and in her eyes he saw the pain that made her shake. That pain was deep inside, not to her physical body. She was devastated by what she'd just done, and Luc had no idea how to make that unhappiness go away.

"We'll deal with everything that has happened."

He tried to reassure her as he glanced around them. "But right now we need to get moving. It's not a good idea to stop for long."

Above them, the sky was a deep, summer blue. Not a cloud in sight. There was no one around: scenting the wind, seeking information from a spirit he'd never before even believed in was now becoming second nature.

Blaze didn't move or respond. Luc cupped her face with one hand. "You're making me a tad nervous, *Ange*. Talk to me."

She bit her lower lip and shook her head. "I cannot do this to you. Maybe if you go, if you are not around me, you will not be like I am. I can feel your fear and resentment. You have every right to hate me for what I've done." She shook her head to stop his denial. "It is my fear as well. I've always been afraid of the things I do. So many times I could have used my anger against others but didn't. Not until today."

"I made you do it." And Luc realized he would do it again. Anything to keep her safe.

"Perhaps I did steal your free will. Maybe your mother's people can get it back."

Luc lifted a brow. "Well, there's not a chance in hell I am leaving you out here."

Blaze lifted her hand. The wind began to blow, clearly at her command. "I will be fine."

Sighing, Luc stood and pulled her upright, keeping his arms around her. "No doubt. But that doesn't change anything." He held on as she struggled.

"You don't want to be here. You don't want me." Tears streaked her face.

"But I am here, and I'm not leaving you." Running his hands down her back, he brushed pine needles from her dress. He threaded his other hand into her hair, needing the comfort of her silky softness.

"Are you hurt?" He couldn't see any injuries, knew it was her mind that had been shattered by the failed merging, but he wanted her to realize that.

"No."

Her silent tears continued to fall. Luc had to do something to snap her out of this. His uncle could be close by. They were on a rise in the land. He needed to get her moving. Luc could make her angry, but given the degree of anger they'd just experienced and the storm that had torn up the land, he didn't think it a wise thing to risk that loss of control again. That left one thing to try. He pulled her back to him and lowered his mouth to hers.

Kissing always seemed to connect them and help them each regain control. He refused to look too deeply into what that meant; he simply closed his mouth over hers, warmed her lips with his own.

Just one simple, comforting kiss. . . . But when Blaze gripped his shoulders hard and leaned in, he couldn't stop himself. His tongue swept over her parted lips then slipped inside.

The fire in him flared to life. His blood hummed in his body, rushing down between his legs. "Damn. I want you. Again."

Blaze shook her head and tried to turn away. Luc

251

wasn't letting go. He needed his angel back, the woman who'd fought for him, come to him, given him life when he'd given up.

"Kiss me, *Ange*. Like before." He demanded it of her. More important than breathing, Luc needed to see fire blazing in her dull eyes, to hear her cries of passion instead of defeat. She was life, was part of him. His hand slipped down her back.

"So soft. Feel me. Let me feel you." His fingers trailed up her thigh, over her hips and over the smooth expanse of her bare behind. He put his heart, his very spirit into the kiss. All his warmth, his feelings, and—to his shock—his love.

He loved her.

Instinct had him swallowing the words, hiding the blinding truth. But as though she could feel what he could not admit aloud, she responded as though something snapped awake in her. With equal fire and passion, her hands trailed over his body, touching him everywhere. Her mouth took his with greed, and as they dueled for control, the heat between them grew. When she nipped him not so gently, Luc felt his loins tighten.

Her fingers raked over his back, slid up beneath his vest, digging in, and when she unwittingly pressed on his wound, he couldn't help the shudder of pain that rippled through him. Lifting his head, Luc stared down into the sheen of stars in her eyes. The blues were a dark, rich shade, the yellows bright and golden like the stars that had surrounded him when they'd merged as one.

Blaze ran her hand over his back. He felt the soothing warmth.

"I hurt you." She looked worried.

He bent his head and chuckled low and soft, and he nuzzled her right ear. "That kiss was worth it."

Blaze smiled sadly. "You are just being nice to stop me from crying."

Luc chuckled. "No such luck. I'm trying to be good. Trying to tell myself that this isn't a good idea." He brushed his mouth tenderly over hers.

Blaze licked her lips. Before Luc, she'd never been held or comforted. "It felt good," she offered shyly. With Luc, all felt right. She felt comforted and loved. Which made perfect sense. He was her spirit mate.

"Let's try this again, to see if it is a good idea." She pulled his head down.

"Why the hell not." Luc pulled her close.

The kiss heated quickly, her arms holding him tightly, his own wrapped just as firmly around her. Their hearts beat as one, and she trembled slightly when his fingers slid up and down her back, feeling every trembling shiver as he deepened the kiss.

Tremors shook him as well. The heat of their kiss started deep in his belly and flowed outward in all directions. She made him feel whole. Complete. She was sweetness and courage. She was his light, her goodness saturating his heart, his spirit. The more he took, the more he wanted to give. Had to give. He couldn't stop. Didn't want to stop. She was his angel and he wanted more. He wanted all of her and he wanted to pour all that was him into her.

Trailing kisses along her jaw, down her throat, he stopped at the gentle swell of her breast beneath her dress. His breathing was harsh, his body tighter than a coiled snake.

Blaze moaned in his ear. Her breath washed over him, and when she opened her eyes, he thought he'd drown in the brilliant blues and golden stars. But even through the desire in her eyes, he saw the cloud of exhaustion. He willed his body to calm because he knew if he didn't stop, he was going to lay her down and make her his. Again and again.

Lifting his head, he rested his forehead on hers. "This is definitely not a good idea."

He pulled back, holding Blaze at arm's length. Before she could protest and fling herself back into his arms, they were interrupted by an arrow.

Red Thunder stayed hidden in the trees. The scene he'd witnessed when the girl had fallen had left him unmoved. He'd watched her stand there like a god, then he'd seen both her and the eagle fall. For a moment he'd been taken back in time.

Fear had dried his mouth and made his legs tremble. But he wasn't that same scared warrior any longer, so he'd quickly banished the fear and kept his goal in mind. To his great disappointment, whatever she'd tried hadn't killed her. He knew she'd tried to do something to the eagle, and that it had failed. And that she was unfortunately still alive.

Several times while the trapper comforted her,

he'd taken aim. Once a spear of sunlight had blinded him. The second time, the wind had sent a leafy branch swaying his way, and then the trapper had followed. Red Thunder didn't care if he killed the man, but he intended to take the girl who'd ruined his life.

Now, when he'd finally had a clear shot, he'd missed. His grip tightened on his bow. That arrow should have hit her. His aim was true.

Above his head, the leaves moved slightly. Had the wind or the gods been responsible for his failed shot? "You cannot hurt me," he called out, his voice soft and steady. Had the gods planned to take revenge for the killing of their children, they would have struck him down long before this. The gods and lesser gods and spirits would not interfere in human life. They could not. If he chose to kill, that was his choice. He'd killed before. He'd killed both a SpiritWalker and a holy man. He still lived.

No, the only person he feared was the girl: he'd seen the power of her storm. Once more he glanced up. The wind was gone. Slowly, he made his way around the rise in the land and picked up the pair's trail.

Storm Warrior hurt like hell. The last thing he'd expected while seeking his sister was to connect with her while in the form of an eagle. He'd been out searching, circling the area from high above to minimize the danger to himself. An eagle flying high was safe from hunters, and no other bird would attack him either.

Raven Mist knelt beside him. She ran her hands over his body. "No broken bones," she said, her voice sharp with worry. "I nearly lost my focus when I saw you fall. What happened?" As he'd fallen, she'd gone into a tight dive to reach him.

"I am fine, little sister. Just bruised." Mind, body and ego. He sat up and stared into the clear blue sky. The last thing he'd expected was for his sister Taya to try and merge her spirit with his. And he'd been too high above the earth to immediately sense her spirit.

He smiled, then let out a satisfied sigh. The pain was worth this discovery. "She is close." Much closer than he'd realized, which meant she was moving toward him, away from where he'd witnessed her storm.

Raven Mist sat back on her heels. "Are you sure?" Her voice shook with emotion.

Storm Warrior stood and helped his sister to her feet. "She tried to merge minds with me."

A small hawk dived down toward them. At the last moment, it flared its wings back, spread its tailfeathers and thrust out its talons. In a blur of motion, the hawk shifted and Thunder Hawk was running toward them.

Raven Mist filled their brother in while Storm Warrior searched the sky with his eyes. Had Taya merged with another bird? Where was she? Was she all right? "Our sister is close," he repeated.

"Where?" Thunder Hawk demanded.

Shoving his hands onto his hips, Storm Warrior

shook his head. He'd been within sight of her, had to have been for her to try and merge minds with him. "I don't know. The shock of her trying that was so unexpected that I lost control."

He frowned at the subsequent silence. His siblings knew he never lost control or focus. One of the first rules learned as a child was to guard one's spirit. First lessons were in controlling thought and emotions, and later, if a SpiritWalker was so gifted, they were taught to shift forms.

Storm Warrior glanced at his brother and sister. The three of them had been blessed. He wondered about Taya. Could she shift shape? He was eager to get reacquainted with his young sister. He wondered how she'd changed.

"You could have been killed!" his sister said, her voice a fierce whisper. "Why did she not sense that you were not a bird? She should have known that you were a SpiritWalker."

"I do not know." The shock was still hitting him hard; it was as though an invisible hand had struck him in the chest. He remembered falling, and had barely managed to regain his focus before striking the earth.

Seeing that Raven Mist was upset, he gently lifted her chin. "It is a risk we take whenever we shift shape. You know this."

While in the form of a bird or animal, they were just as vulnerable as the form they took. His parents were proof of the dangers. They'd been shot out of the sky with arrows. All the abilities in the world didn't change the fact that SpiritWalkers were mortal. They might be descended from gods, but they were as vulnerable as any other creature who walked upon the earth.

"Now what?"

Storm Warrior studied his brother and sister. "We continue our search."

As he moved away, Raven Mist stopped him. "Did she recognize you?"

Frowning, Storm Warrior shook his head. "No. But I felt something else. Someone. There are others connected to her, and I sense they are all in danger. Taya needs us."

"Then we will find her." Raven Mist took off running and leapt high into the air, shifting shape to that of a sleek, shiny black bird. Her flapping wings took her soaring over the trees.

Thunder Hawk followed, becoming a hawk once again. Storm Warrior waited to be sure they were safe in their flights across the sky, then he closed his eyes, called up the spirit of the eagle, lifted his hands and leaped straight up into the air. His huge, powerful wings took him far up into the blue.

Wi was well satisfied with the events taking place below. What had been taken from the three would soon return. The four were strong and gifted, and the girl and her spirit mate were safe. All would be well.

Skan also decided that every material thing should have a shadow, and every shadow of every thing was to be its spirit and with it always.

CHAPTER TWELVE

Blaze and Luc threaded their way through the dense forest. They'd run to put distance between them and the enemy, and had now slowed to cover their trail. The first reaction was to keep running blindly, but they both knew that making noise would just allow whoever was behind them to stay on their trail.

"I thought those warriors took off." Luc pushed himself carefully through a shrub then stepped lightly between a patch of ferns. "Damn, how could I be so foolish as to let my guard down?"

Blaze placed her feet between the light and airy ferns without disturbing the ground or breaking any branches. Inside, her heart was hammering. The forest was so thick, the ground covered with layers of rotting leaves and vegetation: it was near impossible to leave no trace of their presence.

"I didn't sense the enemy. I should have known he was close." Once she recognized a scent, she normally remembered it.

Luc glanced over his shoulder. "We were a bit busy," he reminded her. He held his knife in his hand and moved cautiously.

Blaze stopped as the wind carried to her a strangely familiar smell.

"Come on, Blaze. No time to waste." Luc pulled her to him, his voice taut with worry.

"Wait. I know that scent." Blaze turned and stood still, letting her mind sort through the mixture of odors in the air. Off to the south, there was another village. The scent of wood smoke and cooking drifted lazily up from it.

A badger waddled in the brush not far from them, and farther out, there were more warriors. She sensed these, but they were too far away for her to identify. The danger lay much closer than either she or Luc had guessed.

Another tug to her arm. "Yeah. It's my uncle. Move it."

She pulled free. "No. It's not him. It's not the warriors with him, either. It's someone else. The scent of death is on him, but not as strong." She bent down and put her hands on the ground.

Life from the earth flowed up into her arms. She felt movements and the vibration of life as she connected, her eyes closed, her brows drawn tight in concentration. "He moves fast."

"Yeah, so let's go," Luc ordered.

Blaze focused on the vibrations, felt the subtle difference in one foot and another, the extra weight

placed on the right heel, the force of that heel striking the ground. "I can feel his steps," she breathed.

Her heart gave a jump. How many times had she
felt this person coming to wake her or fetch her in
the night while she slept? Many times his scent
alone had woken her, and right now, that scent was
growing stronger even as the truth exploded in her
mind. She knew this scent as well as she knew her
own, because it belonged to her "father." The
bearskin he wore was old and carried with it the
scents of his smudging, his sweat, and years of use.

"No! It can't be." She turned startled eyes to Luc.
"It is my father!"

Luc clenched the knife in his hand. He reached
down to once again pull Blaze up. "We need to
move." His eyes snapped dangerously.

Blaze stared up into the tree. "I need to be sure."
She knew in her heart that she was right, but her
mind refused to believe that the man who'd raised
her would try to kill her, no matter what had come
before.

"It can't be him. Can't be . . ." Her voice trailed
off as she called upon the spirit of a wildcat, easily
sprang up to a thick branch then started climbing.

Down below, Luc glared up at her. "Damn it,
Blaze!" he hissed.

Ignoring him, she climbed nimbly. She'd been
climbing trees and rocks all her life and quickly
made her way to a high perch in a fork of the tree.
Unsurprised to see Luc joining her, she shifted and

peered down. She felt his heat, the beat of his heart and the air moving through his lungs. His fear—not for himself but for her—surrounded her. She blocked it out, needing to focus. But part of her wanted to revel in his concern.

Nothing moved. In silence they waited. With her hands gripping the rough bark of the tree, she let the hum of life flow into her. The roots of the tree went deep and were spread wide. The first tremors of human steps came from the west.

"He comes." She whispered the words. Red Thunder's scent was growing closer, stronger. The cold hard truth blazed in her mind when she saw him appear, moving cautiously, holding an arrow notched and ready to let fly.

Luc felt exposed, like a raccoon in a tree. They were high above the ground but the foliage wasn't thick enough to shield him and he didn't think he could do another merge. He held himself still. One hand slipped around Blaze's waist, the other gripped the branch overhead to keep them from falling.

In sight below was a warrior wearing a thick bearskin. The snarling head pointed almost straight up, and made Luc think the dead animal was staring at them. In silence, he and Blaze watched the man pass beneath. Luc held his breath, not daring to breathe.

His body pulsed with fear. All the warrior below had to do was stop and glance up, then he and his angel were as good as dead. If not from the arrow, then from the fall. They were sitting ducks.

Calm yourself. The voice slipped into his mind.

Startled, Luc stared down at the shiny top of Blaze's head. Had she said that? Or was it another voice from a spirit? Damn, he wished everyone would stay out of his mind.

I am connected with you, body, heart and soul, as you are with me. The tone was haughty and completely unrepentant.

He recognized her voice.

Dammit, Ange, *you nearly made me fall from the tree. I thought we had to merge to share thoughts*. Like when they'd shielded themselves from the warrior or become one when they'd made love. He wasn't sure he liked her just being able to slip into his mind anytime, and he wasn't sure he could take too many more of these surprises. But now was not the time to worry. First he had to survive. Then he could deal with it.

Block me, Trapper.

Her voice was a soft challenge. Was she laughing at his fears? *Careful*, Ange. *How about free will? How about asking*?

Luc studied the land below. Time slowed to a crawl. He felt Blaze trembling in front of him, watching the warrior beneath. She held on to her control with sheer iron will.

We need to get out of here. I wish you knew how to fly. Unconsciously he sent his voice into her mind, keeping the connection between them open. He didn't dare speak; even a whisper might be heard.

Immediately he felt her pain, and he realized that he'd reminded her of how her parents had died: flying with this hunter below. He felt the buzz of anger grow in her. Heat flared around them.

No! No storms! He made the command as strong as he knew how. In his arms, Blaze was stiff and unyielding.

He deserves to die. She held her head up, her eyes blazing with fury. *Like that, I could kill him.* She silently snapped her fingers.

No. No storms. No killing. He did not kill your parents on purpose. Luc kept a watchful eye on the warrior below who searched for tracks. His blood ran cold. When the man discovered that their tracks ended at this tree, he'd look up. *Now would be a good time for you to do something. Besides a storm.*

You reject what you are, yet you freely use this gift of the gods? She seemed surprised.

Luc narrowed his eyes and his fingers dug into the tree bark. He tried to ignore her question, but her voice captured him just as her eyes did. With each passing moment what she'd done seemed to matter less. He wanted her, needed *her* above all else. The pull of his angel made him doubt everything he'd ever felt. He fought it the only way he knew. Denial. Until he knew for sure what he felt was real, he had no choice but to deny the rest.

Don't have much choice, Ange.

There is always choice. Either we accept or we deny.

We love or we hate. Hide from the truth or embrace it. Tell me, Trapper, that you do not have love in your heart, that we are not connected. You have been gifted by the gods. Blaze met his gaze boldly. *I love you.*

The pull on his heart was so strong that Luc nearly cried out. *How do I know if what I feel is true? Have you stolen my heart, taken my love against my will?*

I could never do that. You know that is not true. Her voice was full of hurt.

Luc shook his head. *That is the problem,* Ange. *I don't know. Now stay out of my head.*

Using his thoughts to talk to her, calling up storms, using power to shield himself—none of it sounded so bad. And flying and running through the forest? There was much he could do with these gifts and abilities Blaze had given him. It was that thought which gave him the strength to resist, and to use his own wits to try to get them out of harm's way.

His mouth tightened. His knife was in its sheath at his side. He put one hand on the hilt, ready to draw and throw. But with so many branches and leaves in the path from him to the warrior, Luc knew he wouldn't have a clear, clean shot. His hand trailed down as his mind raced with possibilities. The pine cone nearby gave him an idea.

He carefully picked one, weighed it in his palm, three fingers curved around it. Lifting his hand he slowly drew back, aimed through an opening in the canopy of leaves then let the cone sail.

It flew through the leaves without touching a single one, arced high then began its descent. Several ravens took to the air, disturbed by what landed with a soft thud just out of sight.

Luc sighed with relief as Blaze's father whirled around then crept off in the direction of sound. Waiting until he was sure the man was gone, he silently climbed down and caught Blaze when she dangled from the branch.

She slumped in his arms. *My father hates me so much that he's willing to kill me,* she said.

The hurt, betrayal and pain in her words nearly drove Luc to his knees. He wanted to hold her, to comfort her and assure her it wasn't her fault. But now wasn't the time.

Snap out of it, Ange. We've got to get out of here. And stay out of my mind.

He lay flat on his belly beneath a pile of brush he'd built. Old Man Rock was within sight and Connie's bastards were up there hiding in a supply cave. As far as he could tell, Luc and the woman had not arrived.

Twisting, he chugged back a swallow of whiskey then went back to his study of the cold, useless stone in his palm. What was he going to do if Luc and the woman didn't show up? Alex and Travers wouldn't wait much longer for the rest of their family to join them; they'd take those girls to the Indian whore's tribe.

That, he couldn't allow. Once there he hadn't a chance in hell in getting his hands on any of them. Smirking, he shook his head.

Connie had been a fool to send them here, thinking no one knew of this cave; but he'd overheard Travers and Luc talking about it one day. Like the rest of them, he knew this land, recognized instantly the landmark they'd referred to. It had taken him a while to find the cave, as it was neatly hidden and could be easily blocked to keep animals out. But earlier he'd inched forward, scouting it out to be sure they'd arrived, and he had seen Travers standing in the entrance.

He'd been tempted to show himself. None of them would suspect that he was behind the attack. All he had to say was that Connie was injured and that they were to come with their uncle, that he would take them to their father.

But he'd resisted. Alex and Travers each had a rifle, and if they were nervous, they might not let him or anyone else up there. So he'd come up with another plan. He'd wait until they left.

Frowning, he slapped an insect off his face. He might get only one chance to get what he wanted. There were enough supplies stashed up there to allow the kids to hide longer than he'd planned to wait, but they didn't have any water. They had to come down sooner or later, and when one did, he'd grab the brat. How hard could it be?

He was a patient man. Always so patient. Hadn't he proved that many times over the years? He always got what he wanted, and now was no different. Greed made him endure the bug bites, the sticks and the hunger in his belly. He fingered his gun.

Whatever he wanted, it would all soon be his. One of them would know the words to make this damn rock work, then he'd be free of them all.

Alex huddled in the cave with her brother and her cousins. "There is nothing to be afraid of." She tried to reassure the twins who looked frightened. At only eight they were enduring much better than she'd expected.

They'd been here for nearly a day with no sign of Luc, Uncle Conrad or Eagle Woman. Alex glanced at Skye, who was still. The five-year-old looked like a fragile porcelain doll. She hadn't spoken a single word since the night before.

"Luc will come. And your mother and father." Alex hated the helpless feeling of waiting and not knowing what had happened to everyone.

"They should have been here by now." Kangee paced.

Travers stared out the cave entrance, which wasn't much more than a thin, tall crevice. "If they aren't here by morning, we're leaving." He glanced at his sister, clearly worried. "We need water. I'll go down." As he rose to grab a hide flask in the back of the cave: "No." The twins spoke in unison. "There is danger."

Alex stared into two pairs of the most unusual eyes she'd ever seen. "We need water." She chewed her lower lip and glanced at her brother. "Maybe you should wait until it's dark."

"Right. Then I can fall and break my damn neck

getting down there." He grabbed his gun, but before he could leave, Kangee whirled.

"I'm coming with you," she said.

Travers shook his head. "You are *not* coming with me."

Kangee stalked up to him, toe to toe, and lifted her chin. "Fine. Then *you* can come with *me*."

Alex sighed when Kangee slipped out through the entrance. She herself stood. She needed to move. Needed air. She went to the entrance and let the cooling breeze sweep across her face, then slipped out to rest her back against the cave face. One side of the rock was a sheer drop.

She bent over to look below. The tops of the trees looked small, more like blades of grass than a forest. She edged away, feeling a bit queasy at the height. But she had to admit, she'd never seen such beauty nor felt so small until she'd joined her father in this vast wonderful world.

She grinned, glad she'd come, even if her father was still a bit mad at her. He'd pulled her brother Travers into this business two years ago, leaving her with their mother in the whorehouse and a life she'd have done anything to avoid.

Her features turned grim. Even in death, her mother had proved how much she hated Alex. On her deathbed, she'd sold her to the highest bidder. And as Alex had learned, young virgins were not just in demand, but fetched a hefty price.

But Alex had plans for her life, and pleasing men in or out of bed was not one of them. When her father had taken her brother, leaving her behind, she'd vowed to do whatever it took to get out, including stealing. She'd taken her mother's hidden stash of coins, sold the cheap baubles that had been gifted to her mother for lying on her back over the years, and to be sure she had enough, she'd stolen from the nasty witch who owned the cathouse.

No, no one bought or sold Alex like livestock. She'd cut her hair, bought men's clothing and had scouted out the trappers in the saloons. She'd found a group who knew her father and put a huge wad of money down on the table as payment for safe passage.

She shook her head. Money talked. It always would, though she had little other use for it. She didn't want fancy dresses or sparkly stones. Didn't want to be pampered. She just wanted her freedom, and now that she had it, she'd die before she gave it up.

Moving carefully, she checked out the other two sides. Nothing moved but some deer in the brush. On the final side, she gave a quick glance then flattened herself quickly against the stone wall. A single, solitary shadow was moving.

She held her breath, then let it out when she saw that it was just her brother. Kangee was behind him, and even from up here she could hear them arguing.

"Fools." Shaking her head, she was ready to go back inside when she spotted a burly figure wearing a fox-fur cap step out of the bushes and smash the butt of a rifle into Travers's head, then point the gun at Kangee.

"Oh no!" She jumped back and bumped into

Skye, who'd just come out of the cave. "Skye, baby, get back in the cave. All of you!" She stared at the twins. "We must be very quiet."

As Alex carried Skye back inside, the little girl's eyes darkened. So did the sun.

All spirits are connected. All are related. All belong to and travel the path of life. All are part of the circle of life.

CHAPTER THIRTEEN

The sun was slowly dimming over the land when Blaze and Luc caught sight of Old Man Rock. The formation of stones rose high above the trees, a rock throne. A flock of ravens flew around it, creating a dark halo that matched the way Blaze was feeling. She was furious, hurt and confused.

Her father hated her enough to try to kill her. Even now, he was pursuing. She felt him. He was not close enough to spot, which was good, because that meant he couldn't aim his arrows at their backs. But she and Luc didn't dare stop to rest. They moved forward, snaking around trees, circling in tighter arcs around the mountain, but never taking too much time to do so. Time was not their friend.

Then there was Luc. She glared at his back. She was foolishly in love with this man who wanted no part of what she was. His rejection of that hurt. Unbearably. Sometime during the day between kisses and loving, she'd allowed herself to believe he loved her, thought she'd felt it in him and that he would stay with her. That he'd be as she was.

But he hadn't changed his mind. He didn't want her. Not in the way she needed to be wanted. All her life she'd sought acceptance and love. Once more it was to be denied her, and the pain of his rejection made putting one foot in front of the other difficult. Tears blurred her sight, making it hard to see the individual fronds and small patches of low-growing plants.

The trees had thinned, the undergrowth thickened. Small pines grew in the hope of reaching the great heights of many of the other giant trees stretched over the land. Realizing it was going to be impossible to hide their tracks, Luc had sped up.

Blaze followed blindly, her mind like a windstorm, twisting, twirling and knocking her thoughts and emotions from one side to the other. She loved this trapper, felt that they were meant to be. They were two spirits joined as one. Her heart and soul belonged to him. Without him, her spirit would wither and die. But . . .

The ground went from level to a slight incline. As she walked, she considered Red Thunder. Him, she hated. Not so much for killing her parents. Luc was right; he'd have had no idea at the time. It had been a tragic accident, but instead of taking responsibility, he'd hidden the truth. He'd lied and he'd used her and everyone else to get what he wanted.

Love clashed with fury, which spread out into hurt. Grief rolled with desire and acceptance. So much had happened in such a short time. It seemed like forever since Wise Owl had given her that clear crystal which had led her to her green-eyed trapper. Finding him and saving his life had given her knowledge that she'd yearned to hear all her life.

No more would she doubt what she was or be afraid of it. Whether he knew it or not, Luc had given her a precious gift when he'd told her she was a SpiritWalker. Soon, she vowed, she'd be among others.

Instead of being happy, the realization suddenly made her sad, for what good was this knowledge without the man she loved and wanted to share this new discovery with? He didn't want that part of her, had rejected the closeness, the bonding of their minds and spirits.

Since fleeing from her father, Luc hadn't spoken. Not a single word. Aloud or in her mind. And she hadn't tried to talk to him. She'd followed silently, blocking her emotions and pain, and when the sadness grew overwhelming, she tried to grab onto her hurt and fury.

He might not want her gift, to be a SpiritWalker, but he'd proven himself very adept at using what was available to him. Even now, whether he realized it or not, he was blocking her—yet at the same time, the love she sensed he felt for her threaded them closer, tightening the bond.

He thought she controlled him, blamed her for the love he felt and believed that she had taken his free will from him.

Foolish man, she growled, deliberately shoving the words at him. Could he not believe in love?

Stay out of my mind.

Blaze stopped, her hands on her hips. "You're not being reasonable. I cannot make you love me. I do *not* control how you feel, Trapper."

"And I'm supposed to believe that? You changed me once—maybe without meaning to. You could do so again."

Shoving past Luc, Blaze let a branch whip back then turned with satisfaction when she heard Luc curse. "I took nothing from you that you were not willing to give. Your spirit accepted me. Of its own free will. That is something even I have always understood, and I did not have family or other Spirit-Walkers to teach me."

"No? So how did you know how to join us?"

Blaze smiled, if grimly. "I followed my heart, Trapper. It is too bad that you cannot listen to your own. It would show you the truth."

Luc glanced at her, sighed then turned away. "Wait here. I'm going to circle back."

Fighting the urge to follow just to make him mad, Blaze leaned against a tree. She needed a moment to herself, anyway. Luc was being stubborn and foolish, and she didn't know how to prove to him that what he felt was as real as the tree at her back. It made her heart ache.

Yes, she wanted to go to him, to plead with him to accept her gift. To accept her and love her as she loved him. There had to be a way for her to prove to him that they were meant to be spirit mates. Her spirit had merged with his, and his with hers. They were two, yet they were also one.

Above her head the sun dimmed, yet it was far from dusk, and there were no clouds in the sky. Something was wrong. Sensations climbed the tree and slid into her. Straightening, she stared up at the mountain.

Red Thunder was still coming. He was far enough behind that his scent had grown fainter, but she knew he could easily catch up once more, and she was prepared. She'd know before he ever got that close again.

No . . . the tremors she felt in the air came from another source. She took several steps toward the mountain. Whatever it was it came from there, not behind her. It came from the mountain where Luc's sisters were supposed to be waiting. She sensed . . .

Luc! She sent his name outward and took off running with the speed and agility of a deer.

Women. What was he going to do about Blaze? Luc knew he'd hurt her, but hadn't been able to help himself. Having her slip so easily into his mind had been too much. If she could do that, she could easily make him believe he loved her.

He knew she was lonely. So was he. The question was, if she had affected him as he feared, would she take his free will away in matters of the heart? And the love in his heart, was it real? Was it pure? He didn't know, so he'd closed himself off from her.

Doubling back down the trail, he drew in a long, deep breath, instinctively seeking Blaze's scent. He stopped. It seemed farther away. *Damn.* He hurried through the brush, suddenly uncaring that he might ruin his false trail.

When he got back to where he'd left Blaze, she was gone. He opened his mind and called out, *Where are you?*

Free will.

The thought came to him. Not from her or the gods or spirits, but from his own heart. Since becoming a SpiritWalker, he'd used the gifts and abilities without much thought. When it was there, he took it.

Was she right? Had he done these things all of his own choice? Or was it because they were "connected?" He ran through the trees, following her scent like a wolf tracking prey.

Blaze! He put all he had into that call, opened his mind fully. No matter what his mind feared or believed, feelings of his heart drove him forward.

At the mountain. Your sisters are in danger. Reach out. Touch Skye. My connection isn't deep enough. Yours will be.

Luc froze. His mind accepted hers, welcomed the information. The silence had been unbearable, and he knew if anything happened to Blaze, he'd be lost. Whether it was real or not didn't matter. He knew that now. He had to go to her. Had to be with her.

Closing his eyes, he pulled forth an image of his baby sister. *Skye. Baby sister of mine. Answer me. Are you all right?*

A moment of silence followed, and he was just about to tell Blaze it wasn't working when he felt a small touch in his mind. There were no words, but the images made him cry out.

He saw Travers lying on the ground, wounded and bleeding, and Kangee tied. And he saw his uncle. Clearly. They were all near the base of Old Man Rock. Quickly he shared the images with Blaze.

Hurry, she replied.

How do I call upon the spirit of the wolf? As he followed her directions, he had no doubt that he was making a choice. Maybe he'd had no choice all along, but he knew he'd do whatever it took to save those he loved. And as he leapt over a fallen log, he considered that he truly loved Blaze. He probably had all along. His heart had been lost when she'd first come to him in her golden splendor.

Stay hidden. He sent the command, but when he didn't feel any response, he ran as fast as he could, tearing across the forest floor. He reached the base of the mountain and froze. *Where are you?* he called out to Blaze, needing to be sure she was safe.

The sound of a stinging slap followed by a cry made him cringe. Staying hidden, he found his Uncle William and his cousins near the base of the mountain.

I am safe. The little ones are safe, as is the older girl with them. I will try to help the others.

No! Stay away. Stay with the others.

Needing to keep his focus, Luc studied the area.

He had his knife, but his uncle had a rifle pointed at Kangee. He tamped down his fury that his uncle could do this to them.

A sudden movement high above made him catch his breath. He spotted Blaze making her way across the top of the Rock. She moved slowly, her body shielded, but he knew she was there. He didn't dare distract her, but as a rock tumbled down, he froze. His uncle whirled. Before William could glance up, Luc made a decision: he strode out of the forest.

Immediately, the rifle was pointed at him. "About time you showed up, boy."

Luc pointed to Travers. "You killed him." His senses weren't sharp enough, honed enough to see if his cousin lived.

"Thought I'd killed you, too," William said, eyeing Luc's bare chest, seeing the faint redness, all that remained of his wound. He half grinned. "I saw what you looked like. You were dead. Got the power yourself, boy? Nice to know. You can tell me how to use this." He held out the green stone. "I know you want to share with your dear sweet old uncle." He jerked his head and motioned for Luc to sit. "Come join our little party."

Luc had little choice. He sat, his mind split between the gun that was back to being pointed at Kangee, and his woman climbing high above them. He didn't know what Blaze planned, but as he'd learned, she was full of surprises.

Make it good, Ange.

* * *

Red Thunder had a perfect shot at his daughter. He held his arrow trained on her. How easy it would be to just end her life. To end the secrets. But as it had done so long ago, the sky began to darken. He held himself still as he watched his daughter staring down at something below.

Moving silently, Red Thunder spotted the trapper who'd been kissing her sitting on the ground to the east with another trapper, one much older and holding a gun on a young girl. The girl was sobbing. Red Thunder's eyes narrowed on the trapper. He was holding a green stone. Red Thunder fisted his own, the one he'd stolen. Maybe he'd learn the secrets of the stone at last.

In the circle of life, it is perhaps man who has the greatest thirst for all that life has to offer. But often, it is man who forgets all that Nature offers him.

CHAPTER FOURTEEN

Luc had to buy time to allow Blaze to do whatever she could. He had no doubt that she'd come up with something, even if it was only a distraction that would allow him to get the gun from his uncle.

"Where are the twins? And Skye?"

William laughed. "They'll join us shortly. You see, now that I have you, everyone will do as I say." He peered into the bushes. "Where's the woman?"

"What woman?"

William reached over and slapped Kangee. She cried out. "No games, boy. Connie's whore. Where is she?" He took a long swallow from his flask.

"You killed them. I haven't seen her since you attacked us."

"Liar. She called up that storm. She was with you." He dropped his flask and shoved the muzzle of the gun hard to Kangee's temple.

"No. The woman with me is not my earth mother. She is another SpiritWalker. She got mad, and she left me back there." Luc carefully shifted his gaze past the figure of Blaze climbing the mountain high above them. *Going to have to do something quick*, Ange. *I'm counting on you.*

"You killed my father and Eagle Woman. And Travers. Why?"

William dangled a polished stone in front of Luc's face. "How does this work? Tell me how to use the magic that makes you turn into an owl and fly."

Luc stared at the stone. It was the one Eagle Woman had given to his father during their marriage ceremony. His father never, ever took it off. He licked his lips. Seeing it was surely proof that his father had died.

Pain and despair filled him. Sitting on the ground, still bound, Kangee was silently sobbing.

William glanced over at her. "Stop the sniveling, girl."

"Leave her alone," Luc ordered.

"You're not in a position to give orders, boy. Now tell me what I want."

"I don't know. And that is the truth."

William's eyes narrowed. "Then make the girl tell me. I heard you before. She's one of them."

"First, tell me why? Why kill my father?"

"He wouldn't share. Never liked to share. Damn bastard. Moment he was born, everything changed. Our mother was nothing but a damn whore after our father died. Connie always ruined everything. You and my dear baby brother were leaving."

"You attacked because we wanted to leave?"

"Albert was angry. He worked hard to keep us together, and then you go and ruin it all."

"That makes no sense. Albert still has you and my cousins." Luc just couldn't understand his uncle's anger.

"Brother Al isn't happy unless he controls everyone. He was furious, and that meant I was going to have to live with him, to deal with it. Like always. I'm tired of taking your father's leavings, cleaning up his messes."

"You could have left. It was your choice to stay." There was that word again. *Choice.* Luc longed to reach out and connect with Blaze, but he didn't dare.

William looked both sad and pained. "No. I got no choice. There's no way to leave. He knows."

"Knows what?" Luc chanced a glance up and saw that Blaze was on the ledge above.

William passed his hand over his forehead. "I did everything for him. He kept us together, raised us. He deserved to have what he wanted, but she was going to ruin it, so I had to take care of her." He stroked his rifle over Kangee's temple.

Frantically Luc tried to think of something he could do that wouldn't bring harm to his cousins. He didn't dare use a storm or the wind, for Blaze was far above them. He glanced at Travers, but his cousin wasn't moving. His uncle's ranting pulled his attention back.

"Women. They ruin everything. They killed my father, tore up my family." William stared into the red stone. "But now it's my turn."

Luc went still. His best bet was to keep the man talking. "Who, uncle . . . ?" he said quietly.

William grinned, his features twisted with hatred. "Connie's mother, the bitch. She was the first. Slept with another man. Got pregnant. The old man was so angry his heart gave out. I saw him. Saw his face go purple, then he dropped. No one knew. Just me. And ma. She was a whore, and she killed my father."

Luc listened and watched. He'd had no idea that his uncle hated Luc's father so much. "She died giving birth to my father."

William sneered, "She died—deserved to die. Then the bastard baby went away. But later, Al brought him back home to be with us, his family, insisted we all stay together. How I hated Connie. He ruined everything. We were happy, just the two of us, Al and me, but I had no choice. Al wanted us all together."

Luc saw a side of his uncle that he'd never before seen: the jealous, unhappy man. "You stayed with Albert and my father. Worked beside them. Why?"

William shrugged. "Needed the money. Al wouldn't give it to me unless I worked for it." He licked his lips and ran a hand over his face. He looked exhausted. "Then Connie decided he wanted to stay with that bitch who birthed you. Meant more work for me. But I always found Connie's stash. He knew, but he never said anything. Couldn't let him leave to stay with that bitch."

He suddenly eyed Luc with glee. "Killed your mother." He stroked the barrel of his gun.

Luc hadn't expected this. He jumped to his feet. "You killed my mother? You murdered her just to keep from working?"

"Yeah. And now you're ruining it all by wanting to leave. Everyone was leaving. Leaving Al. Leaving me. Couldn't allow it." William held the gun pointed right at him.

Fury and pain struck Luc. "You bastard!" Behind his uncle, he saw Kangee trying to scoot away.

"Not me, boy. Just you and your father, 'cause he never married your ma." William's face turned ugly as he laughed. "I followed you, hid in the bushes to see what Connie was up to. Was always good at spying on the bastard. Heard you talking, then saw what your father did. Turned himself into an owl and figured I had a way out. Everyone was leaving, so why not me? I could just fly away. Be free. Get rich."

Kangee had reached Travers. Luc chanced a look at her. He eyed her then the rock cover, telling her silently to get behind the rocks. She did, and then it was just Luc and his uncle.

William laughed and held the stone that had belonged to Luc's father in his hands. Then he frowned. "I don't feel anything. Nothing special." He pointed the gun at Luc. "No more talk. How does this stone work?"

Luc smiled grimly. "It is a gift. It has to be given in free will, and accepted in kind."

Roaring with rage, his uncle lifted the shotgun and took aim at Luc's heart.

High above them, Blaze fought panic as she stared down from the top of Old Man Rock. Below, Luc was in trouble. Lying flat on her belly with her head hanging over the sheer edge, she watched with her heart in her stomach.

Seeing the gun pointed at Luc, she knew he was out of time. The wind carried muffled shouts up to her, but her mind was too torn, too fractured with fear, worry and love for her to concentrate and call upon it to bring the sounds all the way to her.

Anger burned deep inside and struck out, seeking release, but she controlled it. Above all, she had to protect Luc. Standing, she held her arms up high, fingers spread and pointing sharply toward the sky.

"Hear me! Hear me, gods and spirits. All my relations, hear this daughter." She waited, and when she felt the sigh of wind on her face she continued.

"The man I love needs my help. You chose him to be my mate. My spirit mate. You chose him. I accepted him. I wish to give him the gift of life. What he does with it is between him and you. But give me what I need to save his life and the life of your other daughter below."

Blaze felt a crackling in the air. Energy swam

around her, sent her hair flying in all directions. She looked wild. Elemental. Primitive, with sparks flying around her, spiraling from her head, twisting around her body and circling her feet. She was power, she was energy, and she sent bolts of that energy downward like a warrior would throw a lance.

The ground shook with each spear of bright light she threw. Darkness gathered around her, yet she herself shimmered with light. She cast another bolt of light. A tree exploded.

Luc had never been more mesmerized. He glanced at his uncle. "Put the gun down, Uncle. Do it now," he urged.

"No!" William glanced up. "I'll kill him! I'll kill him right now!" he screamed at Blaze. The acrid smoke from the burning tree nearby made his eyes water.

"Stop now, Uncle. Don't do this," Luc begged. Fear bit at him like a dog snapping at his heels. Blaze could so easily strike his uncle down, and he found he didn't want her to do it. She shouldn't have to mete out justice.

He tried to connect with Blaze. He felt her mind, but anger and fury surrounded her.

Let me in, Ange. *Let me in.*

He is going to kill you. Her words blazed with fire.

No. He won't kill me. Luc tried to explain. He had to reach her. The power of her fury was so great, they might all be in danger from it.

He will. The air crackled, and jagged lines of white struck from the sky above.

If he hurts me, Ange, *then you'll just heal me again.*

Would you choose that? Would you come to me of your own free will? Would you choose life as a SpiritWalker?

In a heartbeat. Luc meant it. Life without his *ange* was a world without the sun, sky, moon or stars. It'd be a gray void, filled with emptiness for all eternity.

And the rest—do you accept my gift of your own free will? Will you be my spirit mate? A SpiritWalker?

Yes. Free will. The words echoed in his mind. And in that instant Luc realized that he'd always accepted her of his own free will, all of who she was and what she was. He'd done so when he'd first accepted the gift of life from her.

I chose you before. All of you. I love you. You are my true ange. *The only person for me. My spirit mate. For all time.*

Then let our spirits merge, truly become one. Her voice boomed in his mind.

In his hands, his crystal grew hot. He drew it out, following instinct, and held it up. His uncle gasped. Kangee, peeking out from behind the rocks looked shocked, but Luc ignored everyone, letting the bright sun shine into the stone. The green core glowed as though on fire.

Above him, Blaze had raised her own stone. The blue sparked with fire, and as she stared down at the green incandescence of his, she shuddered with relief. She needed this man. Her trapper. Luc was hers.

The two lights merged, forming a combination

of blues and greens. The colors formed a transparent shield around Luc.

Instinct had driven Blaze to this last step. She'd discovered her inner child, now she had to become it—what she'd been—and put her faith in it.

She stepped to the very edge of the cliff, held out her hands and fell forward.

Life and death are part of the circle of life. Without the winter there would be no spring. Without birth, there would be no life.

CHAPTER FIFTEEN

Luc's heart shot straight up into his throat as Blaze stepped off the cliff. Her figure blurred, then she was gone, and in her place, a large, white-headed eagle was in a sharp dive, heading right for his uncle. Its shriek rent the air, the sound making William jump. But before he could aim and fire, an arrow shot out of the forest.

No!" Luc screamed. The arrow was aimed at Blaze. Before it struck, another bird, this one also an eagle, flew in front of her. Somehow it managed to pluck the arrow from midair with its talons and then it flew off. In front of Luc, his uncle lifted his rifle.

Luc launched himself forward. He and his uncle fought, hands grasping to gain control of the weapon.

A shadow slid over Luc, and he watched as Blaze flew forward. She struck his uncle with talons outstretched, beak open and shrieking loudly.

"Get back," he yelled as he wrested the gun from his uncle's grip. He tossed it aside.

But William wasn't going to give up. He pulled out his knife and slashed at the eagle. Before Luc could reach him or grab Blaze and shoo her away, a blur of gray fur streaked past. A wolf appeared, sank its teeth into Luc's uncle's throat. Luc recognized the healing wounds of the wolf, and realized it was the same one Blaze had healed. The wolf had killed their enemy.

Holding out his arm to the eagle, Luc sighed when she flapped and landed. He ignored the pain from her talons. "That was some surprise, sweetheart. How about you change back? Don't think I can take any more today."

He felt her in his mind, grinning, and he thrust his arm up, casting his angel back into the air. The eagle lifted her wings, flared her tail and landed smoothly, talons blurring into feet, the brown and white body becoming his beloved.

In her human form, Blaze clung to Luc. His cousin and sisters were running toward them. There was yelling and shouting and lots of hugging and crying. Her heart was racing, but she was happy. She'd done it: come full circle. She'd once believed she could fly, and today, she'd done so to save her mate. Her spirit mate.

Luc tensed and pushed her behind him. "We have company."

Blaze lifted her brow when she saw her chief and two of his warriors. In front of them was Red

Thunder. He stared straight ahead as though she did not exist.

Two Arrows stepped forward. "We have been following your father, child. We were not able to help you. I am glad you are safe." He was staring up into the sky where an eagle circled.

Red Thunder fearfully eyed the eagle, who was circling lower. "She is no child of mine!" he snarled. He grabbed his bow and arrows from around his neck and tossed them away. Then he shoved past the warriors and took off running.

Anger and regret made Blaze want to sob. "You tried to kill me! Why? I did nothing to you!" She called after him.

"You ruined my life! You deserve to die!" he shouted back. He turned and stared at the assembled group with hatred.

Grief welled up in Blaze. "You killed my parents. You did not mean to kill them, I believe, but everything you did since that day has been of your own choosing. I have no pity for you." And she didn't. She felt sad, but her anger had faded.

Above her head, the eagle went into a dive. It landed, transforming into a tall, handsome warrior. Red Thunder's eyes widened as that warrior approached.

"This is the warrior who killed our father?" the warrior asked, turning to Blaze.

Blaze stared at the man. He wore a traditional breechcloth, and had his hair in two long braids with eagle feathers. "Who are you?" she asked.

He held up his hand. "My sister. It is good to finally have found you."

Blaze glanced around. Was he talking to her? "Who are you? You are the one who saved me from that arrow!"

The warrior bowed. "I am Storm Warrior. Your brother." He turned back to Red Thunder, who all of a sudden looked frightened. "I believe you took something from our father," he said. His voice was low and dark.

Red Thunder grabbed hold of his medicine pouch. "Stay away." He tried to flee, but the other warriors of his tribe had circled behind him. They jumped forward and grabbed his arms.

Storm Warrior stepped forward and yanked the medicine pouch from around Red Thunder's neck. He opened it and dumped the contents onto the ground.

Everyone crowded close as Blaze's brother picked up a shiny red stone. "This was the soul stone of our father—stolen by this man when he stole you."

Chief Two Arrows came forward. He too bent down, and he picked up an eagle bone whistle. "This belonged to my father, the shaman, husband to Wise Owl." He whirled around and faced Red Thunder. "Where did you get this?"

Blaze spoke up. "That is the whistle he used to summon me."

The chief turned it over and held it out to Blaze. "These symbols . . . this belonged to my father. How long has he had this, child?"

Blaze stared at her father in horror. He'd started to use that whistle about the time the old shaman died. She realized: "You killed him. Why?"

Red Thunder glared at all of them. "He knew what you were."

Chief Two Arrows fisted his hand around the whistle, overcome by grief. "You will die for your crimes." He motioned for his two warriors to take him away.

Luc put his arm around Blaze's shoulders. She said, "Nothing was as it seemed."

Storm Warrior returned to her, and he put his hand on her shoulder and looked deep into her eyes. Blaze held her breath as long forgotten memories surfaced. Her heart and her spirit knew he spoke the truth. He was her brother. "I do not remember your name. I thought I would know it."

Storm Warrior grinned. "I believe at the time I had a different name. It has changed many times."

Blaze stared into her brother's silvery eyes. Of course. Boys as they grew into warriors often changed their names—often after doing something great. "I remember you. I do." The memories were vague, but they were there.

She glanced behind her brother and saw two more birds flying down toward her. She wasn't too surprised when they both shifted smoothly into humans, but her eyes widened.

Storm Warrior smiled. "Raven Mist and Thunder Hawk. Your brother and sister."

Raven Mist came forward. "You are Taya."

Blaze hesitated. "I was Taya," she said.

"And now?" Thunder Hawk looked surprised.

Hesitating, Blaze wasn't sure. Taya was the child, but she was a child no longer. Blaze was a name given to her by a people afraid of her, though in part due to the man who'd stolen her from her family.

"I believe it is the right of a woman's husband to give his wife a name that befits her." Luc rose behind her.

Storm Warrior frowned. "You are her husband?"

Luc put his arm around Blaze and drew her close. "We will be wed. Soon." He glanced down at her. "If she'll have me."

Blaze grinned. "You are mine, Trapper," she said. She glanced from Luc to her brother. "You may consider this man my husband."

Storm Warrior nodded. "Then, indeed, he has the right to bestow upon you a new name."

Blaze turned to Luc, touched that he seemed to understand how she felt. "What would my trapper wish to call me?" she asked.

Luc slid a hand around her neck and stared into her eyes—her beautiful, exotic and wonderfully mesmerizing eyes. "You are my angel—here on earth and in heaven—but I do not think I want anyone else calling you that." He cradled her head in his hands and smiled at her. Blaze stared at him, her love shining in her eyes.

"Blaze is a name that fits you. You are the flame in my heart and soul, the blue fire that first drew me to you. My soul stone had the blue of your eyes, the fire of your spirit. You also came to me as an angel, and with your light and the love in your heart you saved my life. You'll always be my beautiful, blazing angel of light." He paused as tears streamed down her face and over his thumbs. You're are my *Ange*. My angel. But that is a name I reserve just for myself to use.

"Would you hate it if I asked you to keep the name Blaze? Be the blue light for all. Let your love and goodness be a bright beacon for all in need."

She hugged him tightly, her tears soaking his shoulder. The name, one given to her as a young girl because of her eyes took on a new and wonderful meaning. She wasn't a curse, something to be feared, but a light to lead the way. When she pulled back, she stared into his eyes. His words had touched her deeply, as all she'd ever wanted was to help others, to use her gifts for the good of all.

"What about me, *Ange?*" Luc cupped the side of her face gently, his thumb catching a tear. "Do I get a new name?"

Blaze smiled impishly. "You shall always be Trapper when you anger me."

Luc smiled. "Call me what you wish, as long as you love me as I love you."

"With all my heart and soul, Trapper. However, I choose to gift you with a new name."

She paused, her expression serious. Bestowing a name was an honor. Her heart swelled with love and joy that he'd trust her to give him a new name. She took her time. The name she chose had to reflect the essence of the person he was. Who he was not just to her, but to all her people. She began speaking, the words flowing from her heart:

"We rode high together. You showed me the heavens when we joined as one. We met on a path of stars when you came to me of your own free will as I choose to come to you. You shall be Star Walker."

"That's nice, *Ange*. Beautiful. Like you." He pulled her to him and, ignoring the happy shouting around them, he kissed her long and deep.

*Joy and sadness, love and hate, light and dark. All add
to the balance and color of life.*

CHAPTER SIXTEEN

Luc's happiness was overshadowed by his missing
parents. Holding his father's soul stone, he realized
the man was gone. He had to be.

"I'm so sorry, Star Walker." Blaze put her hand
on his arm.

"It'll take me a while to get used to the new
name, *Ange*." He glanced at the stone. "I wish he
was here. He'd have loved you," he remarked. He
blinked rapidly. He'd gained so much, but at a high
price.

Across from him, Alex and Travers, who had a
huge bandage around his head, sat with the girls.
Alex spoke. "I'm so sorry, Luc."

Luc nodded. Alex had felt guilty for not coming
down to help, but he'd assured her that choosing to
stay and protect the girls had been the right thing to
do. "Thanks, Alex."

"He is here."

Luc glanced at Skye. He drew his sister into his

arms. "You're right, Skye. Our father is here, in our hearts."

"No." She wiggled down. "He is *here*." She ran over to the bushes and parted them to reveal the wounded wolf, who was watching them with sad eyes.

Luc frowned and shook his head. "I wish it were true, Skye. But he hasn't changed. If this were our father, he would have returned to us a man, not remained a wolf."

"Unless he is unable to take back his body," Storm Warrior suggested. He looked thoughtful.

Luc glanced up. "Explain."

"If his mate is gone, he cannot shift. He needs her love, her spirit, for they are merged as one."

Sadness filled Luc. He held on to his own soul stone, the one that carried the spirit of his angel, as hers carried his. He stared down at the stone, then glanced at Blaze. He knew he had a lot to learn about being a SpiritWalker. So did she. Her eyes mirrored his sadness.

Skye stared up at her big brother. "My mother's spirit still lives," she said. She took the leather necklace from Luc's hand and slipped it over the head of the wolf.

Minutes passed, but nothing happened. Luc let his breath out slowly. "That was a good idea," he started to tell his sister. Then he gasped. The outline of the wolf blurred and faded until a man stood in its place.

"*Mon Pere!*"

Luc's father let out a long breath. He swayed for a

moment, then bent down to scoop his crying daughters into his arms.

"You are alive?" Beside him, Blaze wept.

Conrad reached out and drew Luc in for a hug. "Thank you." Then he turned to Blaze. "And thank *you*. I would have died had you not healed me."

"You led me to Star Walker. It is I who must thank *you*."

"*Mon Pere*, I am sorry—"

Luc's father shook his head. "No. She is alive. I do not know where she is, but she is out there. Alive." He stared down at his girls. "We'll find her. Somehow, we'll find her."

Blaze and Luc walked off a distance to give father and daughters time alone. Moving through the fallen dark, finally alone with the woman who had won his heart, soul and spirit, Luc stopped and stared into her eyes.

"That was some performance today, sweetheart."

Blaze grinned. "It was fun. I think I will like flying. I will teach you."

Luc laughed softly. "I'll do anything to make you happy. Just promise me one thing."

"What?" Blaze stepped back, her eyes wary.

He pulled her back into his arms. "Promise never to get mad at me."

Blaze sighed, and he kissed her. Then she laughed. "No promises, Trapper."

Pulling her close again, Luc whispered, "I love you, *Ange*."

Blaze threaded her fingers into his hair. "As I love you, Star Walker."

They kissed and held each other tight, and an owl flew above their heads. He circled silently for a moment, spotted his eagle bone whistle around the girl's neck and knew peace. Catching a current of air, the old shaman soared higher and higher. He'd been trapped on the earth until justice could be had, and now he was free at last to go to the spirit world.

We walk in circles. Take the time to balance the circle of your life. Spend time with Mother Nature, gaze with awe at the stars and sky. Be as one with the world upon which we walk, and enjoy all that we have been given.

EPILOGUE

Two bald eagles flew over the shimmering lake, the smaller one trying to stay protectively near his mate. The female let out a series of shrill cries as she dipped her talons into the water and sent a spray up into the air.

Miye kinyan! I fly.

The voice of the little girl once known as Taya rang in the ears of the woman she'd become. Blaze was a SpiritWalker, a child of the gods. She could shift shapes and soar across the brilliant blue sky. The cool droplets of water beaded on her feathers. Above her, she felt the soft brush of her mate's wing tip across her back.

Sighing, she left the water and soared, catching a current of air. With her wings outstretched, her talons up, she let herself be carried high. *I love this*, she said, connecting with her love, her spirit mate. She tightened her turn until she was flying next to her green-eyed trapper.

Star Walker. They'd started off as two distant spirits, but were now one heart, one soul, one spirit.

I want you. She let her need for him blaze from her, and when he faltered in his flight, she let out another shriek, this one amused.

You did that on purpose. Star Walker tipped his wings back and, with one lazy yet strong downward stroke, rose above his mate.

Blaze felt his love and his answering need. Glancing down, she sighed then went into a steep dive. At the last moment she pulled, thrust her talons out and slowed her descent with her wings. She landed, not on talons, but on her own two feet. It was a perfect, seamless transformation. She turned. Star Walker followed. His landing was as perfect as her own.

"Damn it, *Ange*. You know I hate it when you do that."

Blaze grinned, feeling a bit breathless—as she always did after one of their flights. She loved the speed, the feel of the air swishing past. "I know, Trapper." She went to him and put her arms around his neck. "But do you hate this?"

She kissed him, softly and tenderly, a sweet, loving mating of mouths. He wrapped his hands around her and pulled her close.

"Let me show you how I feel." He drew her tighter against him. His kiss was anything but sweet and tender. It was fierce, full of love and need. When he pulled back, she was breathless.

"What do you think, *Ange*?"

"I think you need to finish what you started, Trapper of mine."

"*Miye kinyan!* I fly." The new voice made Blaze grin. It was full of youth and joy. "Later, of course," she added.

She ignored her husband's groan, turned to scoop their young daughter into her arms. Their son joined them, shouldering his small bow and arrow. At only six winters, he was fiercely protective of his young sister who'd just turned three.

Staring into young Kaya's eyes, Blaze saw herself mirrored in the blue and green. Her daughter had the eyes of a SpiritWalker.

"Full circle," she murmured, remembering that summer years past where she'd learned the truth about herself and her parents.

"Full circle, sweetheart." Star Walker took his daughter and held her out to his son. "Now, we have unfinished business," he murmured in his wife's ear. He eyed his son and jerked his head.

"Come on, little sister." Keeping the little girl's hand firmly in his, the boy led his sibling back into the forest toward the village.

Blaze watched them go with love filling her heart. Taking her husband's hand, she led him up to her old cave. She and her family lived in a longhouse in the village now. As a holy woman, she had a place. She belonged, was respected and honored. But she still loved her cave, and came here often when she needed time alone.

Turning into Star Walker's embrace, she let him

kiss her long and hard. He led her to a pile of furs in the back. Kneeling, she took one of his hands in her own. "I have a gift for you."

With his eyes full of love and desire, he cupped one side of her face with his other hand. "*Ange. You* are my gift. You are all I need."

Smiling, she placed her hand onto her belly and let the life growing inside her flow into him.

"Another child?"

She nodded. "Are you happy?"

He grinned. "But you're not going to be. No more flying or shifting shape for you for a bit."

Blaze fell into his arms with a sigh. "Then I'll just have to fly with you, Trapper."

"That you will, *Ange*. That you will," he whispered. Then he laid her down and covered her body with his.

Connie Mason

Highland Warrior

She is far too shapely to be a seasoned warrior, but she is just as deadly. As she engages him on the battlefield, Ross knows her for a MacKay, longtime enemies of his clan. Soon this flame-haired virago will be his wife, given to him by her father in a desperate effort to end generations of feuding. Of all her family, Gillian MacKay is the least willing to make peace. Her fiery temper challenges Ross's mastery while her lush body taunts his masculinity. Both politics and pride demand that he tame her, but he will do it his way—with a scorching seduction that will sweep away her defenses and win her heart.

The Sword & the Sheath

BONNIE VANAK

From a young age, Fatima knew she must do battle. She knew this, her destiny, because every fiber of her body cried out for it—just as every fiber cries out for Tarik, the impossibly handsome "White Falcon," her friend and next in line to lead her tribe. She has been trained by her father to be the future sheikh's bodyguard. Yet, women of the Khamsin are not warriors, and the sons of sheikhs do not wish to have their lives saved by women any more than they wish to fall in love with childhood friends. Tradition be damned; she will fulfill her destiny. And Tarik will love her forever.

Blood Moon

✠ ✠ ✠

Dawn Thompson

Jon Hyde-White is changed. Soon he will cease to be an earl's second son and become a ravening monster. Already lust grows, begging him to drink blood—and the blood of his fiancée Cassandra Thorpe will be sweetest of all. Is that not why the blasphemous creature Sebastian bursts upon them from the London shadows? But Sebastian's evil task remains incomplete, and neither Jon nor Cassandra is beyond hope. One chance remains—in faraway Moldavia, in a secret brotherhood, in an ancient ritual and in the power of love.

The WARRIOR TRAINER

GERRI RUSSELL

Scotia's duty is to protect the Stone of Destiny—the key to Scotland's salvation, and the reason she and the women who guarded the Stone before her had become the best warriors in the world. Yet those women had never met a man like Ian MacKinnon.

He's journeyed to her castle to learn her legendary skills so he can exact vengeance against the English. His viciousness on the battlefield stands in stark contrast to his tenderness in the bedroom. But he will soon move on, leaving Scotia to face a conflict for which she has no training: her duty to the Stone versus her desire to follow her heart.